Offside

D1371288

The stories so far. Other books in the Team Mates series (in order):

Offside

Paul Cockburn

First published in 1998 by
Virgin Books
an imprint of Virgin Publishing Ltd
332 Ladbroke Grove
London W10 5AH

Copyright © Paul Cockburn 1998

The right of Paul Cockburn to be identified as the author
of this work has been asserted by him in accordance
with the Copyright, Designs and Patents Act 1988

A catalogue record for this book is available from the
British Library.

ISBN 0 7535 0053 1

Typeset by Galleon Typesetting, Ipswich
Printed and bound by
BPC Paperbacks Ltd, Aylesbury

First published in Great Britain in 1996 by
Virgin Books
an imprint of Virgin Publishing Ltd
332 Ladbroke Grove
London W10 5AH

A catalogue record for this book is available from the
British Library.

ISBN 0 7535 0053 1

Typeset by Galleon Typesetting, Ipswich
Printed and bound by
BPC Paperbacks Ltd, Aylesbury

One

The others were all calculating the odds. On the face of it, things didn't look too good.

Nicky, though, kept his attention on just one of the hard faces closing in around him. It was a face he knew well — square, brutish and ugly, with icy-cold blue eyes. A fuzz of blond hair covered the guy's skull (which was a new look, it hadn't been that short before).

Nicky brushed his hand through his own hair, smoothing the fringe away from his eyes. He was grinning uncontrollably. His friends might be nervous, but Nicky was in complete control.

'Hello, Bennett,' he called, managing to say the other guy's name as if it was a swear word.

Bennett's expression hardened. He and Nicky went back a long way.

'Fiorentini,' he scowled. 'You're a long way from home turf.'

Nicky took a quick glance around, as if to remind himself where he was. 'I don't remember Loam Park being Blackmoor's patch,' he replied.

Bennett laughed, making it seem more like a snarl.

'Maybe it is now,' he boasted, with a quick gesture to his mates. His confidence was starting to return. When he and his gang had first found Nicky and the others loitering in Loam Park, Bennett hadn't known what to do. Even though there were a dozen boys wearing the black jackets of Blackmoor School and just half that number in dark blue, he hadn't known what to make of Nicky and his mates being here. Loam Park was a long way from Spirebrook Comprehensive. It was far enough away from Blackmoor, but Bennett and his pals had their reasons for being here.

There were a couple of other things troubling Bennett about the situation. One, he wasn't sure how he felt about Nicky.

True, Nicky was a snivelling 'Brooker – and the feud between Blackmoor and Spirebrook had been going on for years. However, Bennett and Fiorentini had also been team mates for a year, playing for the same team in Oldcester's District Youth League. OK, they hadn't become close friends but a team mate was still a mate. Second, it seemed odd seeing Nicky without his shadow. Bennett looked again at Nicky's companions. Where, he wondered, was Chris Stephens?

He knew most of the others. Phil Lucas, the quiet one from the West Indies was at the front; the short brat with the dark hair beside Lucas was MacIntyre; the crazy-looking one with the haircut from hell and the chewing gum was Fuller; and the fit, lean hard one at the back with the hair like rusted wire was Russell Jones. They all played football for Spirebrook; in addition, Bennett knew Jones and MacIntyre from another team they turned out for, the Riverside Colts.

The Colts were big rivals of the team Bennett (and Nicky) played for. So, that was a double reason for disliking them.

Bennett turned his attention back to Nicky. Once again, he found himself wondering what Fiorentini was doing here without Stephens to hold his hand. Something was wrong . . .

The rest of the Blackmoor lads were getting impatient. There was no doubt in their minds. Twelve of them, six lousy 'Brookers. They were hungry to get it on.

Standing about five or six metres in front of Bennett, Nicky knew the Blackmoron was struggling to decide what to do. He grinned. Opportunities like this didn't come round very often and this was one to be enjoyed to the fullest.

'We heard you guys were hanging around over here,' he called. 'It got us curious.'

Bennett's eyes narrowed. Had their little secret been rumbled?

'Why? What's it to do with you?'

Nicky hesitated for just a moment, wondering whether to come clean. It seemed a shame to spoil the moment by just *telling* Bennett what they knew, about how the Blackmorons had managed to get a key to a staff door at the small cinema on Gainsbury Road, about how they had been sneaking in to watch Certificate (18) films in the afternoons after school. Nicky liked moments of drama like this. He didn't want to throw it away.

2

'We brought someone along you ought to meet,' he said. He turned and put his arm round the shoulder of the sixth 'Brooker in the group. He was almost as tall as Nicky, though he looked a year or two younger. He had a serious, smooth face and small, grey-blue eyes. He looked restless, as if he had a coiled spring inside waiting to drive him into action.

'This is Bob James,' Nicky said by way of introduction. 'He moved up this way over the summer. He got through the trials at United – perhaps you remember him?'

Nicky saw Bennett stiffen, clenching his fists. He'd hoped reminding the Blackmoor student of the trials would yank his chain hard. Bennett had been on the youth team books of the city's Premiership club, Oldcester United, until a year or so ago. He'd lost his place, but had tried to get it back that year. Nicky, Russell and the absent Chris Stephens had been there too – and they had all found places in the United youth team. Bennett had not.

'His dad managed to get his job transferred to Oldcester over the summer, so that Bobby could take his place in the squad. He'll go to the new school when it opens next Easter, but for now he's at Spirebrook, same as us.'

Bennett didn't reply; what was all this to him? On the other hand, anyone who willingly pulled on Spirebrook blue was his enemy. James getting through the United trial while he had failed only made things worse.

Behind Bennett, some of the other Blackmorons weren't able to keep so quiet. All this waiting was driving them nuts. Whispers were flying among them – who cared why the 'Brookers were here, let's just get them!

Nicky pointed out James's jacket. Bennett looked closer. It had the Spirebrook badge on the pocket, but now that he was concentrating, he could see that it was actually the wrong colour. The 'Brook jacket was dark, sure, but it was definitely blue. The jacket James was wearing was the colour of black ink.

'See this?' Nicky said. 'It's his old school jacket. It wasn't worth buying him a new one for just a couple of terms, so his mum just sewed our badge on the old jacket.'

Even Bennett was losing patience with this long-winded explanation. He took half a step forward. 'Get to the point, Fiorentini,' he snarled.

3

Nicky sighed, not wanting to waste a moment of suspense. All the same, he knew the Blackmorons were beginning to lose the plot, so he hurried towards the finish.

'So, his mum started a new job as well. It was OK for a week or two, but then some real berks started causing trouble. The manager saw their jackets and thought they were the same as this. He'd only ever seen Bobby's in the dark, see . . .'

Bennett's eyes were glazing over. Nicky speeded up even more.

'So, this manager thought the kids got in with the help of Bobby's mum. He gave her the sack. Now, why don't you take a wild guess at where this job of hers was?'

Bennett's face paled, as if he was being faced in class with a question he'd never be able to answer. Blackmoor School had a reputation for 'attracting' some of the stupidest kids in the city (a reputation, in fairness, that didn't extend far beyond the gates of Spirebrook Comp). Bennett didn't take his shoes and socks off to count up to twenty, but that was only because he couldn't easily count to ten in the first place.

Nicky sighed. He could tell Bennett had lost the plot.

'The cinema, dummy! Don't you get it? Your scam has been rumbled.'

That was much easier to understand. Bennett's eyes glistened like broken glass. The colour came back into his face and spit flew off his lips as he growled angrily back at Nicky.

'You grassed us up, you . . .' he cursed.

Nicky smiled broadly, his teeth flashing, glad that Bennett had finally seen the light, even if the point had been drilled into his head with six-inch nails.

'You know the score, Bennett,' he whispered. 'I'll do anything, anywhere, anytime, to score against a Blackmoron. And we owed you, big time, for that stunt you pulled at our school last Easter.'

Everyone knew what he was talking about. Bennett's mates had sneaked on to the Spirebrook site one evening during a school disco. They ambushed Chris Stephens, and were about to tie him to the gym apparatus naked when they had been caught in turn by Nicky and the rest of his year group.

'We stuffed you sideways that night, Bennett,' said Nicky, ignoring the fact that Bennett hadn't actually been there himself. Some of those behind him had been, though.

4

'The way I hear it,' Bennett replied, 'there were twice as many of you as there were of us. Now the tables are turned.'

He was advancing now, on the brink of breaking into a run. His hands stretched out towards Nicky's face.

'Get them, lads!' he roared, and the Blackmoor gang surged forward like a wall of water from a ruptured dam.

Nicky saw it coming. The way Bennett's voice had suddenly hardened, the way he had lifted his fists. Even before the enemy came storming towards him, Nicky was turning away.

One of the advantages Nicky had on the football pitch was his explosive acceleration. From a standing start, he could be moving flat out in just a few strides. Right now, it meant that although he was a metre and a half behind his mates as he turned, he was actually level with Russell Jones before anyone else had covered twenty metres. Leading the way along the path, Nicky gritted his teeth and poured on the power.

The sounds from behind made sure he didn't slacken the pace. As they saw their enemies fleeing, the Blackmorons had screamed in triumph. That scream had turned into a howl of frustration as they saw the 'Brookers were getting away.

Loam Park wasn't so much a park as a small corridor of grass, trees and paths connecting two main streets in the south-west of the city. In the direction the Spirebrook lads were fleeing, the ground was slightly downhill. People out walking their dogs or just using the short-cut looked up in amazement as Nicky, with the others close on his heels, flew past.

Bennett had managed a bit of a jump start on his mates and was pounding along the tarmac path, almost tripping over in his enthusiasm to get hold of Nicky (or any of the other 'Brookers, come to that!). He was tall and long-striding, but the enemy seemed to stay just out of reach. He growled angrily as he ran — it was just his luck that the six blue-jacketed cowards in front of him were all quick runners. Bennett was no slouch, but he was falling further behind. The other guys from his school were even further back.

The path flattened out. They were nearing the exit from the park, where a pair of gates led directly on to Gainsbury Road. It was five o'clock on a September weekday after-noon. Rush hour traffic was building up. People crowded the pavements; shoppers jostled each other with plastic carrier bags; suits trudged slowly towards the car parks and bus stops.

Bennett grinned slightly when he saw them. The crowds would slow the 'Brookers down. It didn't worry him to carry on their dispute in the middle of a crowded street. In fact, an audience might be even better. It would show everyone around here which school was the hardest!

But, just before the gates, the 'Brookers swerved sharply left. Bennett almost managed to collar MacIntyre as they took the corner, but he was moving so fast that he needed both hands for balance as he skidded on the path. MacIntyre ducked under his flailing fist, his eyes wide with fear for just a moment before he skipped away again.

Bennett was breathing hard, but he set off again with new determination. The 'Brookers were now on a dirt path, running parallel to the main road. Bennett took a look back to his left, where his mates were cutting the corner to save time. Nicky and his mates had just lost half their lead.

What was more, they were heading for disaster. Bennett knew this better than anyone. The path led to a group of trees, then petered out. Beyond the trees, there was a pathetic bed of trampled flowers before a low wall and beyond that, there was a gap through the wall. The 'Brookers would never all get through before Bennett caught up.

His heart jumped. He was going to make Fiorentini pay!

That moment of triumph lasted for about half a second. Bennett remembered how it was that he knew about the wall and the hole in it – this was the way he and his mates got to the cinema. The back door they used was just twenty metres from the gap, across an alley.

If Nicky and the others knew about the cinema scam, they knew this was the way the Blackmoor posse came from their school along Canal Avenue, into Loam Park and through the gap in the wall . . .

In that instant, Bennett instinctively knew it was a trap. He would never let it be said that he had been suckered.

Unfortunately, his instincts were running about three seconds too late. He was in the middle of the trees now, with the rest of his mates just behind. The broken wall lay ahead. Just as he suspected, the 'Brookers didn't try to dive through the narrow gap. They stopped and turned, grinning with undisguised glee. And suddenly there were rather a lot of them too . . .

'Hey, Bennett!' came a voice. Bennett halted and looked up. 'Stephens . . .' he snarled.

The face he had missed earlier was above him in the branches of a tree. Chris Stephens' face was unmistakable, even in the shadows. That mop of blond hair, like an explosion in a mattress factory; the intelligent, bright blue eyes. And that smile. That smile that said 'I've beaten you again.'

Bennett hated that smile.

'Going to the pictures, Bennett?' Chris asked. Bennett could see his enemy had a Super Soaker in his hands. There were other blue jackets all around; some in the trees like Stephens, others on the ground. Some were carrying paper bags. Others had water pistols or the bigger Super Soaker rifles.

An ambush, Bennett groaned inside. The freaking 'Brookers had put one over on them yet again.

Moments later, the bombardment started.

Twenty minutes later Nicky still couldn't stop laughing. Tears rolled down his cheeks, streaking through patches of soot, dirt and flour. Nicky hadn't been able to resist getting more closely entangled with the Blackmorons. Chris and the others had been content to douse them with sticky gunk from the water guns followed by a barrage of flour and dirt. Nicky, on the other hand, had wanted them to get just a flavour of how much worse it could have been. He had steamed into Bennett as his former team mate tried to fight his way out of the trap.

As a consequence, Nicky was the only one of the guys from Spirebrook with a mark on him. The ambush had been a complete success otherwise.

'Oh, man,' Nicky gasped, fighting for breath. 'I am going to miss all this *so much!*'

TWO

'I hate this place! What a dump!!!'

Chris kept silent, sitting on the wall outside the gym, watching as Mr Lea, their PE teacher, tried to get the school bus to start. The rest of the team were standing about looking helpless as well.

Nicky looked at his watch. Then he grabbed Robert James's arm so that he could look at his watch too.

'Aw, man!' he moaned, loudly.

Flea looked up angrily, which stopped Nicky from adding any more to his whining. It's a knack some teachers have — they can reduce a room to silence with just a glare. In Flea's case, it helped no end that the threatening stare was backed up by him being about two metres tall and nearly that much wide. When new students first saw Flea, they never made the mistake of thinking he might teach music or biology. Even in a collar and tie, Mr Lea still looked like he was wearing a torn rugby shirt with blood on the chest.

'Instead of moaning, Fiorentini,' he snapped, 'why don't you go and wait by the gates for the AA? When they get here, you can help them find us.'

'Doughnut is already there, sir,' Nicky replied quickly, flashing his most ingratiating smile. It didn't work.

'Then why don't you go and wait by the gates so you can show Packham the way.'

Chris and a couple of the others tried to choke back their laughter. Nicky's eyes flashed angrily.

Flea buried his head back under the bonnet of the stricken bus once more. Nicky decided this meant he didn't actually have to leave, and came to sit on the wall beside Chris.

'Even if Flea gets the bus started now, we'll still be too late,' he whispered. He held up his watch (as if Chris didn't have a

8

pretty good idea of the time already – Nicky had been counting the minutes for the last hour).

'They said they'd give us some extra time,' Chris reminded his mate.

'It's quarter to five,' Nicky said, just in case Chris had forgotten how to tell the time. 'It'll take us thirty minutes or more to get there – more if the traffic is bad. So, let's say we kick off at half five, that's –' He started to count the time off on his fingers. '– quarter past six half-time, quarter past seven full-time, back here eight o'clock.' He ran his fingers back through his hair. 'My mum will have a fit. We're having lasagne tonight.'

Chris opened his mouth to speak three times in the next ten seconds. On the first occasion, he was going to ask what difference lasagne made to how late it would be before they got back. On the second, he was close to commenting that Mrs Fiorentini never got mad with Nicky, who was her eldest son and the apple of her eye. In fact, hardly anyone over the age of sixteen ever got mad with Nicky, unless you counted teachers. Then, opening his mouth for the last time, Chris was about to remind Nicky that it wasn't as if his dinner would go to waste – Mrs Fiorentini always cooked far too much grub, and if there was ever any threat of there being a mouthful left over, she just invited someone else to stay until it was all gone. In the end, Nicky spoke again before Chris uttered a single word.

'Typical. That heap of bolts should have been condemned years ago. I really hate this dump.'

This time Chris knew just what he wanted to say.

'Nicky, it was only yesterday that you were saying how much you were going to miss Spirebrook.'

'Never!' howled Nicky in protest. Ignoring the fact that there had been two dozen witnesses, he turned to gesture at the dull, grey stone and dirty windows from which Spirebrook had been constructed. 'Look at it . . .' he sighed.

Chris didn't need to look to know just how the school would look on a wet September afternoon. The tired, damp view behind him was etched on to his brain. The cramped classrooms and dark passageways of Spirebrook Comprehensive were something he'd struggle to forget.

It wasn't all bad, though. Spirebrook had one thing going

for it. At the back of the site, sheltered from some retail warehouses by a smart new road and a high wire fence, was a long, curving sports field. It swung round the middle of the three main classroom blocks, past the dining hall and the boiler room, bulging at both ends. Chris imagined the sports field must look like a curved, green peanut from above.

At one end there was a sadly neglected cricket pitch and some cracked and pitted tennis courts. There was a running track near the narrow middle part of the field. During the summer term, that end of the field came to life, but just now, Chris knew, it would be little more than a weed factory.

But up here, by the gym, was the most important part of the school, the centre of Chris's life for years. Two football pitches fitted in neatly between the gym, the fence and the dining room, edged on one side by a path leading to the rear gate. Two gigantic electricity pylons stood like olympic-standard floodlight towers to either side of the pitch nearest the gym, and the wires stretched across one penalty area.

Chris and Nicky had stood under those on one of the first mornings they had spent at Spirebrook, wondering if it would be possible to get a ball over the wires. It was. Since then, plenty of their mates had passed the same 'test'. The most recent had been Russell Jones, who had punted a ball over on the first attempt. Nicky had complained that the wind had gusted just as he thumped the ball, so Russell had kicked it back the other way, against the wind.

Soon, Chris, Nicky and Russell would be leaving Spirebrook behind. At the beginning of the summer, they had come through a trial for Oldcester United and had joined the club's youth squad. For now, that meant training four nights a week at Star Park, United's home ground. But in a few months, they would be moving to a new school, a school for gifted young players that was being built close to the stadium. There would still be teachers, lessons and homework (no matter what Nicky thought!), but there would also be intensive coaching and fitness training.

It was going to be great. Chris couldn't wait for the new school to be opened. But all the same . . .

'I'll miss the old place,' Chris sighed, more to himself than out loud.

Nicky's ears, though, were better than radar.

'Huh!' he snorted. 'I can't wait to get away! This place –'

At the last moment, Nicky stopped. He'd seen the warning glance in Chris's eyes and the way Russell Jones jumped to his feet as if he was going to butt in too. The penny dropped.

'This place isn't so bad, but . . .' He stalled, unable to think quickly enough to get himself out of the hole he was digging. The others watched closely. Not all of them, of course, would be following Chris, Nicky, Rob and Russell to the new school.

'. . . it could do with a new bus,' smiled Chris. Nicky grinned, looking mightily relieved.

'Yeah!' he chuckled.

At that point Flea came to the same conclusion. The boys pretended they hadn't heard him cuss at something under the bonnet and stared up into the sky as he ducked his head out.

'This is pointless. I'll call Mr Evans at St Joseph's and tell him we can't make it. We'll have to concede the game.'

There was a chorus of disappointed groans all round. The senior players were even more disappointed than the guys from lower school. Three weeks into the new season, and their record now read two defeats and one game scratched. After winning the Oldcester Schools League last year, this was a strange way for Spirebrook to start the new campaign.

'This is just bloody typical,' moaned Nicky, louder than anyone else.

Chris got down from where he was sitting and picked up his bag. As far as he could see, there was nothing typical about it. Losing the first three games of the season was going to make it very difficult to hang on to their title. What made it worse was that in just two weeks they were to play their arch-rivals from Blackmoor. If things carried on like this, they might lose. Against the Blackmorons. It didn't bear thinking about.

While Flea slammed the bonnet shut and stomped off into the gym to wait for the AA, the boys from the two teams milled about uncertainly. Some of them were due to be picked up by parents at a later time; others wouldn't be able to get in for another hour or so.

'Well, let's not waste the opportunity,' said Nicky, taking charge. 'We could have a practice game. Who's up for that?'

At first, no-one seemed that keen. After all, they played each other all the time in practice and on the playground – who needed another game?

Then Chris had another idea. 'Isn't it about time Bob won his "cap"?' he said.

The others knew what this meant immediately. Robert James looked around at a ring of smug smiles.

'Oh, oh,' he sighed.

'It's OK,' said Chris, knowing why the new boy was worried. 'This isn't a head down the toilet bowl type of thing. But everyone in this team has had a crack at a little challenge. Now, I know you're only going to be here a couple of terms, but you're a 'Brooker for that long, so you ought to have a go.'

It may have only been the third week of term, but Robert was already a solid fixture with the football crowd. If they'd told him the initiation involved swimming the river, he'd probably have had a go. Instead, they led him out on to the senior football pitch, halting just inside one half. They faced back towards the school.

'This way, do you think?' Chris asked the others.

Various opinions were offered. Nicky wet his fingers and tested the air, although it was obvious from which way the wind was gusting.

'OK, Bob,' said Chris. 'Here's how it is. You have to kick a ball . . .' As he spoke, he lifted his head and arm up towards the wires trailing over their heads '. . . over those wires.'

Robert stretched his neck back to look at the target. The wires were a long way up – he had no way of telling exactly how far, but it was a good way. He breathed a sigh of relief.

'Is that it?' he asked.

He didn't have much doubt that he could do it. Robert James may have been a couple of years younger than Chris and Nicky – who had just moved up into the senior team captained by Griff – but it wasn't that obvious from size alone. In fact, he was several centimetres taller than Mac, who was a year older.

In addition to being tall, Robert was strong. He didn't look too heavy – he wasn't a bruiser like Fuller or Griff – but his arms and legs were powerful, and he was broad-shouldered.

All told, if it wasn't for his slightly younger face, with its innocent blue eyes and clear, pale skin, Robert could easily have passed for being the same age as Chris and his classmates. He had fine, light brown hair, which sort of fell from the top of his head, dead straight. The closest he came to being fashionable was the way he always wore his shirt untucked.

'I can do that,' he said. Then, as he looked down, he saw all the others were backing away. 'What?' he asked.

'Did we mention the fact that it's against the school rules?' asked Chris. He rolled a ball underarm towards Robert's feet.

Now Robert could see what the trick was. Out here on the field, he was in clear sight. The path from the main buildings to the back gate went along the side of the football pitch and the staff car park was just behind the sports hall. The only good thing was that 'Andy' Cole, the head teacher, was off on some course. Robert sighed, then grinned broadly.

It didn't make any difference who he got caught by, he suspected. The trick was to get the ball over the lines first time, without being seen.

His 'mates' had all faded away into the background now, hanging around near the entrance to the dining hall or over by the gym doors. Would they give him any warning if a teacher was approaching? He doubted it somehow.

He looked up again. Fine. He could do this. No problem.

He dropped his jacket to the ground and stepped back a little further to measure the angle. The wind was blowing briskly, flicking at his shirt and hair. Robert figured all he had to worry about was getting the ball up there and it would be blown over the bottom wires anyway. That was all he had to do, right?

He decided against asking. Why make life any more difficult?

He picked up the ball and felt it between his fingers. It was firm and not too light. He bounced it once or twice, dropped it on his instep and flicked it up. It was fine.

Taking it in hand again, Robert took one last look around and measured a three step run-up, starting almost on the halfway line. He took a deep breath, ran in and let fly.

He made perfect contact with the ball, lifting it hard and high. He knew it was a 'winner' right off. It cleared the bottom cable by three or four metres, the wind rushing it forward as it started to descend.

Robert took off from his right foot and punched his fist through the air. First time! He'd passed the test. He could see the others in the distance, watching the ball as it fell. A few of them were clapping.

He felt good for about another two seconds. The ball came

13

down diagonally, driven by the strong wind. It hit the ground and kicked off at an angle, moving really fast. Robert didn't even have time to draw breath before it smashed through one of the dining room windows.

It wasn't the first time one of those windows had been broken and it wouldn't be the last. Most often, of course, there were plenty of potential suspects and the teaching staff were forced to work out who was guilty by the scientific method of picking anyone who was running away.

On this occasion, though, the only possible candidate was Robert James. Which made it just a little unlucky that, at the very moment when the glass was raining to the floor, Ms Robinson, the young geography teacher, came out of Block I on her way to her car.

She looked round at the unexpected noise; Robert looked back. She could see the crowd of other boys in the dining room entrance, some of them staring through at the ball spinning and bouncing off the table legs inside, others open-mouthed with laughter. And she could see Robert alone on the field, under the electricity wires.

No need to call Poirot for help with this case, then.

Given the choice of hanging round while Robert was dragged off to the deputy head teacher, a new guy called Leggett, or legging it themselves, the various members of the Spirebrook Comprehensive School football team decided that they'd sooner be elsewhere.

Those who had been over by the dining hall were the quickest movers. They, after all, were clearly on the scene of the crime. The main path led from the hall to the main gates, and some of them broke personal bests for getting off the school site.

Chris, Nicky and some of the other older boys were in the group by the sports hall. Hidden from Ms Robinson's direct view, they were able to make themselves disappear at a more casual pace. By the time the geography teacher had nabbed James and hauled him off to the school office, they were out of the back gate and walking down the road with all the innocence they could fake, as if it was just a coincidence that they were passing.

Without anyone actually saying anything, they headed for the bridge over the river. There was a small patch of ground over there which had yet to be built on and those boys who lived at this end of the main road – including Nicky and Mac – had adopted it as a place to hang out.

It was as good a place to hide and gather their wits as any. Griff had a ball in his sports bag, which they kicked about between them while they talked.

'That was unlucky, wasn't it?' said Fuller, the first to speak.

Almost everyone knew what Fuller meant. The exception was Russell Jones, who was the most recent arrival in their group before Robert.

'Yeah, getting caught like that . . . he should have moved faster.'

Chris found himself stifling a laugh. There was no way Russell could have known that Fuller was the last one of them to get caught – in fact the only other one there had ever been. He'd been dancing round the field celebrating his success when Mrs Cole had walked up, tapped him on the shoulder and beckoned for him to follow her. Fuller had been given enough extra homework to keep him busy for the next three months (or about ten days for anyone else) and had been banned from the school team for the rest of term.

'I think he meant . . . the way the ball bounced . . .' Nicky spluttered, making a very bad job of hiding his amusement. Fuller was scowling. He wasn't sure whether everyone was laughing at Jones or him.

'Right . . .' said Russell slowly, realising that something was going on. He decided to keep quiet from then on.

'It was a weird bounce, wasn't it?' Mac commented.

'Like a rugby ball,' said Mike 'Geoff' Hurst, one of the senior team's defenders. Chris remembered that he played both sports through the winter.

'Do you think "Andy" will suspend him for the term, like she did with –' Nicky just pulled himself up in time. 'Like she did before?' he added, lamely.

'Who knows?' said Chris. He had Griff's ball at his feet and was flicking it from one to the other, trying to keep it airborne. Nicky watched him with a smile that said he wasn't impressed – Fiorentini was much better at those kinds of ball tricks.

15

'Maybe she'll go easy on him, being a new boy,' he said. 'Maybe she'll realise that he was just going along with the rest of us.'

'Maybe,' agreed Chris, but then he added: 'But if she does, she'll come looking for someone else to blame.'

Nicky took a moment to think this through.

'He's on his own,' he concluded.

Three

⚽

They were on the point of giving up and going home when a group of lads from the new housing estate further up the road came over and asked if they fancied a game. Looking at each other, the 'Brookers realised that they might as well get something going. Anything was better than not playing at all.

Nicky leant over close to Chris's ear and said he recognised a few of the lads. They went to a posh school just up the road, not far from Russell Jones's house. Russell's elder brother, who was now inside, had pinched most of the furniture the Jones family possessed — much of it from the school.

Russell watched the kids from the private school warily.

With the new arrivals, they were thirteen-a-side. Nicky and Griff selected the two teams, arguing about who would take first pick and whether there were any rules about who you could select. Following Griff's first choice — Chris Stephens — Nicky was tempted to try and get both Russell Jones and Mac, who had been Spirebrook's keeper before Jones, into his side. If he could force Griff to play without a proper goalie . . .

Griff picked the tallest of the non-'Brookers, a dark-haired, stocky guy named Bryan Matthews. Chris watched from the side as Bryan took Griff through the best of the others. In the end, most of the guys from over the river were on Griff's team. Nicky had stuck with faces he knew.

The game was a noisy, cramped affair. There wasn't enough room for 10 players, never mind 26, and the ground was uneven and strewn with loose bricks and half-buried concrete.

Passing was impossible, close control was even less likely. As soon as a player received the ball, he was pounced on by two or three defenders. It was only when some of the less committed players became tired and bored that space opened up, allowing a few goals to be scored before the evening closed in.

⊗

'That was interesting,' said Nicky.

Chris, who was walking slightly tenderly after having been on the wrong end of one of Fuller's challenges, looked up at Nicky with just a little annoyance. His friend's mood had swung right back round again, aided, no doubt, by the fact that he had been on the winning team and had scored twice.

'I suppose,' Chris muttered, lifting his bag higher on his shoulder. They were getting close to the junction where they would split up; Chris to continue along the main road for a distance while Nicky turned right and climbed the hill to his house.

'Didn't you enjoy it?' asked Nicky.

Chris bit his lip after thinking of some sarcastic answer. Taking a deep breath, he went with a different reply instead.

'I'd sooner have played for real. A chance to get some points on the board would have counted for more than a kick-about.'

Nicky made a kind of laughing, spluttering sound, which was meant to show that he thought this was a rather obvious thing to have said. Chris didn't rise to the bait.

'What I meant,' Nicky continued after a short pause, 'was that it was interesting to watch some of the others in a game like that. It was different from training or League games . . .'

Chris knew Nicky well enough to realise that he was about to get one of Nicky's instant-fix ideas. Fiorentini had never captained a school side, but that was just an oversight as far as he was concerned. Nicky never missed a chance to show who was really in charge.

'Give me an example,' said Chris, knowing he would get one anyway.

'OK,' said Nicky. 'What's been wrong with Spirebrook all season?'

Chris sighed. It didn't look as if he was going to be able to escape easily; they were going to have to go through an in-depth analysis of who or what was at fault. Chris thought about pointing out to Nicky that 'all season' consisted of two defeats and a scratched game, but knew this wouldn't make any difference.

'Not much,' he replied. 'A bit of bad luck, I guess. Perhaps we're not as tight as we could be . . .'

'Aha!' cried Nicky, who had clearly heard the answer he wanted. 'That's right. Too many goals let in at the back!'

Chris knew this wasn't quite what he had said, but he was almost prepared to let it pass.

'Two-one and one-nil, Nicky. Hardly thrashings, are they? You could as easily say we've not been scoring enough at the other end.'

Nicky wasn't going to have that. His face folded in a deep frown.

'Get real,' he said. 'We're not the problem.'

Chris could see Nicky's turning coming closer. Perhaps it would be best to just let Nicky get whatever was bothering him off his chest.

'So, what are you suggesting?'

'Think about the three goals, Chris.' That was easy enough. A deflected free kick in the 1–0 defeat, plus a sloppy goal from a deep cross and a fast counter-attack in the game the week before. They had very little in common, except for one thing.

'Russell wasn't at fault in any of them,' Chris said quickly, in case that was where Nicky's thinking was leading.

'Of course not!' erupted Nicky, as if Chris was being deliberately dense. 'It was the defence! That's where the weak link is.'

The upper school team had broadly the same defence that had been put together in the junior team two years before. Bruise, Griff, Fuller and Packham playing as a flat back four had played well together until the two central defenders had moved up into the senior team. Now they were all reunited. By rights, they should have been a pretty good unit still.

But, now that Nicky had put the thought into Chris's mind, there were a few problems. Steve 'Bruise' Brewster was a good player – and a good mate – but he picked up more silly illnesses and injuries than the rest of the team put together. His normal cover was Mike Hurst, but he was more interested in rugby than proper football and was absent a lot of the time.

Mac, Marshy and Sean Dolan had all been tried out at right back, but not convincingly. Each of them was a better player in midfield anyway, providing a bit of bite alongside the creative skills of Nicky and Jazz.

In addition, Griff and Fuller had grown a lot over the last two years. Not in height, so much, but definitely in weight and bulk. Griff was looking downright heavy, and Fuller had a kind of junior Gladiators look about him. Neither was very quick any more, and they couldn't jump to save their lives.

The more Chris thought about it, the more he realised Fiorentini might have a point. But a good defence doesn't become rubbish overnight. That back four might not be as good as it was, but it was still better than a lot of others in the league.

'So, what are you getting at, Nicky?'

They had reached the bottom of Church Hill, the road which climbed up to Nicky's street. The traffic was louder here, since the road opposite was the new road on to the retail estate, and there was a large, new supermarket on the corner. They were both talking that little bit louder, which made them sound that little bit more aggressive and determined.

Nicky flicked his eyes away for just a moment, as if he was annoyed that Chris still hadn't reached the same conclusion he had.

'All right,' he said at last. 'That system you were trying out with the Colts at the end of last season.'

At last Chris felt the penny drop. He had spent a season with the Colts, a team run by a guy called Iain Walsh, who was in turn a mate of Sean Priest, the Oldcester United youth team boss. It was a so-called secret that Priest had set up the Colts so some of the promising players who didn't make it on to the youth scheme could train with an experienced coach. Walsh had taken over an old youth club team, moved their HQ to a proper pitch at the university and had recruited the best players he could find on the west of the city. Chris, Mac and Russell Jones were all Colts.

That is, they had been. Chris and Russell, now that they had been accepted on to United's books, had to resign from the Colts over the summer. Football Association rules meant that the only team, other than United, they could play for was Spirebrook Comp. And when the new school was built . . .

Chris shook his head, trying to get back to the point. At the end of last season, Walsh had adopted the system England had employed before the Euro 96 finals. Three at the back, with a defensive midfield player tidying up in front of them and providing a starting point for counter-attacks.

It had looked good for England (even if they hadn't used it much in the European Championships), but it had done wonders for the Colts. With five men across midfield, including guys like Mac who could get back and tackle, they had used just one pure defender at centre back. The wing backs were encouraged to get forward, as were the midfield. The Colts could go from ten men back to six players in attack in three or four passes.

Chris remembered some of the games they had won with that system. Then he tried to imagine Doughnut, Griff and the others working the same way.

'That can't work at school,' he said. 'We'd need three new defenders.'

'Exactly,' said Nicky, as if Chris had just agreed with the point he had been wanting to make all along.

Chris knew trouble was coming from that moment on.

Four

Chris was slowly getting used to the new rhythm of his life. School was much the same. He was getting on OK with all the subjects he had selected, with the possible exception of maths and foreign languages. Chris could count goals in Italian and French, but that was about it.

Football had changed dramatically, of course. Tuesdays and Wednesdays now belonged to the school team; practice one night, matches the next. Some Wednesdays there were also Oldcester United games to watch. Chris, his father and Nicky went to almost every home match, using season tickets they bought without fail every season. Many of the away games were on Sky, which Nicky had at home.

Thursdays and Fridays belonged to Oldcester United too, in this case training with the youth team. Saturdays either meant going to Star Park to watch football or going to play football, and there were training sessions and matches on Sundays too.

For the first time in his life, Chris could eat, sleep and breathe football almost seven days a week. It was heaven.

That Wednesday after the abandoned visit to St Joseph's, Oldcester were due to play Spurs in a Premiership match at Star Park. However, by lunchtime, Chris couldn't see the game taking place. It had been raining all morning; a heavy, soaking downpour.

It was so dark in the classrooms that every light in the school was on. Looking through the window, Chris could see students in other classrooms, looking equally fed up.

The bell rang, saving Chris's class from any more maths, and they trooped out to eat lunch. Chris, Nicky and Jazz gathered at the lockers, pulling out lunch boxes and paper bags. The usual trading took place.

'Tell Jazz about the idea we had yesterday,' said Nicky

suddenly, having failed to swap his pastrami sandwich for some lamb in pitta bread that Jazz had brought. They walked out towards the playing fields.

Chris looked up from his bag as they went through the doors. He had cheese and tomato. Again. Somehow, eating alongside Jazz (whose father ran a grocery store and whose cousin had a Balti restaurant) and Nicky (whose mother practically owned Tescos) always left him feeling ordinary. It was about one day in two hundred that either of them ever wanted to swap for something his father had made.

'What was that?' he replied, his mind not quite in gear.

'We said we'd talk to Flea about making some changes in the team,' Nicky said, taking a huge bite from a massive hunk of ciabatta bread stuffed with meat as he walked along under the covered way.

Chris halted just before he took a bite from his own food.

'Did we?' he coughed.

Out of the corner of his eye, he noticed the look of alarm on Jazz's face too. Flea wasn't against taking advice from his players. In fact, he spoke with the captains of the school teams before every game. However, each time Nicky introduced an idea, it turned into a battle of wills. Flea might be a teacher, two metres tall and weighing the same as a Ford Transit, but Nicky was a Fiorentini. That made it about even.

'The three man defence thing,' Nicky said as they reached the edge of the playground. He scowled as he realised that the rain was keeping everybody under shelter and that all the seats were taken. 'We said we ought to try it,' he added.

Jazz's face lost the look of panic it had worn for a few seconds. Nicky had introduced the idea in just the right way. As a Colts player, Jazz knew the system well. They had continued to use it this season, and even though the Colts had lost Chris, Rory Blackstone and Russell to Oldcester United, they had still won three of their first four games.

'That might be a good idea,' Jazz agreed. Nicky grinned at Chris. Then he noticed a couple of Year Two students who were foolish enough to leave their seat for a moment while they dropped some rubbish in a bin. He pounced on the empty seat at once. By the time the Year Two lads returned, Nicky was firmly in place, munching through his food as if he had been there for hours.

23

The younger boys wandered off. Chris and Jazz wandered over to join Nicky, both feeling just a little guilty. Nicky turned to face Javinder Ray with renewed confidence.

'I thought we could try out the new system in practice next Tuesday, and if it worked OK, we could start using it in a few games.' Jazz nodded enthusiastically. Chris, who was pulling a can of Virgin Cola from his bag, knew Jazz hadn't yet seen the trap Nicky was luring him into. 'We just need to have a word with Flea, and get him to let us give it a go.'

Jazz didn't mind that idea. He hadn't been in trouble with the PE teacher for weeks.

'Then we have to explain it to Griff,' Nicky continued, and Jazz thought about that for a moment. The truth started to dawn on him. Whatever lights were turning on in Jazz's mind, though were immediately dimmed. A heavy shadow fell on the three of them.

'Explain what to Griff?' asked Fuller.

No-one hated a wet lunch hour more than Fuller, who thought sitting around on the edges of a damp playground was even more boring than being in class. He had wandered over after watching Nicky pull the seat-grabbing stunt with the Year Two boys. He'd had it in mind to try and pull the same gag on Nicky if he got the chance, but the snatch of conversation he overheard sounded a lot more promising.

Jazz looked up, startled. He started to splutter something about not really knowing what was going on. Chris remained silent. That left Nicky, who had never quite learnt how far Fuller could be pushed before his natural thuggish character burst through.

'We want to try out some new ideas in the team,' Nicky explained, ensuring that Chris and Jazz were as caught up in the argument as he was.

'You're not the captain,' said Fuller, sharply. 'Griff is.'

Nicky sighed. 'That's why we want a word with him.'

Fuller looked around, left and right. A wolf-like smile spread across his lips. 'Then let's call him over,' he said.

Chris almost abandoned his 'keep quiet' policy, but it was too late. Fuller bellowed across the playground to Griff, who was sitting under the shelter of the covered walkway between the sports hall and Block 1. Griff wandered over, followed by some of the other members of the team, including Phil Lucas and Sean Dolan. Mac appeared from the other direction with Russell and Robert James.

Oh, good, thought Chris. The gang's all here.

'What's the matter?' snapped Griff, who didn't appear to be in a very good mood. Perhaps he knew that any discussion that had Nicky at the centre had to be a bad thing. Chris had the same impression.

'Nicky's got something he wants to talk to you about,' Fuller said, with a thick smirk stuck to his face, just as if his mouth muscles were stuck.

'Yeah?' asked Griff, grittily.

If this had been Chris's problem (which was a big if, right away), he might have thought about letting the matter drop when he heard the hard edge to Griff's voice. He looked across at Nicky and guessed that his mate was having the same kind of second thoughts. Fiorentini might not have been the most sensitive person in the world, but even he could spot that Griff was in no mood to be told how the defence was to blame for all Spirebrook's problems.

Unfortunately, Fuller — who won even fewer awards for sensitivity — had seen the same thing. And nothing suited him better than to have Griff and Nicky fall out.

'It's to do with the team,' he announced. Then, realising that players from various Spirebrook teams were there, he added: 'the football team.'

A couple of girls at the back of the group sighed and walked away, but they were the only ones. About twenty others hung on, hoping that a miserable lunch hour was about to liven up.

'Yeah?' said Griff, and his voice managed to sound even uglier. 'What's on your mind, Fiorentini?'

Back down, Chris whispered in his mind. Back down. On the pitch, he and Nicky shared a kind of telepathy. Each knew exactly what the other was thinking. However, that mind-link never seemed to work away from football. Nicky didn't back down. In fact, given that he had an audience hanging on his every word (or so he thought), he sat on the arm of the bench and started to lay out his plan.

'OK. It's no big secret that we've not had a very good start to the season,' he said.

'Our team's doing all right,' Mac pointed out. At least the lower school had a 4–0 win and a squeaky draw to their credit.

Nicky ignored him. 'Now, this week was just because of the stupid bus, but that still means we don't have a point after three games. And, don't forget, the Blackmorons will be here in a fortnight.'

'And everyone knows they've been stirred up,' snarled Fuller.

Nicky ignored him too. 'So, we were just talking about what's wrong and what we can do to change things round.'

'Is that right?' asked Griff. His voice sounded icy cold.

'Yeah,' said Nicky. 'Look, it can't be that we're not good enough players, can it? I mean, three players in the United youth squad, another couple in the Colts. Tell me another school with that many players doing so well.'

There was a ripple of agreement through the crowd. The 'Brook had every right to feel good about its football team. Nicky wasn't telling them anything they didn't know.

'So, what's the problem?' muttered Griff. He hadn't failed to notice that Nicky's list of the team's strengths didn't include the captain.

'Well, maybe we're just not playing to our strengths,' Nicky continued, which Chris had to admit was the most diplomatic way of putting it. 'We were thinking maybe we need a change of system.'

There was still nothing wrong with that. People were listening closely, wondering what Nicky was going to suggest.

'We quite like the idea of adopting the system England used before Euro 96. Five across midfield – two wide, two central, and one guy sweeping up just in front of the defence.' The buzz of comment grew louder. Nicky flicked his eyes round the players most likely to make up a midfield like that – Jazz wide on the left, Marsh sweeping, Dolan and Hurst in the centre. Add himself on the right, and that was your five. Other people were making the same guess.

On the fringe of that group, Mac was wide-eyed with excitement. Even though he was a year younger than the age break for the senior team, there was no rule against him playing in the older group. And he was playing in the sweeper position for the Colts this season. If Marshy couldn't handle it, perhaps he could step up?

In those first few seconds, at least, everyone was talking quite positively about Nicky's suggestion. Everyone liked the idea of taking a leaf out of England's book. The midfielders liked it best of all. Dolan and Marsh tended to slip in and out of the team, now here they were being 'offered' key roles.

Griff and Nicky were looking directly at each other, Chris realised. Griff was slowly working out that – unless Nicky was suggesting playing with just one up front – that left only three places for defenders. If they were going to copy England, just who were going to shadow Pearce, Adams and Neville?

'Do you see?' Nicky was explaining, scratching his forefinger across the palm of his left hand as if he was drawing little diagrams. 'It's much more flexible. Sean, Marshy and Hurst can all help tighten up the defence. Then, going forward, me and Jazz can play out wide to stretch the defence, while Marsh or "Geoff" pushes up through the middle behind Chris and Phil.'

Griff lifted his eyes from Nicky's hand. 'What do you mean, "tighten up the defence"?' he growled.

The buzz of conversation silenced almost immediately. Chris could hear the rain splattering down on to the playground like shrapnel.

'Oh, come on, Griff,' said Nicky, as if he still had everyone behind him. 'Don't take it the wrong way. I just mean we'd have extra cover to avoid giving away the kind of goals we've –'

He didn't finish, but then he didn't need to. Everyone knew what Nicky was finally getting round to saying. Griff had heard the words of the whole sentence in his head before Nicky had got as far as 'I just mean . . .' He leant forward aggressively. The group around him spread out a little.

'What? You little jerk! Are you trying to blame it all on us?'

Griff's voice had become very loud and very shrill. No-one liked the sound of it. Even Nicky was starting to wonder if this discussion was going to turn out like he'd planned.

'No . . . that is . . .' he began.

'You'd better not be!' Griff roared. 'I've carried this team for years. While you were doing all that pretty boy stuff out on the sideline, I was making sure we kept the game tight. You want to remember who won the ball before it came out to you, Nicky, because you sure as hell never won it much yourself.'

Fuller yelled his agreement from alongside. Things were far from under control now and Chris knew he couldn't let matters continue the way they were headed. He took a deep breath and joined in.

'Griff, hang on,' he said. Griff opened his mouth to tell him to back off, but Chris kept going. 'Everyone's losing sight of the ball here. We've only had two games, and two narrow defeats. We all know we can put half a dozen goals past both King Edward's and Blackmoor, and then we'll be off and running. The only thing holding this team back at the moment is that luck hasn't been going our way.'

People had shut up to listen as Chris spoke, and there was a moment when he thought he'd calmed the situation down. But what often happens when a third person gets involved in a dispute between two others is that they both suddenly realise the things they have in common, and turn on the new arrival for butting in.

'Luck?' screeched Griff. 'You make your own luck in football, Chris.'

'Yeah,' snapped Nicky immediately. 'Luck is when a ball goes in off a post instead of bouncing back out. But when the ball keeps going in your end, or when you can't score at the other, that isn't luck, it's skill.'

Chris had heard Nicky's theories about luck often enough, although he had never had it thrown at him like this before.

'You're both talking rubbish. Sometimes, a perfectly good team can have a run of bad luck where results go against them for no reason.'

'There's always a reason,' Griff said, dismissing Chris's argument with a wave of his hand, although he didn't bother to tell anyone what that reason might be. 'Nicky's right. Luck's all about one-offs. If a team starts losing two or three games in a row, it's because of something else.'

'My point exactly,' said Nicky. 'If we make a few changes . . .'

Griff's eyes narrowed, as if he had just remembered that Nicky, not Chris, was supposed to be the target of his anger.

'OK, smart-mouth,' he said. 'You've picked the rest of the team – now, what about defence?'

There was another silence as others in the crowd did the maths and worked out that all four of the regular defenders were standing there, and that there were only three places left under Nicky's plan. A few of them gave Fuller more room.

Nicky was still confident he could win the argument by good logic alone. 'Well, there's nothing wrong with what Russell's been doing . . .' he began.

'Thanks a lot,' muttered Jones, which attracted a few chuckles from that end of the scrum.

'But we have to make changes if we move to a back three. The players have to be quick on their feet, because they have a lot more ground to cover...'

Griff could see the way this was going. 'What about height at the back?' he growled.

'Sure,' said Nicky, 'but think about what England did. One big centre back, and two wing backs capable of pushing up on the flanks. So, what we're looking at is...'

He paused for just a second. Griff and Fuller were very close. Both of them had worked out that they didn't qualify as nippy wing-backs.

'Perhaps the individuals don't matter,' Nicky concluded lamely.

That wasn't going to fly. Griff leant a little nearer.

'Spit it out,' he growled.

Chris could see that Nicky knew Griff wasn't going to be happy with what he heard. He tried the mental communication thing again. Just lie to him! he urged in his head.

But Nicky must have had his internal e-mail switched off, along with the rest of his brain. Chris knew he was about to spill the beans.

'OK, my money's on Doughnut on the left, one of you in the middle...'

Flicking his head, he indicated that the choice he was offering was between Griff and Fuller. Neither looked very happy. Chris was watching Griff closely, sure that the older boy was going to thump Nicky for suggesting he was only a 50/50 pick for the team. Instead, it was Fuller who reacted quickest.

Chris was annoyed he didn't see it coming. Fuller was the more naturally violent of the two.

Nicky, to his credit, guessed right. Ignoring Griff's threatening growl and upraised fist, he watched for Fuller to lose control and wasn't disappointed.

'You little jerk, Fiorentini!' Fuller yelled, and his fist came out of the crowd like a motorbike slicing through traffic. One second the road was safe enough, the next second, WHAM!!!

The best thing to be said about the next few seconds was that at least one of the selection problems was solved.

29

Five

— ⚽ —

The phone rang while Chris was getting changed.

His father answered it, but Chris instinctively knew it was for him. Sure enough, his father called upstairs.

'It's Bob James.'

Chris came down to the hall, pulling his baseball jacket over his United replica shirt, and dragging the fingers of one hand through his hair, as if his unruly mop might just lie flat for a change.

His father had changed too, and was pulling on his trainers. He tapped the glass of his watch to remind Chris of the time. They didn't have long if they were going to get to Star Park for the kick off.

'You and Bob teaming up a bit?' Chris's father asked, holding the receiver against his chest.

Chris had reached the bottom of the stairs. He pulled his own trainers out from under the hall table.

'A bit, I guess,' said Chris. 'It's a bit funny for him at school, knowing that he's only going to be there until Easter.'

His father nodded, understanding. All the same, he whispered at Chris to hurry, then handed the phone over and walked into the kitchen.

'Hi,' said Chris.

'I wish people wouldn't call me that,' Robert replied. Chris was caught out for a moment. Did James think Chris had called him 'hi'?

'I don't like "Bob",' said Bob, after a short pause. 'Or "Bobby".'

Chris tried to get his head together, wondering if his father had got it wrong and that it was someone else calling to talk *about* Bob.

'Can we start this again?' he pleaded.

30

'Oh, sorry . . .'

Chris was convinced it had to be James. The voice sounded a year or two younger than the rest of the guys, and it had a soft, southern accent, which made it sound unusual.

'Forget it,' said Chris. 'Is something wrong?'

'Wrong? Why do you think something's wrong?'

Chris sighed. He didn't really know Robert James very well yet, but he hoped his new team mate wasn't the kind of guy who rang up to complain about how people said his name.

'Look, I'm sorry,' said Chris, quietly. 'But I don't have long. I'm off to the game at Star Park.'

'Oh, right,' came the reply. 'I just wondered if you'd heard the news.'

Quite possibly, thought Chris. Depends what news you mean. In the meantime, he took a guess.

'You mean about Fuller going to hospital? Yeah; broken hand, and at least six weeks in plaster. He might not be able to play much before Christmas.'

Chris didn't know whether to laugh or cry about that. Nicky had seemed so unaware of the hostility he was causing it was just like he'd turned into Superman when Fuller threw the punch at him, moving so fast no-one could see him. Afterwards, Mac had been sure that Fuller had smashed his hand on Nicky's chin, not on the hard brick wall behind where Fiorentini had been sitting.

Fuller's hand had turned purple before their eyes, swelling up so that it looked like he was wearing lurid boxing gloves. He'd been whisked off to hospital while the rest of the team had been hauled off to see 'Andy' Cole. Given the choice between searing pain and several hours in casualty, or facing the head teacher for a grilling on what had gone down, Chris wondered if Fuller hadn't got off lightly.

Still, for once, Chris could rightly claim to have been more or less uninvolved. He'd been silent throughout the whole conversation, barring that one attempt to get the others to see sense. After all the times he'd wound up in deep trouble through something that Nicky had done, it was quite unusual for Chris to be able to look his head teacher in the eye and say that he hadn't been to blame at all.

All of which meant that Chris didn't feel any great need to go over events again just because Robert James had called up out of the blue. However, his concentration was soon switched back on again as he heard James's reply.

'No, not that – the break-in at the youth club at Riverside.'

'What?' cried Chris. His mind raced through all kinds of wild thoughts, from 'who cares?' to 'what did they take?' to 'how does Bob – or whatever he wants to be called – James know?'

Chris got the answers in a flood of excited conversation, during which his father reappeared from the kitchen with his keys in his hand, jacket over his shoulders and a 'come on!' look on his face.

'You know we've been living in Compton Street, renting a place until our new house is ready to move into?' James asked. Chris hurried him along with his mind. The telepathy actually worked better with James than it had with Nicky. 'OK. Well, you know Iain Walsh lives just four doors down from me, in the corner house with the red door?' Save the home decoration, Bobby, Chris screamed in his head, knowing quite well where the Riverside Colts' coach lived. 'OK. He came home about twenty minutes ago while I was helping my dad get some stuff he'd brought from our old house out of the car; you know, some books and clothing . . .' ARGGGHHH!!! Get to the point! 'Well, anyway, Walsh was talking to Sean Priest outside his house, and I overheard him say someone had broken into the youth club. It must have been about six o'clock.'

Chris broke the flow of Bob's report in case he got any more detail about time zones or the accuracy of his watch.

'What happened?'

'They smashed a window! Apparently, they cleaned out the slot machines, ripped the cloth on the pool table and generally knocked the place about.' Chris bit his lip angrily. He'd never used the youth club much, which was just a base for the football team as far as he was concerned. In fact, the last time he'd been there had been after the Colts had won the District Youth League just after Easter.

Chris felt a small twinge in the back of his skull. The bad news wasn't over yet.

'Walsh said they also took some cash and a laptop computer from the office,' James was continuing. 'But the worst thing is, they broke into the trophy cabinet in the main hall.'

Oh, oh.

'They've nicked the League trophy, Chris. They've nicked the shield you won.'

Eleven minutes into the game, Piet van Brost smacked a free kick past Ian Walker and United were in the lead. From that moment on, Spurs came at them with a vengeance and really should have got at least a draw, but Sheringham had one of those nights when everything he hit flew right into the keeper's belly, and Anderton was kept out of the game by some good defensive work by a new defender called Kemp, signed from non-League football over the summer.

It was a close thing, but Oldcester United survived. The win put them smack in the middle of the early Premiership table. It was too early to say that they couldn't be relegated straight back down to Nationwide League football, but United had made an OK start.

'I think we'll be in Europe next season,' grinned Nicky, satisfied with what he'd seen. As always, they were waiting for the crush to die down before they left their seats in the Easter Road Stand. Nicky was always supremely confident at the beginning of a new season. He'd made the same prediction two years ago when Oldcester went down.

Chris's father was more pessimistic. 'We need to do more at home than scrape one-nil wins to make the top five,' he said.

'Why?' asked Nicky. 'That's all Arsenal ever do.' Nicky, who had a mind for soccer trivia like a steel trap, knew that the Gunners had the evil eye over Oldcester. Five 1–0 wins in the last six meetings. Never mind that United had beaten them 5–0 in 1994/5 to even the goal difference out a bit, that still meant Arsenal had taken fifteen of eighteen points.

It had always been Oldcester's problem over the years. They never seemed to be able to manage late winners the way that Manchester United or Liverpool did, or to hang on to a narrow lead like Arsenal. Too many drawn games they should have won, and too many last-minute defeats. The local paper had calculated that United might have finished ten places higher in 1995/6 if football matches only lasted 80 minutes instead of 90.

33

But no-one bought season tickets at Star Park because they expected to win everything in sight. They came because, when all was said and done, supporting Oldcester was something that crept into the blood of the people who lived there. The first time local people pulled on a red and blue shirt, they were infected with a disease. The symptoms were simple. Against all logic, suffering Oldcester supporters started each season believing this could be *the* year when United would lift a Cup or finish in the top three. And they kept believing that until January or February.

Chris couldn't imagine what it must feel like to support one of the bigger clubs, one of those who genuinely had a chance of winning something each year. He thought it was probably rather boring.

Nicky was worse. If you didn't support your local team, you were some kind of traitor in Nicky's eyes. Chris remembered the way Nicky had gone on at Pete Baynham for supporting Leeds in the year United had gone down. Leeds had managed a trip to Wembley, but that still hadn't stopped Nicky getting on Baynham's case.

Chris took a moment to wonder how his former team mate was getting on up north. In the next moment, he found himself wondering who Bob James supported, and how long it would be before Nicky gave him the treatment.

From there, it was easy to go back to the break-in at the youth club. Chris felt a dark cloud gathering in his soul.

Lifting that trophy was the proudest moment in Chris's footballing life so far. Well, perhaps there had been some other equally solid moments, but winning the League in his first — and only — season with the Colts had been an achievement Chris would remember for years. When the game that clinched it was over, Sean Priest and the League secretary had presented them with the shield. Chris had got his hands on it right after the Colts' captain, Zak.

They'd gone back to the youth club for a bit of a celebration and the shield had been locked up in a glass cabinet Walsh had bought specially. Afterwards, there had been so many other things to think about — such as a one-off Cup challenge, and the return leg of an exchange visit to America. Chris hadn't thought much about winning the Championship. And now, of course, he wasn't a Colts' player anyway.

But hearing that the trophy had gone reminded Chris of that day, and how good it had felt. He imagined Zak and the others would be gutted.

'What's on your mind?' Nicky asked, nudging Chris with his elbow. 'This thing at Riverside?'

'I guess,' said Chris, turning to face Nicky (aware that his father was sitting right behind him). 'It's just bugging me a little, that's all.'

Nicky nodded, thoughtfully. Winning with the Colts was one of the few things they hadn't shared, since Nicky had been playing for another team. 'Maybe it'll turn up. I mean, what use is it to anyone else?'

There was that. It was just a plain wooden shield with a gilded silver mount and a plaque for the names of the winning teams. It hardly seemed worth the trouble of taking . . .

'What?' said Nicky, reading the look which was firming up on Chris's face.

Chris glared at him, and tried to indicate with his eyes that he didn't want his father to think he was taking a particular interest in the affair. Nicky — luckily — caught on just in time and made a big point of opening his programme to check some vital fact he hadn't read ten times already.

Chris used the next few minutes to try and get his mind straight. Some very curious thoughts were starting to swarm around in there. About the only thing he had clear in his brain by the time his father suggested they should head for the exit was that this curious run of ill-fortune that had gripped Spirebrook seemed to be catching.

Six

— ⚽ —

Chris moved in on goal like a big cat stalking prey. He was perfectly balanced, the ball just ahead of him. The keeper knew he could go left or right, and shoot with deadly skill from either foot. He came forward slowly, wary of being chipped, trying to make himself a big target, trying to make Chris commit himself one way or the other.

There! That was it, the first sign of what Chris was going to do. The striker was still twenty metres out, but he had moved the ball out on to his slightly stronger right foot. Chris was going to try and beat him from there.

Russell stopped moving forward, and came up on to his toes. He was a good keeper, the kind who gets into a striker's head and works out what is coming before the other player knows himself. He was medium height, slender and wiry, very quick both in his reactions and movement.

One-on-one, Russell Jones believed he had a better than even chance. Nothing would give him more satisfaction than to beat out this shot of Chris's and keep his afternoon's unbeaten rec–

Russell realised he'd been suckered just a moment too late. As Chris brought his foot forward, it wasn't to shoot but to steer the ball to the left. Chris accelerated quickly, moving just wide of the penalty spot. As quickly as he could, Russell scampered across the goal to try and smother the ball, but Chris had him cold. The ball was fired in low, under Russell's body as he hit the floor.

'Good, good!!' yelled the coach from the touchline. 'OK, next!'

Chris circled round to the side at a run, slowing gradually. Once he was walking along the sideline, he looked back to see Russell was already back on his goal-line waiting for the next player to run at him. Jones just had time to flash him a smile of congratulations before he had to take guard again.

'Nice,' said Sean as Chris came close. 'I was just about to shout at you for rushing things when you pulled that stunt.'

'I've given up trying to beat Russell from twenty metres out,' said Chris. 'He's stopped too many of them recently.'

Sean Priest nodded, scratched his beard and watched the next player coming in. It was Rory Blackstone, another one of the Colts who had come up to join the United youth squad. His face was split with a wide grin. This kind of one-on-one thing wasn't playing to Rory's strengths, but he gave it his best shot, hitting the kind of long shot that Chris had been bluffing he would try. Russell slammed against the grass as he beat it out with his wrists.

'Don't rush it, Rory!' Sean called. 'Get in closer!'

Rory signalled back to Priest that he understood, turning away to walk to the far sideline. He was still grinning broadly, but then it took a lot more than one missed chance to throw Rory out of a good mood.

'He got eight goals from eight headers earlier; he can afford to smile' Chris said, mostly to himself. He was remembering the drill they had followed earlier, with the coaches firing in crosses from both sides. Chris had managed seven, smacking the third chance high over the bar.

'He had a good five-a-side yesterday too,' said Sean. 'He's a lot quicker than he looks. He just has to start believing in himself a bit more. Half the time, I get the impression Rory still thinks being here is a big mistake, and that he's going to wake up soon and find it was all a dream.'

Chris grinned and watched as Russell narrowly missed stopping a shot from one of the fifteen-year-olds. Both he and Sean clapped the effort.

The trials at the beginning of the summer seemed a long time ago now – at least to Chris. The memory of how frightened he had been of failing to make the cut had faded. All he could remember now was how determined he had been on the day, and how good it had felt when Sean had told him that he had won his place at United.

Chris had never wanted anything else.

Without meaning to, he touched the club badge in the centre of his chest. Out on the edge of his mind, there were other dreams: about playing for United in the Premiership; about being a full-time professional. He and Nicky had talked about what it would be like to step out on to Star Park's lush green grass in front of 25,000 fans. In Nicky's imagination, the games were always vital FA Cup ties or do-or-die six-pointers to clinch the Championship. Nicky had dreams of pulling on an England shirt, playing in the European Championships or the World Cup. Chris's dreams rarely went so far.

Just as he was thinking of Nicky, Chris realised that it was his team mate's turn to run the shoot-out against Russell. With a relaxed, easy first step, Nicky took the ball across halfway and closed in on Jones's goal. His pace was steady, almost cautious.

Russell wasn't taken in by that. He knew Nicky was one of the quickest players United had found, capable of an electric change of pace. Russell had seen plenty of Nicky's tricks before. He came just a few steps off his line to narrow the angle until Nicky was almost into the area, then he took off quickly, hoping to close Nicky down before he could think up some stunt.

Too late. Chris realised that Nicky must have had this trick in mind from the moment he stepped up to take his turn. He hit the brakes, like he'd reached the end of a leash. He trapped the ball under his right foot, dragged it back and flicked it up knee-high on his toe. Russell was still four or five metres away, closing quickly. Nicky dinked the ball over his head.

Russell had no chance to stop, never mind get back. All he could do was slow down a little, turn and watch as the ball sailed over his head.

The ball cleared Russell by several metres. Unfortunately for Nicky, it also went about three metres over the bar. By then Russell had almost collided with him, and they both stumbled back, laughing.

Chris was laughing too. The only person who didn't seem to find it particularly funny was Sean Priest (although Chris was sure there had been a short smile on his face too).

'Nicky! What was that supposed to be?!'

Nicky looked hurt, although the flashing grin was still in place.

'I tried to chip him, Sean,' he said. Russell raised his eyebrows, as if to admit that he'd stood no chance of reaching the attempt.

'Think you'd be able to get away with a drag back like that in a real game?' Priest demanded, walking on to the pitch. 'You should have tried going round him, or slotting the ball to his right – Russell was showing too much of his near post.'

'I didn't notice . . .' Nicky said, and the way he said it suggested that he thought this was a good thing to say . . .

'Then try looking!' yelled Sean. Nicky recoiled as if he'd been hit. The grin vanished.

No-one knew quite what to say. Priest blew his whistle to bring the practice to an end, even though there were a few guys still to take their last run on goal. The others walked off towards the changing rooms, leaving Nicky and Russell on the pitch facing Priest's wrath. Chris remained where he was. The four of them were soon the only ones left.

'Go and get changed, Russell,' Priest demanded. The keeper moved off slowly, as if he was stuck to Nicky with glue. He was still only a few metres away when Priest started getting stuck into Fiorentini.

'Nicky, have you any idea where you are?'

Nicky looked around very quickly, as if there was a small chance that he'd been transported to another planet while he was watching Sean. That had to be the only explanation for a question like that. Nicky knew he was lousy at geography, but even he couldn't get lost while standing still. No, they were still at the London Road training ground.

That was too obvious an answer, so Nicky didn't say anything.

'You've been coming to practice with the youth team – what? – for three weeks now,' Priest continued. 'I expected you to treat it as a bit of a laugh for the first couple of weeks. After all, it's quite a thing just getting here, isn't it?'

'I guess,' said Nicky, quietly. He had no idea where this was leading.

'But it's time to move on,' Priest said, some of the anger draining from his voice. He was standing back a little from Nicky, so that he wasn't towering over him. It let the two of them look each other in the eye.

'What do you mean?' asked Nicky.

Priest thought for a moment before he answered, scratching his beard. Chris listened hard from the touchline as the coach explained.

39

'You're a good player, Nicky. You've got good speed, excellent ball control . . . and the understanding between you and Chris is really spooky.'

Nicky's lips curled for a fraction of a second, as if he was going to grin and see it had been a joke all along. Sean's cool blue eyes were still perfectly serious, though. Nicky stifled his laughter in his throat. The word 'but' was a racing certainty to be the next thing he heard.

'But you have to decide how far that talent is going to take you. If getting into the youth squad is all you want, if this is as far as your ambition goes, then you're actually wasting everybody's time.'

Chris knew Priest couldn't possibly believe that. Nicky's dreams were always larger than anyone else's. Priest had to be trying to draw Nicky out . . .

Nicky didn't see it so clearly. 'No!' he protested. 'This is just the beginning! I want to be a professional football player.'

Priest actually smiled this time. 'Good,' he replied. 'Then you want to start acting like one. And that means taking practice seriously. A laugh and a joke is fine, but you have to prove that you can do the work as well.'

Nicky gulped. The sessions at United were the most physically taxing exercise he had ever had (and not just him; after the first session, Chris almost didn't have the energy to walk out to his father's car). Was Sean suggesting things were going to get worse?

Priest read his mind. 'That's right, Nicky. What we've done so far is just the beginning. After a season training with us, you won't recognise your body. And the physical side is just one thing. I want to get into your mind.'

He stepped closer and picked up the practice ball. 'Let's try again. I'll go in goal this time.'

He rolled the ball back towards the halfway line, then turned his back on Nicky and marched towards the goal. Nicky hesitated. He looked over to where Chris was squatting on his haunches on the sideline. Chris shrugged.

'Yeah, right,' muttered Nicky to himself. 'Go for it.'

He jogged back and collected the ball. When Priest signalled he was ready, Nicky bit his lip, thought through his options and set off.

'Go on, Nicky!' he heard Chris shout.

He moved in steadily, a little quicker than he had against Russell. At first he came straight forward, but then as Priest took the first steps off his line, Nicky slipped a little more to the right, hoping to confuse Priest about the angles.

Priest was no goalkeeper. He was just a shade heavier than in his days playing as a mean defender for United (among others), and a touch slower too. Nicky fancied his chances going round the coach.

He increased his speed, then gave a kind of hitch kick as he reached the edge of the box, trying to push the ball into space ahead of him, wide of Priest's advance.

Priest dived to his left as Nicky and the ball went round him. Nicky hurdled over the coach's arm, chased the ball down and struck it towards goal. The angle, though, had ended up just a little tight. The ball hit the side netting.

Nicky groaned, looking back quickly to where Priest had fallen. The coach was picking himself up, having watched the ball go wide.

'Better,' said Priest.

Nicky was stunned. 'I missed,' he reminded Priest.

Priest didn't seem that worried. 'Tell me,' he said. 'Why didn't you try that drag-back chip thing with me?'

'You'd see it coming,' said Nicky.

'Aside from that.'

Nicky pushed back a strand of his hair. 'Well, it'd never work, would it? I mean, you're taller than Russell . . .'

Priest nodded as if some great point had been made, then waited to see if Nicky had got it.

'So . . .' Nicky began.

Priest put him out of his misery. 'You said you wanted to become a professional footballer. Well, in the Premiership, believe it or not, the goalkeepers are more my size than Russell's.'

A light came on behind Nicky's dark eyes.

'Ah!' he said.

'Yeah?' asked Priest, making sure that Nicky really was up to speed. 'You understand? There's no point teaching you how to beat other kids your age, even if that is all you get to play against for now. We have to teach you the skills that will let you beat Seaman or Schmeichel or someone like that.'

Nicky really had got the point now. Or part of it at least.

'So, what you're saying is . . .'

'What I'm saying is, cut out the fancy stuff. If you want to chip the goalkeeper, fine. But no showing off. And don't make up your mind what to do before the move has started. Use your brain, Nicky. Use your eyes and your brain.'

Chris figured the lecture was just about over, and started to wander closer. However, Priest stepped back and fetched the ball from where it had fallen, and rolled it back towards the centre circle once again.

'So, try again, Nicky.'

Nicky opened his mouth as if he was going to say that Priest had made his point, but even he knew better than that. He ran his hand through his hair, gritted his teeth and trotted back to where the ball had rolled to a stop.

'Use your eyes and brain, Nicky!' called Priest as Nicky came forward. 'Find the most certain way to ensure that the ball ends up in the net, not the flashiest.'

There was a flat, concentrated look on Nicky's face that Chris hadn't seen before. He stopped where he was, watching closely. Nicky was moving forward quickly, angling to the right again. In fact, Chris noted, he was moving even wider this time. Chris found himself thinking 'this will never work'. If he tried to go round Priest again, the angle would be even tighter.

Nicky kept the ball close, dribbling with his usual skill and control. Priest came off his line as steadily as before, shutting off the best shooting angles, but not leaving himself open to be chipped. Only when Nicky stormed into the penalty area did Priest commit himself, rushing out quickly.

Nicky let him get very close. Too close, thought Chris. There was no chance to lob Priest now, and little chance Nicky could get round the coach. Was he going to try and slot it under the keeper at the last second?

At that moment, Nicky hit the ball at last. Only it wasn't a shot. Nicky side-footed the ball across the box, to where Chris was standing. Priest threw out a foot, but he didn't get within a metre of the ball.

It rolled across to Chris, who saw the look on Nicky's face. He knew Nicky had played the pass deliberately. Chris stroked the ball into the open goal.

Priest had lost his balance and ended up on his backside. He looked back over his shoulder to the ball rolling into the net.

Chris couldn't read the expression on his face at first. Finally, though, Priest hauled himself off the ground and pounded Nicky on the back of the shoulders with his hand.

'Yes, very funny,' he grinned.

'I used my eyes,' Nicky said, in case Priest had missed it.

'Yes, sure,' said Priest, and he pushed Nicky towards the goal to fetch the ball. 'Very clever. As punishment, you can collect up all the practice balls before you get changed.'

'Aw, man!' wailed Nicky.

Priest's attention was already switching to his next victim.

'And you can help, Stephens,' he said.

Chris flinched, taken completely by surprise.

'Me? What did I do wrong?'

'You were a mile offside,' replied Priest.

43

Seven

⚽

The next few days passed peacefully enough. The training sessions with the youth team were tough, but Chris started to feel his fitness was improving with each week that passed. Nicky settled down, taking practice more seriously. They were beginning to get used to the rest of the guys in their age group as well, and the nucleus of a good team was coming together.

One thing that was going to take a lot of getting used to, though, was that the youth team played so few competitive matches. In fact, so far this season they hadn't played a single game against anyone other than each other.

Also there were all kinds of Football Association regulations that had to be obeyed: rules about keeping records of the amount of time spent in coaching sessions, about registration and a whole load of other stuff. Chris kept his book – the record book of all his training sessions and other football coaching – up to date and made sure that he paid close attention to any 'important' announcements made by Priest or one of the other coaches.

Nicky, though, found it all very frustrating. On Friday, he mentioned it to Priest for the tenth time.

'When are we going to have a game against another club?'

Priest turned to face Nicky. The rest of the squad – all 134 of them – had broken up into small groups to work on their fitness. Nicky was suffering with a small twinge in his leg, so he was doing some light work with Sean.

'I told you, Nicky – we're entertaining Aston Villa next week.'

Nicky's face registered a kind of hurt disappointment, as if he'd hoped that the news would have been more interesting.

'I know about that, sure,' said Nicky, 'but when are we going to play some proper games?'

Priest sighed, and tried to get Nicky involved in the reflex exercises they were working on. All the boys had been given a full fixture list for the season, and, after each training session, Sean made sure they knew what was coming up. However, it was clear that Nicky was still waiting for an answer, as if he couldn't quite believe what he had read.

'It is a proper game, Nicky. At least, you'd better take it seriously.'

Nicky wasn't going to fall into that trap.

'Yeah, of course, but what I mean is . . .' He stopped, trying to find the right words for what he wanted to say. 'It's just that none of the games you've fixed up are what I'd call *real* games. I mean, we're not in any kind of League or anything. That's what I don't understand.'

Just along from where Priest and Nicky were talking, Chris pulled up from some sprint training. Resting his hands on his knees, he tried to fill his lungs with air. As he straightened up, he could overhear the conversation between Nicky and the United coach.

'Nicky, how many more times are we going to have to go through this? The point of the School of Excellence programme is to provide you with the best *training* possible, not to have you chasing around in some competitive League. You can get all that playing for your school, so what's the point in still more games? The emphasis here is on coaching and developing your skills.'

'But . . .'

Priest choked off Nicky's interruption. 'It isn't that you won't play matches for United, it's just that we don't play them week in, week out, and we don't worry about results, League tables or Championships. The only exceptions are the National Youth Teams Cup in the spring and a few one-off events.'

'We don't play any real matches at all, except for a couple of Cup ties?'

Priest was almost beside himself with frustration, explaining this to Nicky for what felt like the tenth time.

'There are friendlies all through the season, Nicky. Like the game against Villa next weekend. It's just that the rules are a bit different. We play 30 minutes each way, with free substitution, and no-one bothers with the result.'

Nicky laughed loudly. The only way to make Fiorentini

ignore the result of a game was to blindfold him and lock him in a box while it was played.

'I don't get it,' he said. 'I bet it's not like this at Manchester United.'

Priest wasn't in the mood for another argument with Nicky, or he might have exploded. As it was, he had to speak through gritted teeth as he told Nicky that United had to obey the same rules as everyone else, and those rules were that boys signed up with League clubs weren't supposed to play any competitive games, except for their school.

Nicky was about to ask what would happen at Easter, when he and Chris and the others would be at United full time. Did it mean they wouldn't –

He never got to finish the question. Priest remembered something important he had to tell one of the other coaches on the other side of the ground, and set off at a run. Nicky decided to moan to Chris instead.

'Does it make any sense to you?' he asked.

Chris shrugged. It did seem a little odd, doing all this training and yet playing so few matches, but he understood the point. Oldcester United were trying to bring young players on gradually, not wear them out before they were seventeen. He wondered if he should try to explain this to Nicky once again, but realised he didn't have any appetite for an argument either.

'No,' he replied.

Nicky gestured with his hands to show how crazy he thought it all was, then put his arm round Chris's shoulders so that he could whisper in his ear.

'If we're not going to be in a League with this lot, it makes it even more important that we get things right at Spirebrook.'

Chris nodded. In a way, he actually did agree with Nicky this time.

'We have to get Griff and the others to see sense,' Nicky continued. 'Will you back me up at school on Monday?'

If there had been any way to avoid answering a question like that, Chris would have thought of it. His mind was racing like a Formula 1 car. In the end, though, he just couldn't wriggle out of it.

'Let's see how things turn out,' he said.

Nicky grinned, pretty sure this meant 'yes'. Chris was about to explain to his team mate that it wouldn't do any good if the team split into two camps, but just then 'The Terminator', the toughest guy on Sean's coaching staff, suggested Chris could do a few sit-ups instead of gassing with Nicky.

Nicky shrugged and walked away, limping just that little bit harder than he had all day.

That Saturday, Oldcester managed a point at Goodison Park. Chris followed the game on Radio Five.

It sounded like a good game, with plenty of chances for both sides. It was just the sort of contest United normally lost in the last minute, but this time they finished off the game in style, with a couple of late chances to pinch it.

Chris turned off the radio, feeling pretty good. Oldcester were having a better season than he had hoped for. Too many teams coming up from the First Division got creamed in the Premiership. Oldcester looked like they belonged there. The next hurdle to overcome was a home game against Manchester United next Saturday. It would be a sell-out.

Chris wondered if Oldcester would take revenge for the 5–0 thrashing they'd had off United the year they went down. Up in Chris's wardrobe – getting a bit small to wear – was a Manchester United shirt, signed by all the team. It had been given to Chris by Peter Schmeichel, the United keeper, after he and Nicky had gone up to Old Trafford for a look around.

Schmeichel had left the shirt at Star Park on the night they walloped Oldcester. As well as the autographs, there was a PS written near the bottom.

It read '5–0. Ho, ho!'

It was a private ambition of Chris's to give Peter a shirt in return one day, with the same joke written on it as a PPS. It would be even better if Schmeichel could actually be in goal when it happened.

Thanks to his new job at a computer superstore, Chris's father had to work late every other Saturday, making up for the time he took off to see United's home games. Alone in the house, having tackled his chores and homework, Chris was wondering what to do for the next couple of hours. He thought about going round to Nicky's, but the prospect didn't interest him as much as it normally did. If he rolled up at the

Fiorentini house at teatime, Nicky's mother would make sure that he never wanted to eat pizza again.

In addition, Nicky would only be interested in talking about his 'big idea' and how they could persuade (a) Flea, (b) Griff and (c) the rest of the 'Brook team that the big idea would turn their season around in an instant. Just recently, Nicky was like a broken record on that particular subject. Chris really wasn't in the mood for any more of it.

So – what to do instead? Chris had just about decided that an hour or so on the Internet might be favourite when the phone rang.

Chris picked it up and said 'hi'. This time, he recognised the voice at the other end right away.

'Chris?' it asked.

'Hey, Bob,' said Chris. As soon as the words left his lips he remembered that Bob actually didn't want to be called Bob. The only trouble was that he hadn't got around to saying what name he would be happy with instead.

There was a short hesitation at the other end of the line.

'Good result today, huh?'

'Yeah,' said Chris, assuming Bob was talking about United. The conversation halted there, as if United's point at Everton was the only possible topic. It took Chris a moment to remember Bob had rung him, which presumably meant there was a reason for the call.

'So . . .' he began, searching for a clue as to what they were supposed to be talking about.

'Can I talk to you for a minute?' Bob asked. Chris took a deep breath, fighting the temptation to tell him that talking was just what they were doing.

'I guess,' he said. 'What's the problem, Bob?'

Once again, it was almost like *hearing* Bob flinch at the other end of the line. Chris decided that he'd better get this name thing straight right now.

'Look, I'm sorry – I mean, I know you told me you don't like being called Bob. It's just that . . . well . . . what do you want to be called?'

'My friends – I mean my old friends – used to call me Rob. Or Robbie.'

That was it? Chris couldn't believe it.

'OK,' he said, slowly. 'I think we could remember that.'

'Like Robbie Fowler,' Bob – Robbie – explained, as if Chris could possibly have missed the point.

'OK.'

'Or RJ. That's what my dad calls me sometimes.'

'OK.' Chris could feel himself starting to go numb. Chris was starting to realise that if he ever had to talk to James on the phone again, his brain would start dribbling out through his ears. He glanced at his watch. Still only five to five. It felt like he'd been on the phone for hours.

Out of nowhere, a thought popped into his head.

'Actually, Russell Jones is an RJ as well. I mean, those are his initials – no-one actually calls him that. It might be a bit confusing, you know? Like, when Russell first started playing for Spirebrook, we had another guy called Jones in midfield. Alistair Jones – do you know him? He doesn't play much now. He's into computers and stuff.'

Chris's mouth continued to operate on auto-pilot, spewing out this drivel, while his brain was shrieking NO!! He knew why he was talking like this; one of Chris's pet hates were those long silences you sometimes get when you talk to people on the phone. Chris always tried to fill the gaps.

He got the impression this time, though, that he was gabbling on like this to prevent James from talking instead.

'Uh, sure . . .' he heard James break in. 'Listen, I need to have a word with you.' What? thought Chris, desperately. You mean this isn't enough?

James realised at the same moment that this didn't make sense. 'I mean in person. Me and Mac. We both want to talk to you about something.'

'Mac?' asked Chris, completely taken by surprise.

'Yeah. He said we could meet round at his house. Would that be OK?'

'Um . . .' stalled Chris, but he didn't manage to think of an excuse quickly enough, so he followed this up with 'sure'.

'OK. I'll see you there in twenty minutes,' said James, and with that the phone went dead.

'What? Toni – ?' Chris was still opening his mouth to try and get out of the arrangement when he realised he was talking to a dialling tone. He put the phone down and shook his head, trying to clear it of the mental garbage it had filled up with in the last few minutes.

Was Robbie James the most boring person in the world, or what?

'I'm going out, mum,' said James, pulling on his jacket.

'OK,' his mother called from the kitchen. 'Don't be late.'

'No problem. I'm going to Donald MacIntyre's house — I've left his number by the phone.'

'Was that who you were speaking to just now?'

'Uh, no,' said James, pausing at the door. 'That was Chris Stephens, the guy at football I was telling you about.'

'Oh. Right. Yes. The one you said was pretty clever, right?'

James quickly thought through the conversation he'd just had with Chris Stephens. He couldn't believe what a jerk the older boy had been.

'I don't think so, mum,' he said. 'I must have been thinking of someone else . . .'

Eight

Chris hadn't been counting on going out that evening, but that was just the beginning of the surprises waiting for him.

For example, the only reason he had spent the afternoon at home alone was because he hadn't been able to face the idea of listening to Nicky trying to take over Spirebrook's football team. Chris had no time for all the politics in sport; as far as he was concerned, the manager picked the team, the captain led them on the field, and that was that. He'd never understood how it was that a bunch of directors who'd never played the game could end up firing a decent manager just because a few results went the wrong way.

Fortunately, that had never been the way Oldcester United operated. Dennis Lively, the mountain-sized chairman of the club, liked to say he never fired a manager – although a few had slipped away by 'mutual agreement'. For the last few years, the manager had been Phil Parkes, the ex-QPR, West Ham and England keeper. It had been a strange choice in the beginning, but Lively said he liked having a goalkeeper in charge.

'He hates letting anything go past him,' the chairman had told the press. Parkes had done a pretty good job, too. Even though Oldcester had found themselves relegated in Parkes' fourth season, Lively had stuck with him, and United had bounced right back.

Chris believed in sticking with people who didn't mess you around. That was why he was struggling with Nicky's determination to challenge Griff's captaincy and Flea's handling of the team. The same combination had worked well a couple of years before; a few duff games didn't change that.

Chris was thinking about all this when he left his house, having scribbled a note to tell his father where he was going, in

51

case he didn't get back first. He felt guilty for avoiding Nicky. In fact, he almost went back inside to give him a call.

Out in the street, Chris was distracted by the weather. The afternoon had been OK, but as Chris walked to the end of his street, turning on to the main road that ran between Spirebrook and the city centre, he realised it was turning quite chilly. By the time he reached the turning he took towards school each morning, dark storm clouds were rolling down from the north.

He had visions of getting caught in a downpour. For a brief moment he thought about turning back, but instead he hurried his step. In the same instant, the traffic on the main road stopped at the pelican crossing. Chris instinctively crossed to the other side and took the side street that led towards school.

It was marginally quicker this way. He could skip over the wall by the school's front gate, cross the playing fields and nip out through one of half a dozen gaps in the back fence along the new road. It wasn't likely anyone would be around to see him break the school's rules and it might just save him thirty seconds out in the rain.

Life's like that. The smallest decisions can sometimes have big effects. Chris hadn't consciously decided to take the short-cut until the crossing stopped the traffic and he felt the cold wind of the approaching storm on his back. This was maybe the second time in his life he had taken this route towards Church Hill, where Nicky and Mac both lived.

After today, he would never take that route again.

It wasn't far from Nicky's house to Mac's — just a short haul up the hill and into Sailing Ship View, the highest point in Spirebrook, and the poshest. Mac's father was a surveyor for Oldcester City Council. His mum owned her own business. The three of them lived in this big old house, with a gate across the drive and trees in the front garden. At the back, the house overlooked the river and fields. One of Nicky's sisters had once had a pony that she used to ride out that way; Nicky thought it must be pretty cool to just be able to hop over your back fence and be out in the country.

Not that he was jealous of Mac in any way. The Fiorentinis

lived in a big house too. The difference was, they had to. In addition to Nicky, his parents, his grandmother, his sisters and his baby brother, there were always other people staying at the house. For some time, a cousin who worked at a TV studio in the city had occupied the spare room. She was supposed to have been moving out for months, but nothing happened. More recently, a girlfriend of one of Uncle Fabian's sons, who was studying at the university just down the road, had moved in as well, sharing the same room.

The pair of them had been pestering Nicky about a trade. They were after his large bedroom at the back of the house. It would be nice, Nicky thought as he wandered into Sailing Ship View, to be able to jump over the back fence and get away from them all sometimes. When Mac had called him (right after James had called Chris, as it turned out), he'd been glad of an excuse to get out. But he couldn't live in a street as quiet as this. It would drive him nuts.

Nicky went up to the door and rang the bell. Mac let him in. Bob James was already there, he saw. To Nicky's surprise, so was Jazz.

'Hey Jazz,' he called across the room as soon as he saw the tall, dark-skinned midfielder. The group had gathered in the conservatory at the back of the house. Dark clouds rolled by overhead, but the coming storm looked like it might skirt by Spirebrook and dump its weather on Blackmoor instead.

There were biscuits and cans of drink. Not quite the spread his mum would have laid out, but Nicky decided he could last out the hour or so until tea. He cracked the tab on a can of Virgin Cola, and sat down beside Jazz.

'Why are you here?' he asked, digging his mate in the ribs.

'I told my dad I had to pick up some books for homework,' Jazz replied, looking around at the others shiftily. He hated telling even the smallest untruth to his father. In fact, he hadn't agreed to come over until Mac remembered there was a geography textbook in his bedroom he had borrowed from Jazz about nine months before . . .

'Who's watching the shop?' asked Nicky.

'My sister,' groaned Jazz. 'And she's bound to make a mess of things, so I'd like to get back pretty soon.'

'Suits me,' said Nicky, with a glance round at the others. 'I have to be home before seven anyway. So, who are we waiting for besides Chris?'

'No-one,' said Mac, with a glance at his watch. 'I couldn't get in touch with Russell.' No wonder, there was no phone at the Jones's house.

Nicky thought through the rest of the team. 'Did you try Phil Lucas?'

Mac nodded. 'He didn't want to come. I don't think he's comfortable with talking about the team behind Griff's back.' Mac's grimace showed he was fairly uncomfortable with the idea too. 'I know he and Fuller don't get on . . .' he added, in case anyone got the idea Chris's strike partner was on the other side.

'Just Chris, then,' said Nicky, nodding as if he was satisfied with five for and one abstaining as a first head count.

'I hope he's not long,' muttered Mac, with another look at the time.

'He'll be here,' said Nicky, confidently. 'We can always rely on Chris.'

Mac knew. He was counting on it. With Chris there to balance Nicky's wild ideas, maybe this would seem less like a bunch of traitors plotting a coup and more like what Mac had hoped it would be – a chance to discuss how they could get the others in the team to agree to some changes.

'Hey, Bob!' smiled Nicky, gesturing with his head in James's direction. The younger boy twitched a little, but smiled back.

'Good result today, eh?' said Nicky, turning away to face the others. He rubbed his hands with satisfaction.

'Chelsea –' started Jazz, before Nicky cut him short.

'Looks to me like we could easily have a place in Europe next season,' Nicky continued, turning his voice up a little to drown Jazz out. He hadn't forgiven Jazz for adopting Chelsea as his favourite team. That kind of thing was worse than being a traitor in Nicky's eyes.

'I hear you and Chris have season tickets,' said James from the side.

Nicky looked back round at the younger boy, then changed the way he was sitting, fed up of pivoting back and forth to keep all the others in view.

'That's right,' he said. 'Do you go?'

James shrugged. 'My brother and I might go to a few games,' he replied, 'when he comes up to visit.'

Nicky didn't ask when that might be. He had no reason to want to understand the workings of Bob James's family.

'We get spare tickets sometimes,' Nicky announced. 'You know, when some of the people we sit near can't get to a game, or whatever.' Jazz and Mac looked at each other, and both of them tried to hide the smiles that crossed their faces. Nicky made this announcement to just about everyone he met. If they all took him up on his 'generous' offer, he'd fill the whole Easter Road Stand.

James didn't seem so keen to swallow the bait, however.

'I'm not sure . . .' he said.

'What?' demanded Nicky. 'Have you got problems with your family as well?' This was a reference to Jazz, whose father had never allowed him to go to a proper League match. Despite all Chris and Nicky's pressure, Jazz had only visited Star Park for a friendly and on the day Spirebrook had played there in the County Schools Cup Final.

'I'm not sure Chris likes me that much,' James muttered, so low that Nicky didn't hear him properly. He didn't add that his opinion of the striker had changed a great deal after their earlier phone call.

'Where is Chris, anyway?' asked Mac, impatiently.

'It's taking him long enough,' agreed Jazz.

Mac decided to take a look out the front. Church Hill was steep, but it ran as straight as an arrow. From the end of his road, Mac could look down all the way to the supermarket. The odds that Chris would come from any other direction were slender indeed.

Nicky was going to wait until Chris arrived, or at least until Mac got back, before he started outlining exactly how he wanted to play things with Griff and Flea, but the biscuits ran out and his attention started to drift.

'Here's what I've been thinking,' he said. The other two looked at him, their faces a mixture of interest and worry. Robert James might have been at Spirebrook for only a few weeks, but even he knew that when he heard the words 'Nicky' and 'thinking' in the same sentence, it was time to worry.

'Now that Fuller's out for a few weeks, I'm pretty sure

55

we've won the argument about playing three at the back.'

'I'm not so sure,' said Jazz. 'After school on Friday, they were talking about moving Marsh back alongside Griff, or asking Alistair Jones if he'd —'

Nicky cut him off sharply. The last thing he wanted to hear was someone else's plan (just in case it was a good one, thought Jazz).

'But that's not going to work, is it?' He didn't allow anyone to answer. 'And besides, this isn't about finding someone to cover for Fuller, it's about changing the team. A five-man midfield would work better. We want three guys at the back who can cut it. Packham — yeah, he's probably OK at left back. But Griff's too slow and Bruise is — well —'

Jazz had a look on his face that was approaching horror. He was quite keen on trying the new formation — he figured it would make playing in midfield even more exciting. Although Jazz had a reputation for being a soft tackler, he actually enjoyed getting stuck in when he could. And he wasn't scared of the extra work in the new scheme either.

But what did worry him was the idea of telling Griff he didn't have a place in this new plan. Griff was the captain! He was also bad-tempered (although not as bad as Fuller) and the kind who held a grudge for years.

Up until now, Jazz hadn't realised just how far Nicky was prepared to go. Suddenly, he felt really nervous about what he was hearing.

'But who . . .?' he spluttered. Then it struck him. Why else was Bob James here?

'Think about it,' said Nicky. 'He's good enough to play for Oldcester, so he has to be good enough for us.'

Jazz couldn't argue with that. And it would be pointless to remind Nicky that James *was* playing for Spirebrook already, in the junior team. All the same, Jazz felt he had to try.

'But he's only Year —'

Nicky cut him off yet again, as if he was getting used to guessing which argument Jazz was going to try before Jazz had worked it out himself.

'Yeah, yeah. But there's no rule says you have to be a *minimum* age to play in the seniors. Look at Mac, he's a year younger than us, but no-one's against him moving up to play for the upper school XI.'

Jazz didn't remember it being quite that cut and dried, but he didn't want to be deflected. At the same time, it was really awkward talking about this with Bob James just sitting there, looking embarrassed.

'But he'll be up against guys three, four years older . . .'

Nicky frowned and shook his head, the answer to that obstacle at the front of his mind.

'You haven't seen the way we train at United,' he explained smugly. 'Chris can tell you; half the sessions we're all pitched in together. The other night, Sean had us running American-style shoot-outs. The keepers were rotated round so that one minute you were going up against some kid of nine or ten, the next against someone fifteen. And that's leaving out how often you have to take on Sean or the Terminator.' He looked across at James. 'Am I right?'

Jazz rested his elbows on his knees, steepling his long fingers together and staring past them. His eyes were burning with an intense light as he tried to get his head round what Nicky was proposing. Every objection he had raised was being shot down in flames. But it just didn't *feel* right.

'Is Chris with you on this?' Jazz asked, looking up at last.

'You can ask him yourself,' smiled Nicky, then his lips flattened out when he remembered that, of course, Jazz couldn't do that just yet. 'Where is he anyway?' he snapped.

Right on cue, Mac ran back into the conservatory.

'Hey, guys,' he said in a rush. 'You want to come see this.'

Nicky's broad grin returned. 'What? Chris wearing something dopey?'

Mac didn't laugh. 'No,' he said. 'I think the school's on fire.'

Nine

⚽

Chris moved quickly as he jumped up on to the front garden wall of the house immediately outside the school gates. He'd never had to face the owner himself, but it was a well-known fact among the 'Brookers that the guy used to go mental when people so much as sat on his wall. There were some sad, rusty strands of barbed wire hanging down the fence to prove there were other people as well who thought kids didn't belong in school when the gates were closed.

Most of the wire must have been put up before the war, however, and it had long since become useless. A security firm had their logo on a plastic card fixed to the gate, but their visits were so rare, that the guy in the corner house had called the police the last time they turned up, thinking they were breaking in . . .

Chris kept his eyes fixed on the guy's front door until he had safely vaulted the fence. Chris landed lightly on the grass inside the school grounds. He was just thinking that it was an odd thing to be bunking *into* school when the smell hit his nostrils.

It was a sharp, bitter, smoky smell. At first Chris wondered if the caretaker was burning leaves, but it was too early for that. The guy from the council who mowed the lawns (a nice name for some rolling weed beds between the buildings) wasn't a likely candidate either.

So . . .

Chris looked around. Now that he was concentrating, he could see a small twist of smoke spiralling up from behind Block 2 (the only name the students ever used for the Tennyson building, one of the three ugly, two-floored class-room blocks). There was an area there called the Quad, a paved courtyard bounded by the dining hall and Blocks 2 and 3. The office of the head of upper school (a guy named Mr

Palmer), the staff common room and the sixth form study room were side-by-side portacabins on the fourth side (a fact which had never amused the sixth form).

This wasn't country Chris came to very often. Chris had been through the Quad before, but the older boys regarded it as their personal patch, and Chris had no interest in running foul of the A-level brigade.

It wasn't likely that any of them were here today, however. And even if it were them, a few fags weren't going to make a column of smoke like that.

Chris's instincts were humming. Trouble. He could smell it a mile off. And right now it smelled of fire.

Chris followed the path from the gates into the centre of the school complex, then turned between the boiler room and the dining block. He couldn't see anything ahead of him, but there were voices, echoing off the walls, whooping with excitement. Chris moved a little quicker, but he tried to stay light on his feet so that no-one would hear him.

As he got closer, more and more of the Quad came into view. A puff of wind filled the area with a dirty, brown smoke, making it hard to make out much, but Chris thought it looked as if the fire was strongest to the left, at the corner of the Quad between the temporary huts and Block 3, the Newton Building, where the best science labs in the schools were. Had a fire started in one of the labs, caused by some leftover experiment? Chris quickened his pace still further, almost at the entrance to the Quad, under the bridge between the upper floors of the dining hall and Block 2.

That was when he saw a shadow running across the back of the Quad. Someone was moving quickly, even more quickly than Chris himself. The smoke hid the person's identity, but Chris got the idea it was someone about his own height. A curling fist of thick black smoke wafted into his face, making him choke, and he ground to a halt in the passageway.

The sooty fog cleared a moment later. Instantly, Chris saw the situation – the fire was burning inside Palmer's portacabin. It looked serious. A window was broken and smoke and fire were belching through the open hole.

In that same second, Chris saw someone running on the far side of the Quad, along the path in front of Block 3, then another, just ahead of the first. The darkening sky and the shrouding smoke hid their faces from clear view, but Chris saw that it was a couple of lads, about his own age. Neither triggered anything in his memory.

He opened his mouth to yell, but the words never came out. As the first sound was rising in his throat, the air was knocked from Chris's lungs as someone clattered into him from the side, bowling him over. Chris threw out a hand as he went down and fastened it on the guy's jacket, some flimsy piece of nylon, like a shell suit top.

They both hit the floor, but Chris didn't manage to avoid being at the bottom of the pile. The guy's elbow hit him just under the ribs, driving the last ounce of breath from his body. Chris felt close to vomiting.

'Let go!' yelled the other guy, his voice thin and squeaky. He was struggling to get free, his head thrashing from side to side as he pulled his body away from Chris's grip. All Chris could make out was that the boy had dark skin, as if he had been out in the sun. His face was hidden by the hood of the bright jacket. Even so, Chris had the impression that he ought to recognise him, but he couldn't quite figure out where from.

A wild blow from the guy's left arm knocked Chris's grip free. The boy got to his knees, dragging himself away. Chris tried to knock his legs from under him, but didn't make firm enough contact. The guy stumbled, but didn't fall. Chris was being pulled over on to his stomach as he tried to hang on — he had just one last chance.

Once again, he lunged out with his hand, this time trying to get hold of the guy's right arm. His fingers slithered down the slippery surface of the jacket, then snagged on something for the briefest moment. He felt it come loose, then his hands were scraping across the paving stones of the Quad as his quarry broke free.

Smoke gusted and swirled around, driven by the freshening wind around the coming rainstorm. It blanketed the Quad like a fog.

As Chris came upright again, he found he could barely see five metres in front of his face. Even so, he was determined that the kid he'd had his hands on wasn't going to escape.

He took a deep breath to replace the oxygen he had lost when the kid had got lucky with his elbow. Big mistake. He

60

took in more smoke than air, and almost retched as the acid taste poisoned his mouth. His eyes filled with stinging water. All the same, he forced himself to run quickly in the direction he had seen the others take – towards the gap between Blocks 2 and 3.

As soon as he stumbled out past Newton, the atmosphere cleared, as if by magic. The smoke was rising up behind him, free to escape now that it wasn't trapped by the buildings of the Quad and the gusting breeze. Chris sucked in some real, clean air and looked up.

Forty metres away and vanishing fast, the gang of strangers was heading for the gate. Chris gave chase after them, even though his head was swimming and their lead was good enough to give them time to get over the gate.

Fuddled by the smoke, his brain was holding up a hand for his attention. There's no way the guy in the shell suit can have got that far ahead, it was saying. He must have gone another way . . .

The answer flashed up right away. Shell Suit had gone out of the Quad the way Chris had come in, past the dining hall. Immediately, Chris changed course, giving up the idea of chasing the others towards the gate. He stayed tight to the outside of Block 2, past what seemed like an endless row of windows opening on to identical classrooms.

You're mine, chump, Chris promised himself long before he caught sight of his target again. He glanced to the side, where the last of the others was just learning that not all of the barbed wire had fallen off the wall. 'Forget them,' Chris told himself, 'stay focused.'

He got his reward the moment he rounded the corner of the building. Shell Suit – and that was what he was wearing, a lurid, pale blue hooded jacket over a shirt and jeans – appeared from the passage between Block 2 and the dining hall, turning towards the gate. He saw Chris come round the corner like a Cruise missile and his eyes opened wide. He issued a kind of terrified squeak.

'Yeah – you want to be scared!' yelled Chris, and he revved up a little more as he thundered towards his prey.

The eyes were all he could make out clearly under the hood, but Chris was sure he was no 'Brooker. He was an outsider. Strangely, though, the guy didn't look as trapped as

61

he should have, which made Chris think again that he ought to know who he was.

No matter. Chris was between him and the gates. The guy didn't so much as take a look around before he took off again, sprinting along the covered way towards Block 1. My territory, thought Chris.

The only thing that worried Chris was that he was running short of breath. Having had the wind knocked out of him and replaced by fumes, he wasn't firing on all cylinders. But now his target was close, he found just enough energy to keep going, cutting the corner across the rolling lawns — or mud-heaps, as they were normally known.

The main doors into Block 1 were just ahead. They'd be locked, Chris knew, but he hoped the guy would try them anyway. It would give him just enough time to —

No luck. The boy suddenly veered left, almost heading straight back towards Chris. He dropped down the slope that led to where the huge rubbish bins were stored.

He vanished almost right away. One of the dull mounds of earth that counted for landscape gardening at Spirebrook Comprehensive lay between Chris and the path. He changed course to go over it. That was when he found he must be more tired than he'd realised. His left foot slipped on the packed earth at the bottom of the slope and Chris went down.

It was hardly a bad fall, but Chris was shattered. He tried to slow his breathing, to take in measured lungfuls of cool air. All the time he was down on his hands and knees, Chris knew the guy could be slipping away, but there was nothing he could do about it.

As he recovered, he felt the first spots of rain on his back.

The distant wail of a siren, closing fast, stirred him to get up again. He felt a little more clear-headed at last. He dragged himself over the mound and dropped down on to the path, angling quickly towards the wooden enclosure where the bins were kept. Nothing. He followed the path round to the side of Block 1, where 'Andy' Cole's office was; nothing there either.

Shell Suit seemed to know his way around.

The sirens were getting closer. It suddenly occurred to Chris that there was no way fire engines could get in. The gates blocked the only driveway, and they were solid and locked tight. By the time they bust them open or whatever, the fire could easily destroy the portacabins, and maybe Block 3 too.

Chris was no big fan of chemistry, but there were limits.

It annoyed him to give up searching for Shell Suit, but in his present state, he'd never be able to catch the guy even if he did see him again. And whether his quarry knew his way round the site or not, sooner or later he'd find one of the holes in the back fence, or nip over the wall into someone's garden. Chris had no way of knowing where to look, whereas he knew exactly where the fire was – and how bad it was getting.

There were extinguishers in the Quad. Chris knew how to use them, having been shown by his father (there was a small one on the wall in their kitchen). All Chris had to do was buy the fire brigade some time.

He picked up his feet, which felt as heavy as stone, and set off back towards the other buildings. The wind was gusting more than ever, and the black clouds overhead were getting serious about dumping some rain on to Spirebrook. The space between the dining room and Block 2 was darker than ever.

The changing wind was keeping the passage clear of smoke, though, and Chris stumbled into the Quad without filling his mouth with its filthy taste again. The fire was in charge of Mr Palmer's office, and tasting the outside of the neighbouring hut, the sixth form common room, blistering the paint.

Chris broke open a fire box and dragged out the heavy extinguisher. Kneeling to keep under the smoke, he aimed the nozzle at the paintwork on the corner of the common room and hit the trigger.

It was fiercely hot and the smoke was grim. Chris managed to keep the worst of the fire's effects off the common room and even forced the flames back from the window of Mr Palmer's office. He hoped the fire brigade would get through the gates soon. The extinguisher wouldn't last forever.

In fact, it was just starting to splutter when the wind lifted the smoke away as if it was a heavy black curtain. Chris had a brief view of the space between the two huts and beyond.

'Damn!' he yelled. Across the playing field, past the corner of the tennis courts at the narrow part of the site, he'd caught a flash of someone in a bright blue top, slipping under the mesh of the fence.

'I'll have you yet,' growled Chris. If the guy didn't spot him coming, perhaps he could close right up and turn it into a sprint rather than a long-distance haul.

He tossed the extinguisher to one side. 'You're mine!' he whispered to himself, certain that nothing could stop him catching Shell Suit this time.

'You're nicked,' said the policeman.

Ten

Everyone was talking at once. The fire officer was repeating to every single person who asked that the fire had been started deliberately; 'Andy' Cole, fetched from her house on the other side of the university, was asking about damage and insurance and safety and . . .; Chris's father, very red-faced (with embarrassment or anger, it was hard to tell) at having been summoned from work, was demanding to know if Chris was being arrested; and two fifth-form girls who had wandered on to the site to stick their noses in were asking hopefully if school might be closed on Monday. Even the policeman's radio, fastened to his breast pocket like an oversized pen, was chattering away, barely one word in ten making any sense. Perhaps, thought Chris, the police sent you on a special course to understand radio static.

The only two people with nothing to say were Chris, who had become rapidly fed up with trying to explain, and the policeman, who was grinning like the guy in Taggart after he's solved another hideously complicated crime.

Yeah, thought Chris, another victory for the forces of law and order.

It was cruel luck that the first policeman on the scene was the local ninny who had convinced himself over the last year that Chris and Nicky were at the centre of every crime, real or imagined, that went off in Spirebrook. He'd had the handcuffs ready the moment he entered the Quad and saw Chris flinging the extinguisher away.

Chris had tried explaining. Now he was just fed up. Sooner or later the copper would have to admit Chris wasn't the right guy, so all he had to do was wait PC Plod out.

They were all parked in the dining room, which Mrs Cole had opened up now that the rain was here to stay.

65

'Hang on,' came a voice, 'I can clear this up.'

Perfect.

Nicky slipped past the copper at the door with a body swerve that would have left the German defence looking stupid and walked over towards the group of adults (and one teenaged prisoner). Jazz, trying to come in behind Nicky, got grabbed, but that just left the young PC with more boys than hands, so Mac and Robbie James strolled in unhindered.

Like synchronised swimmers, Chris, his father and Mrs Cole rolled their eyes up to heaven. Nicky Fiorentini swaggered across the room like a last-minute witness in a murder trial. The two girls giggled. Nicky flashed a grin at them until he recognised who they were.

The older policeman didn't react in the same way as the others when he saw the dark-haired boy stride towards him. He was grinning, a satisfied, oh-you-think-so? smile. Chris imagined he had expected to see Nicky appear.

'I might have guessed you'd be here as well,' the copper said, without even a trace of a smile. He stretched his hands across his rather broad belly.

Nicky didn't look at all worried by the policeman's manner. In fact, he seemed alarmingly confident. Experience had shown Chris this either meant Nicky was in control, or things were about to go pear-shaped in a big way.

'Is this anything to do with you, Nicky?' asked Mrs Cole, with a tired note in her voice.

'No,' said Nicky, continuing before anyone suggested this meant it was none of his business. 'Chris wasn't involved in setting the fire, either.'

'Has anyone said he was?' asked the large copper. He smirked as if his case had just been proved for him completely.

'Then why is he still here?' asked Nicky. Chris's father had been making the same point for the last hour.

'Your mate was found at the fire, having just emptied the only fire extinguisher available on another building. He's been trying to tell us he saw some other boys he didn't recognise, and that he chased one but lost sight of him.' He made a kind of coughing sound to show how much he believed *that* story. It had been just Chris's luck that the nosy-parker who lived outside the school gates hadn't been in all day — there were no witnesses yet who'd seen any sign of these other boys.

66

Nicky replied with a mocking noise of his own. 'Is that all? That hardly proves he set fire to the school.'

'Then why was he here?' the policeman demanded, his lip curled to show there was no answer Chris could give that would satisfy *him*.

'Yes, why was he here on a Saturday?' echoed Mrs Cole.

'Taking a short cut,' said Nicky, 'on his way to meet me.'

'Was I?' asked Chris, realising too late that this wasn't the smartest thing he could have said. Luckily, Nicky saw it too, and cleared the matter up before anyone else could speak.

'A few of us were round Mac's house, and Chris was on his way there. Coming through the school is a short cut.'

'Really?' said Mrs Cole, in her hardest, most accusing voice.

'Sure,' smiled Nicky, 'we do it all the time.'

Thanks, Nicky, thought Chris. He could see from Mrs Cole's face that this wasn't the last he was going to hear of that fact. Nicky was too busy getting in the cop's face to notice.

'So, what does that prove?' the policeman said.

Nicky turned towards Mrs Cole. 'You don't really believe Chris would set fire to the school, do you?' he asked.

Chris was disappointed that she couldn't answer 'no' right away. 'Well . . .' she said, then she closed her mouth and looked at Chris with a worried expression. It was clear she didn't want to think it was true, but she couldn't be certain.

'Look,' Nicky continued, 'it's obvious it wasn't Chris.'

Mrs Cole raised her eyebrows; it wasn't obvious to her. The policeman looked away and chuckled; it would *never* be obvious to him.

'The fire was in Mr Palmer's office, right?' asked Nicky. Mrs Cole nodded. 'Where the sports trophies are kept, right?' The head's eyes widened. 'So why would Chris want to destroy the football cups?'

Mrs Cole looked around quickly at the fire officer.

'Were the trophies OK? They were on a shelf at the back of the room.'

The guy was thinking carefully about what he'd seen, rubbing his smoke-blackened face with his hand. 'I don't remember seeing any trophies,' he said. 'Not on the wall, at least.'

The cop's teeth gleamed as he grinned broadly. 'Nicked, I bet,' he said, with glee. 'The fire was just a diversion to cover the robbery.' He was looking at Chris as he said it.

Nicky was grinning as well. He already knew why the trophies hadn't been on the shelf.

'It's the weekend, Mrs Cole,' he said, calmly. 'Mr Palmer locks them away in the steel cupboard.'

Mrs Cole's face registered the fact that she'd remembered this at the same second Nicky spoke. 'Of course!' she cried.

'I remember seeing a steel cupboard at the back of the room,' the fire officer recalled. 'The fire didn't damage that at all. The contents should be OK, so long as they don't mind getting a little warm.'

Nicky smirked and made a big point of getting in the policeman's face. 'Chris would have known the trophies were in the cupboard, if he'd been trying to nick them – not that he'd have any reason to. I doubt you could break into that cupboard with an axe.'

There was one small flaw in Nicky's argument. Originally he'd been arguing that the proof Chris hadn't started the fire was that he wouldn't want to destroy the trophies. Now he was arguing that Chris couldn't have been trying to *steal* the trophies, because he'd have known they were locked up in the cupboard, safe from all harm.

No-one noticed, except Chris. Mrs Cole shrugged at the policeman, as if she was satisfied that the argument was closed. Chris's father was looking both relieved and angry, and demanded to know if they could leave now.

The copper's eyes sparkled as if he was fighting back the urge to cry. Chris knew he was trying to find some new way to get on his case, but failing.

'Fine,' he growled. 'If your head teacher is satisfied, then I suppose I have to be.' He leant forward, his nose almost touching Chris's. 'But I don't buy any of this guff about there being anyone else here.'

Chris felt his father's hand on his shoulder and stood up. Getting out of here would be good enough. He didn't care what the copper thought.

Nicky didn't either, but he didn't miss a chance to rub his victory in.

'You just can't stand being wrong, can you?' he jeered.

'Nicky . . .' said Mr Stephens, trying to steer all the boys from the room.

The policeman switched his aim to Chris's father.

'You want to teach your kid some respect, mate,' he said. 'These two are running wild, and it's up to you –' He swung his eyes round to catch Mrs Cole with the same sentence '– to keep them out of trouble. If it were my brat, I'd –'

John Stephens wasn't a getting angry kind of father (except with Chris, now and again . . .). The smart money would have been on Mrs Cole making a point. Instead, though, Chris's father took two quick strides across the room and bent forward so that his steely eyes were on a level with the copper's.

'But they're not your kids, are they? You know nothing about them. They're not running wild; they're just lads who are stupid about football and too nosy for their own good. None of them is a thief; never has been, never will be.'

It was just as well Russell Jones wasn't there. It was too good a speech to be ruined by a small inaccuracy like that.

'Stupid, blind, ignorant coppers like you are more trouble than these lads any day. And you know what really gets my goat? You know?'

The policeman didn't care to guess.

'When my lad's made it big, and he's playing for Oldcester United, you'll be sitting on your fat behind in the canteen bragging about how you knew him when he was a kid. And each week you'll wonder why it is you never get any free tickets to the game.'

John Stephens stepped back, his point made.

'The only reason I don't report you is that you've been made to look like a chump in front of one of your own this time.' He indicated the younger policeman at the door. 'I'm hoping he's a better copper than you'll ever be.'

With that, he turned on his heel and stormed out through the door, sweeping the lads ahead of him like a shepherd on overdrive. He didn't even allow Nicky to have the last word.

Now, that really was a neat trick.

Outside, in the cool evening air, Mr Stephens' temper disappeared as rapidly as the storm that had passed by earlier. He stood on the step pulling on his coat.

'What a chump,' he said. That was his last comment on the matter.

As they prepared to move on, the boys noticed a solitary

69

figure at the end of the passage. He had his hands thrust into the pockets of a tatty leather jacket that was several sizes too big. The fire crews were winding up their hoses and sweeping water towards the drains. Nicky wanted to look.

'Leave it, eh?' said Mr Stephens. 'I ought to get you guys home.'

'Aw – just a quick look, OK?' said Nicky, and he set off towards the Quad without waiting for an answer.

Chris looked up at his father. 'Just as well we're not out of control, eh?' he said.

They followed Nicky to the Quad. Now the excitement had died down, it didn't look so bad. Most of the damage was centred behind one window, the one that had been broken. There was extensive damage to the carpet and furnishings, but the room wasn't the burnt-out wreck Chris expected.

The lone spectator (before they arrived) turned out to be Russell Jones, who had been on the other side of the river when he saw the fire's smoke from the yard of his house. Russell had thought nothing of a two mile jog via the bridge to come and take a look.

Chris told him what had happened.

'Looks like you did some good with that extinguisher,' he commented.

Chris's father didn't seem to be in the mood to hand out medals just yet. 'You should have left it to the fire brigade.'

'But they couldn't get through the gates,' said Chris. Of course, that didn't make a lot of sense, bearing in mind that there were three or four fire-fighters still here.

'The gates have special locks,' Chris's father said. 'The fire brigade use a master key. And if that fails, they have cutters that could snap those gates off at the hinges.'

'Oh,' remarked Chris. So much for being the hero, then.

'Let's go,' said his father. He made a point of grabbing Nicky's collar.

Chris and Russell brought up the rear. Just as they were leaving the Quad, close to the entrance into the passageway, Chris saw something glint. One of the firefighters had shone a torch their way for just an instant, and the beam of light had caught something lying on the floor by the wall. Instinctively, Chris bent and picked it up.

Chris used the light from the dining room to inspect his find.

It was a wristwatch, a cheap LCD job. It had a plastic strap, made to look like leather, with plastic studs that were supposed to look like metal. The strap had snapped at the point where it was fastened to the watch itself.

This was the same high quality as the strap (and it was twenty minutes slow), but it was more unusual. For one thing, it was a diamond shape. The ends were pointed, and the cheap gilding had worn away where it had been rubbing against its owner's wrist.

Second, it was bright red, with small numbers around the outer edge, leaving room for a badly drawn footballer in red kit and a logo. The footballer's skin was painted yellow, as if he was Chinese. It didn't say where it had been made. No-one in their right mind would have wanted to admit it.

The clincher was that the logo behind the yellow-skinned footballer's head, read LIVERPOL. Clearly, whoever had bought the watch wasn't very good at spelling, in common with the people who made it.

Chris quickly stuffed the watch in the pocket of his jacket. He had no doubt this was what he had felt fall away when he grabbed Shell Suit by the arm.

As they walked away, he considered his find. Liverpool are a great club, and they have keen fans all over the country, including Oldcester. Tracking down one who might enjoy setting fires wasn't going to be easy.

But finding a Liverpol supporter? That was a different matter.

Eleven

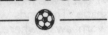

The lads from Villa were good, especially at the back. The younger teams had looked pretty useful against their United counterparts, especially the Under-11s, who had banged in a lot of goals. It was just as well almost no-one was keeping count.

The first defeat Villa suffered (according to Nicky, who couldn't help keeping score) was against Robert James's mob. They played two thirty-minute halves, nine-a-side on a smaller pitch. The Villa boys were gifted, but they didn't seem as fit as James and his mates.

Robert played a great game in defence, mopping up just about anything that came down the Villa left. His tackling was perfectly timed, every time. Late on, he hit a crossfield pass that set up a goal.

Nicky wandered back from the other pitch, where the age group above James's were going down in flames. Having heard the cheering, he had decided to come and support a winning United team.

'Good one, Bob!' he yelled as the United players ran back after the goal. James looked over to the sideline, embarrassed.

Nicky sat down beside Chris, Jazz and Rory Blackstone, who had been watching the game from the beginning, and discussing how they might get on.

'How long before we start?' asked Nicky.

Chris picked up the watch that was lying on the ground between his feet. 'Half an hour,' he replied.

Nicky was about to insist that must be wrong, when he saw Chris was looking at the counterfeit watch he had found. So far, all anyone knew about the watch was that Chris claimed he was looking for the owner.

'Funny,' Nicky said. 'Haven't you set that thing right, yet?'

'The control is broken,' said Chris, who had tried to

72

correct the time that morning.

Nicky sniffed, which summed up how he felt about the cheap watch. 'You told Rory about our adventure?' he asked. Chris wondered how it had become 'theirs' — he'd been the one almost arrested.

'A queer business,' Rory commented, leaning back. 'First the youth club, and then your school.'

'You think there's a connection?' asked Jazz, who didn't.

Rory shrugged. He tugged at his earlobe and scratched his head before he put anything into words. 'It's a bit of a coincidence otherwise, isn't it?'

Nicky didn't believe in coincidence. Even so, he didn't see why anyone would have both wrecked a youth club and set fire to a school. The only link was Chris and the other three 'Brookers who had played for the Colts, Russell Jones, Jazz and Mac.

'It's probably just some thieves who are breaking into the softer targets round here,' he decided. 'Maybe they know someone who can melt down silver.'

Chris was looking at the cheap watch. 'Get real, Nicky. There wasn't enough real silver on the shield they took to be worth stealing.'

'Yeah, but wasn't there a laptop taken?' Nicky asked.

Chris nodded. 'But the guys who set the fire didn't take the computer from Mr Palmer's office — there can't be a connection!'

Nicky tried to laugh that off by rubbishing the cheap 386 machine that sat on Palmer's desk, but he had to concede that it didn't make a lot of sense.

Out on the pitch, Robert James was retreating steadily in front of one of the Villa players. The guy looked as if he would rather pass than take James on, but there was no-one open. Finally, he tried beating James on the outside.

James struck like a cobra.

'Ouch!' muttered Jazz.

'Your man's quick, isn't he?' observed Rory.

'Strong too,' Nicky agreed. 'Hey, Rory — would you say James looks older than he is?'

Chris knew where this was going.

'He's tall, that's for sure,' replied Rory, who had no idea of Nicky's agenda. He pointed out a couple of the other lads

73

playing in front of them; James was way taller than any of them. 'But his face makes him look about ten. It's like he's out of scale, or something.'

He chuckled, and was about to make another observation when he realised Fiorentini had turned to face Chris and Jazz, with a what did I tell you? look on his face.

'Yeah, yeah . . .' muttered Chris.

With the ball out of play, the coaches minding the match decided to rotate a few players on and off the field. Robert James was one of them — he'd made his point pretty convincingly.

Chris and the others were sitting just along from where the substitutes were parked. James joined his team mates, picking up his track suit and pulling it on. Nicky waved him over.

'Good game!' he called. James was delighted with the praise.

'We were lucky!' he called back, taking a few hesitant steps towards them (Chris knew he had realised he ought to stay with the rest of his team, but he couldn't resist coming to see what else Nicky might have to say).

'I've told you, Bob, there's no such thing as luck,' said Nicky.

James's face fell slightly, although whether that was because he'd been called Bob or because Nicky had changed his tone, Chris couldn't say. James froze where he was, halfway between his team mates and the group around Nicky.

'I don't know,' he replied. 'This business at the school . . .'

Nicky's face wrinkled in a mocking smile. 'That was a fire, Bob. Nothing to do with luck.'

Chris nearly said that Nicky was lucky not to have been involved (no matter what Fiorentini thought), but he knew Nicky wouldn't get the point.

James was moving closer once more.

'No, but I mean, it's like the school team is going through a patch of bad luck. Like it's been jinxed.'

Nicky narrowed his eyes. 'Jinxed?' he repeated.

With one last look past his shoulder, James came the final few steps over to the others and sat down at the end of the line, beside Nicky.

'You know, like someone has put a curse on us,' he hissed.

Anyone who had too many conversations with Nicky (and one conversation could be too many) soon discovered that what he believed and disbelieved didn't always fall into neat packages. Nicky didn't believe in God, but he did believe there was something 'holy' about his family's priest. He said he wasn't superstitious, but he always checked to make sure Chris went through his good luck pre-match routine. He didn't believe that there were ghosts, aliens or supernatural powers, but after each episode of *The X-Files* Nicky insisted that the government was covering up all kinds of secrets.

So, in the world according to Nicky, it made perfect sense for there to be no such thing as luck, but for curses to be real.

'You think we've been cursed?' he asked, eyes wide.

'Not exactly,' replied James, who hadn't expected to be taken so literally. 'But I wonder if we haven't attracted some kind of evil spirit.'

Nicky's eyes almost came out on stalks. Jazz was also leaning further forward, taking an active interest. The only negative noise came from Russell Jones, who was at the back of the group, tying his laces for the tenth time.

'What do you mean — evil spirit?' asked Nicky, ignoring Russell's mocking laughter.

'Well, I don't mean a ghost or anything,' James replied.

'I bet Chris is glad you said that,' chuckled Russell, a remark that passed way over Robert James's head. He hadn't been part of the group when Chris had convinced himself he was being coached by a ghost.

'I just mean . . . well, sometimes bad things keep happening to the same people. As if they are attracting it, like a magnet.'

James looked along the line of faces turned in his direction.

'Go on,' Nicky insisted.

'Well, you have to find out what the magnet is and get rid of it,' said James, quietly. 'It's the opposite of a good luck charm, in a way,' he explained, unhelpfully. 'We just have to work out what it is.'

Nicky still looked doubtful about this 'curse' business, but the idea that all they had to do was get rid of some kind of unlucky charm appealed to him greatly. Nicky liked his answers to be straightforward.

'Well, that sounds easy enough,' he said.

'It would be,' said Mac, 'if we knew what to look for.'

Nicky was a lot less satisfied with that answer.

Chris decided to change the subject. All this talk about curses, evil spirits and other stuff wasn't getting them anywhere.

75

The others were losing sight of the fact that this huge problem amounted to the 'Brook losing two games. In that time, nearly everything else had gone right, except, maybe, for the incidents at the youth club and the school.

Chris decided to focus on them. At least they were real — there was physical evidence that something had happened and someone was to blame.

He turned the watch over between his fingers and showed it to Rory.

'Have you ever seen this before?' he asked.

Rory bent closer to examine the watch.

'They've spelt Liverpool wrong,' he said, as if there was any chance Chris hadn't noticed.

'I know,' Chris replied.

'So your man's likely to be a Liverpool supporter who can't read too well,' Rory continued, close to the world record for stating the obvious to people who already knew.

Nicky was about to make one of his offensive jokes. Chris held up a hand to stop him before the first words came out which caused Nicky to act as if he was desperately offended.

'There are probably dozens — hundreds — of Liverpool fans in the city,' Chris said. 'It's just a shame we don't know any.'

'Me neither,' said Rory, with a sad note in his voice. 'Still, you could ask Steve Taylor,' he added.

'Why?' asked Chris.

'Because he's one.'

Several hours later Chris realised that Rory hadn't made a lot of sense at the end of that conversation. It took him another day to realise that actually there was a strange kind of logic to it. Steve Taylor was one of the assistant coaches, working directly under Sean Priest. Liverpool born and bred, he had played for United up until 1988 and then joined the coaching staff. What Rory was actually saying was that he knew Taylor was a Liverpool supporter, but that was about all he knew.

Russell and Mac were still arguing about lucky charms. Chris left them to it and went to have a word with Taylor. The current round of games were coming to an end and there would be a fifteen minute gap before Chris's match kicked off. Plenty of time to see if Taylor knew anything about the watch — and for the others to get bored of their conversation about 'evil spirits'.

It took a while to track him down. By the time Chris found Taylor, he was just finishing a post-match talk with the Under-12s, who had managed a good draw after falling 2–0 behind. The coach wasn't worried about the result at all, though. He was concentrating on how the team had played, and the way they had come back at the Villa team in the second half.

'It was just like I told you at half-time, wasn't it? By pushing up quickly, you didn't allow them so much room. They had to play a few more risky passes and we won a lot more possession.'

He fixed his attention on a couple of individuals, two lads who played in central midfield. 'You two did well, but you have to be more patient. Keep the ball active, pass it wide, pass it between yourselves. Give the other team the run around. Sooner or later you'll see a better passing option, one that sets up an attack. In the first half, we hit too many hopeful passes and because the strikers kept running into offside positions, we were caught over and over again.'

He stood up, away from the small wipe-off board he had been crouching beside. 'Patience, that's the key. Now, go and cool off, and then be back here to see if the older boys can do any better!' He motioned for the team to get up and head for the showers, then noticed Chris hovering nearby.

'Speaking of whom, here's one of our heroes now. Chris Stephens, isn't it? You're on next, aren't you?'

'Yes,' said Chris, which he hoped answered both questions. 'I just need to ask you something quickly.'

'Sure, only ask it slowly, will you? I might not understand otherwise.' He laughed, which was a good clue that Taylor thought he'd made some kind of joke. Chris laughed as well.

'Have you ever seen one of these before?' he said, holding out the watch.

Taylor took it from him, turning it over in his palm to look at the back as if he was too ashamed to look at the front.

'Yeah,' he said, 'it's a watch.'

Chris sighed, then joined in another bout of chuckling. Scousers were clearly supposed to be natural comedians.

'Liverpool,' said Taylor, disgustedly. 'Honestly, you'd think they could get that right.'

He handed it back to Chris. 'Yeah, I've seen watches like that before,' he said, 'when I was on holiday in Spain early in the

77

summer, there were these couple of lads on the beach selling this junk. A right pair of charlies they were — between the pair of them they didn't have enough brain cells to make up one thick person. They must have picked these watches up dirt cheap from somewhere and thought they were a real bargain.'

'Were there just these Liverpool watches?' asked Chris.

'No, the whole lot was a muck up. They had blue Manchester United watches and red City ones; they had Everton watches with the Spurs badge on; they had RPQ watches . . .' Chris had to think for a moment to work that out.

'I doubt if anyone ever bought any of them,' he concluded, cutting right across Chris's next question, which was going to enquire whether Taylor knew anyone who had.

'How did you get it?' Taylor asked. Chris gave him edited highlights of the events at school. Taylor looked thoughtful and quite serious for a moment.

'You shouldn't have taken it, Chris. It's evidence.'

Chris knew that, but the fact that the copper was convinced he was involved had made Chris keep his distance.

'So, should I hand it in now?' he asked, knowing the answer.

'Yeah, but not to the local police,' replied Taylor. Chris wasn't sure what he meant. 'Seeing as it came from Spain, you should call in Interpol,' added Taylor, with a stupid smile on his face and a gesture towards the watch.

Now that, thought Chris, was quite funny.

At the start of the game, Nicky seemed to have his mind on other things, and the usual chemistry between him and Chris wasn't there. Priest, who was coaching this game himself, called Nicky to the sidelines after ten minutes, gave him a strong talking to, then sent him back on with the strong reminder that both teams could play five substitutes.

Nicky woke up dramatically after that.

But right from the beginning, even when Nicky was below par, the rest of the United team were red hot. The Villa lads came at them, determined to make a game of it, but Russell Jones and the rest of the defence were rock solid. Jazz had one of those games when he seemed to be as unreal as a ghost, losing his marker and finding space all the time. His passing was razor-sharp.

Up front, Chris and Rory combined just like they had done for the Colts last season. Rory was big, bustling and attracted lots of attention. He looked slower than he was, and his markers were constantly being left for dead by his little darts and turns. Even when they did stay tight, Rory was the perfect target man, capable of taking the ball with his back to goal, holding off the defender, then laying it off.

Chris was profiting from both the space Rory created and from his excellent passing. He took one knock down in the box and lashed it into the roof of the net. He took another lay-off and whipped a curling shot that the keeper palmed on to the bar. The Villa lads had no answer to the speed and accuracy of United's attacks.

Once Nicky had his act together, it became even more one-sided. He and Jazz fired passes and crosses in from both sides now. The longer the game went on, the more the two United full backs could come up into the game too. The opposition were being overrun.

No-one was supposed to be keeping score, of course, but everyone knew what it was. Villa might have won four out of the six other games to have been played already, but they weren't going to win this one.

Lads from the younger teams crowded the sidelines. The United players were enjoying the way Chris's team was taking revenge for the defeats they had suffered.

Just after half-time, Chris saw Robert James and his mates whooping and cheering at the Villa end, having just got changed.

Play had stopped while Priest made a substitution. He was bringing on a new boy, a lad who was at the club on a trial basis. Chris grinned at the new arrival, and clapped him on the back as he ran by. He could see that the third striker in the squad was stripping off too, and knew that Sean was going to take either him or Rory off, now that they had proved their point.

The new boy slipped into position and watched as Villa took a throw-in. The ball found its way to the midfield, and the sub was quickest to react when two Villa lads pulled an exchange of passes. Moving like lightning, he threw in a lunging tackle — just as one of the Villa players was turning on one foot to run into space.

There was an ugly, clattering crack as the collision occurred. Everyone winced, fearing the worst. Coaches and physios ran on to the field. The new boy stood back with a horrified expression on his face, looking down at his opposite number.

But it had sounded a lot worse than it turned out. The two players must have cracked their shin pads together or something, because the Villa lad sat up after a moment or two and the coaches were quickly satisfied that he'd suffered no worse than a whacking bruise on his shin, just above the ankle, which was colouring up as they watched. He might not feel like doing any Highland dancing for a while, but he was OK.

As he limped off, the ref turned to the new boy. He was relieved that the incident hadn't proved too serious. At the same time, he wasn't overly impressed with the tackle.

'What's your name, son?' he asked.

A few members of the United team were already starting to smile.

'Charlton,' the boy replied, sheepishly. 'Jack Charlton.'

Chris knew the referee quite well. He was one of a group that ref'd all kinds of local matches, including the District League. Chris had been in games with him before. On the whole, he was OK as refs went, but he had a real bee in his bonnet about boys jerking his chain.

So, when his face clouded up like an approaching thunderstorm, it wasn't a surprise. Along with the others, Chris couldn't help but snicker.

'Are you trying to be funny, kid?' the ref demanded.

'No, really . . .' the boy began.

'Get off!' the ref demanded, and he reached into his pocket to brandish a red card. Suddenly, it wasn't funny any more.

'No, really,' Charlton said, his voice high. Other players on the United side stepped forward too, protesting that he really was called Jack Charlton, his Irish dad (no relation to the footballing brothers) having been in Italy for the 1990 World Cup when the Irish team (under Jack Charlton) had scared the living daylights out of the Italians.

The ref wasn't interested. Even if he believed what he was being told, he wasn't prepared to back down now.

'I'm sending you off for that foul,' he insisted, 'not for having a stupid name.'

Chris could see that Priest was furious, but he said nothing, except when he called his team away from the ref. Sean believed in accepting the ref's decision without protesting.

Finally, the United team backed away. The Villa players looked around among themselves and prepared to take the free kick. On the touchline, Priest was trying to attract the ref's attention as two of the subs stripped off in a hurry.

Moments later, Sean brought Chris and Jazz off, adding a couple of fresher midfield players, to try and hold Villa up in midfield.

'I thought the result didn't matter?' sneered Nicky, who had come to the sideline to listen. He thought Priest was trying to defend United's comfortable lead.

'It doesn't,' said Priest, too busy to lecture Nicky properly. 'But ten men play differently to eleven. We might as well use this opportunity to learn the best way to cope with the opposition having the extra man.'

He glanced sideways at Charlton.

'I guess the other lesson we have to learn is to not have players with famous names,' he grinned. Charlton smiled back weakly, clearly upset that he hadn't even touched the ball during his brief appearance. Later, he showed a lot of bottle by going over to the Villa bench to check on the guy he had tackled.

United were bent badly out of shape by the incident and all the changes, and they didn't command the last quarter of the game in anything like the same way as they had the first 45 minutes. Villa scored quite quickly.

'Looks like the jinx is spreading,' Nicky called.

'It's still four-one,' Chris muttered. Even so, he watched the rest of the game glumly, as Villa roared back at United.

The United players from the other teams were silent now, except for one or two shouts of encouragement after a good tackle or an accurate pass. Chris looked along the line. Some way off, Mac and Robert James were standing together. James looked pale. Mac was saying something to him, leaning forward as if he was trying to make some important point.

A gasp went up, attracting Chris's attention back to the pitch. Tim Williams, one of the United defenders, had just hit a perfect pass to Nicky, wide on the right. The Villa full back had pushed up and their defence was stretched. All Nicky had to do was race down the touchline and hit the cross . . .

A flag was waving on the far side. The ref blew his whistle.

'Offside!' yelled Nicky. 'Are you blind? I was in my own half when that pass was hit!'

The ref waved him away. Nicky said something as he walked past, something which didn't carry to the touchline but which the ref clearly heard.

He blew his whistle and called Nicky over.

'Oh, oh,' muttered Chris.

Some more words were exchanged, which the players on the touchline also didn't hear. They got the gist of the discussion, though. Nicky was on his way to the bench.

'I don't believe this!' yelled Priest.

Nicky's face showed that he wasn't very impressed either. 'What a moron!' he said as he kicked off his boots and slumped on the bench beside Chris.

Several of the other players were very keen to find out just what Nicky had said, but they could see from Priest's face that this wasn't the right time to ask. They backed away as the youth team manager came over.

'Brilliant, Nicky. Did you think this was a good time to see how we'd get on with just nine players?'

Nicky wasn't prepared to be in the wrong.

'I didn't say anything that bad!' he insisted. 'It was just bad luck the old duffer heard me, anyway!'

Priest was almost purple with anger at Nicky's attitude. All he could trust himself to say was: 'I thought you didn't believe in luck!'

'Maybe I've changed my mind,' Nicky muttered. Priest turned away. He would deal with Nicky later.

'You went too far,' said Chris, a few minutes later, hoping Nicky had calmed down. He could easily have been talking about either the pointless spat with the ref or the way Nicky had spoken to Priest.

'Too far?' howled Nicky, missing both points completely. 'I was in my own half! That was never offside . . .'

In the last minute, having made three or four spectacular saves, Russell was beaten by a ball that took a wicked deflection off one of his own defenders. That just seemed to sum up the way things had gone. The United players stalked off the field as if they had just been routed 10–0.

'We'll talk about this later,' said Priest, who still looked very hot under the collar. He went over to have a chat with the ref. Most of the United players were glued to the scene, in case they missed something really exciting, like Sean planting one on the official.

Chris, though, was distracted as Jazz and Robert James came up. Jazz appeared confused, as if there were things he wanted to say, but he didn't know how to begin. James looked ill.

'You OK?' asked Chris.

'I thought I'd better tell you, I've worked out what the jinx is,' James said firmly.

Not this again, thought Chris. He was on the point of telling them what he thought of all the nonsense about a curse when Nicky swung round and demanded to know what it was.

James swallowed hard before he spoke.

'It's me,' he said. 'I'm the bad luck charm.'

Twelve

Nothing any of them said could change James's mind.

'Just think about it,' he said, miserably. 'Spirebrook were playing fine until I joined the school. There's been a break-in and a fire ... And now look at today. You guys were *cruising* through that game until I arrived to watch.'

'That's ridiculous!' Chris insisted. 'People can't be bad luck charms!'

'Actually,' began Mac, but a glare from Chris silenced him at once.

'I know what you mean,' said James, 'but look at the facts.'

'What facts?' Chris yelled. They were sitting on the steps outside the changing rooms at the London Road training ground, waiting for Jazz and Russell. Mac and Chris were on either side of James, who had his bag at his feet. He was staring down at it, his face not quite so pale now that he had got his terrible 'secret' off his chest. He still looked pretty sick.

Nicky was standing off to one side, listening carefully.

Getting no answer, Chris spelt out a few facts of his own.

'One,' he began, using Nicky's technique of counting off points on his fingers. 'We won. Not that it mattered much anyway, but it was a win. In fact, when you look at how some of the other teams did, it was a good win.

'Two, your team didn't do too badly either. So, if you are a jinx, you're making a pretty bad job of it.

'Three, the 'Brook are going through a thin patch, that's all. Three games. And that's just the senior team. Your mob are doing OK.'

'Maybe the curse only affects people around me,' said James, who didn't look like he was being won round.

'So it just picks on the senior team, but not the lower school, who you play for?' scoffed Chris. 'Get real. Look, on

Wednesday, we have an easy game, and next week we play Blackmoor. I bet we mop them both up and all this stuff about 'Brook going through a slump will be ancient history.'

'But what about today?' James moaned.

Chris sighed. The kid wasn't going to see how stupid this all was unless it was jammed all the way down his throat.

'What about it?' demanded Chris. 'Did your jinx affect the whole United squad? No. Did it work when you were playing? No! Did it only work when you were watching? Did it? What happened when you watched the other games?'

There was a slight change in the look on James's face and the sound of his voice. He still looked and sounded miserable, but now it was because it appeared he was being stupid.

'Nothing . . . I guess . . . but . . .'

'But what?'

'Well, maybe I'm just *your* bad luck charm.'

Chris opened his mouth to shoot that stupid idea down in flames as well. The trouble was, he couldn't right away.

'That is so stupid,' he said, stalling for time.

'Maybe, maybe not,' came a low, hard voice from the side. Chris looked up. Nicky's eyes had a glassy, edgy cast about them.

'Nicky . . .' Chris began.

'Just think about it, Chris. One minute we're coasting, then James comes along and we're all over the place. Two jammy goals, that stupid business with Jack, that *moron* saying I was offside and then sending me off . . .'

Chris was furious with Nicky. Just when he was starting to turn James around over this jinx nonsense, Nicky was lapping it all up.

'Hang on, Nicky. That was a stupid misunderstanding.' Chris picked his words carefully. Jack's sending off was a stupid misunderstanding; Nicky's was inevitable, given that Fiorentini had been mouthing off. Still, it couldn't do any harm for Nicky to believe Chris thought the sending off was unfair . . .

'But that's the point, isn't it,' insisted Nicky. He sat down beside Mac. 'It's stupid, it doesn't make sense. How come the ref sent Jack off? How come he sent *me* off? It's like he was hypnotised or possessed or something.'

Chris had heard Nicky blame refs for stupid decisions before, but this took the biscuit.

'Nicky, he sent Jack off because he thought he was having him on. That tackle looked really bad, and I guess he was, you know, a bit rattled.'

'Yeah? And what about him sending me off?'

At certain times in everyone's life, there are difficult decisions to be made, when telling the truth is going to get someone mad, but telling a lie is going to allow something else to go wrong. Chris knew at once that this was one of those times. He wanted to tell Nicky he was at fault, but Nicky wasn't in the mood to listen. So, when what he really wanted to say was 'that was your dumb fault, Nicky,' the words came out slightly differently.

'Yeah, well that was just a bit odd . . .'

Nicky took this as conclusive proof he was right. Chris didn't mind what Nicky thought, though. He turned to see if it was having an effect on James.

It was. If anything, James was more miserable than ever.

'Look,' Nicky was saying. 'Maybe it will wear off, you know?'

Chris jumped on that idea as the best way out of the mess. 'Right!' he said, brightly. 'You'll see. The "jinx" will fade away and we can get back to normal.' And in the meantime, Chris was thinking, we can forget this other nonsense about James playing for the 'Brook senior team in place of Griff. That would do them more good than losing any stupid 'curse'.

James was coming to the same point himself.

'So, I should forget about moving up into the seniors?'

Nicky nodded immediately, then stopped. A dark thought was moving through his mind.

'Of course, that might not be enough . . .' he started to say. Chris could sense that he wasn't going to like what came next, but he couldn't find a way to break in quickly.

'After all, you were playing in the juniors when all this started. Perhaps you need to keep a larger distance.'

'Now, hang on, Nicky,' Chris started, hoping to kill that idea right away by silencing his mate. Unfortunately, it was James who spoke next.

'Yeah, I get it,' the younger boy said, almost choking with emotion. 'The only way we can get this sorted is if I don't play for Spirebrook at all.'

By midday on Monday, Chris was in a pretty strange mood. The business with James had played on his mind for what little was left of the weekend, and he had failed to complete an English assignment that had to be handed in first thing.

Mr Grass, the guy who took Chris's year for English, wasn't prepared to listen to excuses. When the idea of the new School of Excellence at Oldcester United had been raised, Mr Grass had come out against it. He disliked the idea of a purpose-built school aimed at the small minority of kids who could play football well. From the beginning of term, he had made no secret of the fact that he didn't think Chris, Nicky and Jazz should leave to go to the new school after Easter.

He had made their lives as difficult as he could, trying to prove that football was going to get in the way of their proper education. Chris had worked hard — he was pretty good at English anyway — but he knew that missing the deadline for this essay had undone all his good work.

Just before mid-morning break, Grass had handed Chris a note. 'Take this to Mrs Cole,' the teacher said, pushing his spectacles back on his beaky nose.

'You're sending me to the head for being late with one essay?' Chris complained.

'No,' sneered Grass, looking very pleased with himself. 'She wants to see you anyway. This is just a bonus.'

It was no secret what 'Andy' Cole would want him for. Chris had almost managed to forget the fire after everything else that had happened, but it was top priority with Spirebrook's dragon lady.

Chris made his way to her office with a heavy heart. When he reached the outer door, which led into the school secretary's den, he found the door propped open with a box, and Mr Palmer carting stuff back and forth.

'Give me a hand here,' the upper school head demanded.

Chris worked out what was going on quickly enough. While the portacabin was wrecked, Palmer was going to have to move into this outer office, sharing it with Ms Popov, the eccentric school secretary.

It was an unpleasant reminder as to why Chris was here.

He announced who he was to Ms Popov, but she knew well enough already. She buzzed the intercom, and Chris heard Mrs Cole ask for Chris to be sent right in. He put the box he was carrying down on top of a huge pile of papers and went to the inner door. As he went through, closing the door behind him, he heard the whole pile topple off the desk and on to the floor. Looking back, Chris saw the box had contained the school's soccer trophies, rescued from the safe.

It had been a while since Chris had been to see 'Andy' Cole. He hadn't missed the experience. Mrs Cole's room was bare and cold; just a desk, a few chairs, a bookcase and a filing cabinet. Her shoes clicked on the wooden floor.

'Sit down,' she said, bringing some papers to her desk from the filing cabinet. Chris sat down and stared through the window towards the school gates. He knew this wait was part of her plan to make him feel even more uncomfortable. Well, thought Chris, it's worked.

'Chris, I want you to know straight away that I don't think you were directly involved in starting the fire.'

She was sitting back in her chair, looking at Chris through her gold-rimmed glasses. Her cool, pale eyes didn't blink once. She had her hands steepled in front of her nose like she was praying. Chris noticed a small feather stuck to the lapel of her smart grey jacket. He had a private bet with himself that she would see it and remove it before the ordeal was over. Then he played her words through again in his mind. Not 'directly' involved. Wasn't that a long way short of not involved at all?

'No, Mrs Cole,' he said, which was as good – and as bad – an answer as any other. His mind raced through the possible ways this interview might be going from here.

'I'm sorry if it appeared I doubted your word. I was upset.'

'I understand,' replied Chris quietly, relaxing fractionally. This was going far too well.

'All the same, there are some things we need to talk about.'

Chris sighed (making sure the head didn't see). So much for relaxing.

'We haven't needed to have a talk for a little while, Chris, because I thought you'd come to terms with the idea that there has to be a balance between football and school work.'

'I have, Mrs Cole,' Chris insisted.

The head had been looking down at the report on her desk, but now her eyes were turned on Chris like a pair of spotlights.

'Really? Then what were you doing on the school site at the weekend.'

Not only could Chris not see what this had to do with football, but he couldn't see why the head should be wasting time on something so trivial when there was someone out there prepared to burn down part of the school.

'I was just taking a short-cut to Mac's place,' Chris explained, for what seemed like the hundredth time.

'Something you regularly do,' Mrs Cole snapped back without a pause, 'at least according to Mr Fiorentini.'

Chris tried to work out what would be best – denying that what Nicky had said was true, or putting himself in the frame for something he had rarely done before.

He kept silent, which seemed to be the best option. Teachers, though, have this knack of making silence sound like just what they expected to hear.

'I see . . .' said Mrs Cole, turning the report over. The next page had more lines of neat type, more notes in red pen. Was it about him, Chris wondered? Being able to read upside down was a vital skill for a student at Spirebrook Comprehensive. On this occasion, though, the report was just too far away for him to make out what it said.

'You do realise, Chris, that your academic and disciplinary record from this school will go with you to your new school after Easter?'

'Yes, Mrs Cole.'

'And you do understand that they're not going to be any easier on troublemakers there than we are here?'

'Yes, Mrs Cole.'

'So, it isn't true that you've started thinking that you can ignore the rules here, because soon you'll be leaving?'

'No, Mrs Cole!' Chris insisted loudly, although he knew at once that having recently broken the rule about being on the site at the weekend made his firm denial a bit weaker.

'I'm glad to hear it,' the head smiled.

Chris was really confused now. Just what did Mrs Cole believe had been going on here on Saturday?

'Let me tell you what I think happened here on Saturday,' said Mrs Cole, as if she had read his mind. 'I think the boys who attacked Mr Palmer's office were actually trying to harm you. I think someone with a grudge against you thought the fire would get you into trouble.'

Which, seeing as that was what had almost happened,

made a kind of sense. Only the fire had started before Chris had arrived, and there was no way anyone could have known Chris would come that way. He hadn't known himself until he had crossed the main road a few minutes before.

'I don't think that can be it, Mrs Cole,' he replied.

The head wasn't listening. She was reading the report.

'As you know, Chris – you and I have talked about this before – I'm not a big fan of competitive sport in schools. I think it splits the school into two halves – those who are good at games and those who aren't. It encourages some students to be lazy. And I think it causes silly and destructive feuds.'

'Feuds, Mrs Cole?'

'Yes, like this silly war you have going with Blackmoor.'

But that wasn't about football, thought Chris, realising in the same moment that – of course – he had no idea what it was about, not right from the beginning. The most recent thing had been that business over the Blackmorons getting James's mum the sack; before that, the Blackmorons were smarting over their defeat at the school disco rumble; before that . . .

It was a list that could go on forever. And, Chris realised, it would go on into the future for just as long. Right now, he knew, the Blackmorons would be planning their revenge for the ambush in Loam Park. They would be plotting how to pay the 'Brookers back for that defeat . . . unless . . . unless . . .

Unless they already had.

'Chris? Chris, are you listening to me?'

Chris snapped his brain back on-line. 'Yes, Mrs Cole,' he replied.

Her eyes narrowed. She had spotted his mind wander off, and knew exactly what that meant. 'Is there something you'd like to tell me, Chris?'

Chris thought about it. For several, long seconds, he genuinely did consider letting Mrs Cole know what was going through his mind.

Then he answered: 'No, Mrs Cole.'

'I see . . .' the head replied, in a way that proved that she really *did* see. All the same, Chris didn't change his mind. Mrs Cole closed the brown report folder. 'Very well, we'll leave it there. Just think about what I've said.'

'Oh, I will,' said Chris, smiling. And he really meant it, too.

'I don't want you to bring your sporting rivalries through the gates of this school, Chris. This is a place of learning.'

I've learnt a lot here, he thought. Especially in the last few minutes.

'All right,' the head concluded. 'Off you go. I really hope we don't have to have another one of these chats before you go to your new school.'

'Me neither, Mrs Cole,' said Chris, standing up. He turned towards the door. For all kinds of reasons, he was very keen to get outside the office.

Just as he reached for the door, he remembered the note from Mr Grass tucked in his jacket pocket. He froze, one hand on the door knob. It was a strong temptation to carry on, having forgotten the note.

Mrs Cole had noticed Chris stuck to her door. 'Is there something else, Chris?' she asked. 'Something you'd like to tell me after all?'

Chris turned round, pulling the note from his pocket. It appeared that he was going to have another 'chat' with Mrs Cole after all, and sooner than even she could have guessed.

But, thought Chris, I still haven't seen her remove that feather from her lapel. I just know she will.

And if there was one thing that gave Chris almost as much pleasure as football, it was being right.

Thirteen

Chris spent the next part of the lunch break thinking things through alone. He found a quiet spot on the field behind the tennis courts and ate his sandwiches slowly while he digested the thoughts running through his brain. Once he had it straight in his own mind, he went looking for Nicky and the others.

Just about everyone involved with the school football teams was involved in a wild game on the playground behind Block 3. As soon as he caught sight of Chris, Nicky hoofed the ball on to the grass.

'Your throw!' he yelled at Fuller. 'And we bring Chris on!'

Fuller scowled, but didn't say anything as he lumbered after the ball. Chris noticed the heavy plaster cast on his hand. Fuller clearly hadn't realised that being told to avoid playing football applied to games in the playground.

While he shook his head in despair, Nicky jogged over.

'Come on, get your jacket off. Where have you been? We're nine-six down!'

Apparently, Nicky had picked Chris for his team even though he wasn't around. Chris smiled despite himself.

'I can't play,' said Chris.

'We all know that!' yelled Bruise from nearby.

Chris ignored him.

'What do you mean?' asked Nicky, with concern in his eye.

'I mean I can't play,' said Chris. ' "Andy" Cole has barred me from playing football until after I get that English assignment in, and not even then unless I get at least a "B".'

'Oh!' scoffed Nicky, dismissively. Getting barred from playground football didn't sound like much of a punishment. For a second, Nicky considered not bothering with the maths homework they'd been set before lunch.

Then the penny dropped.

'Oh!' said Nicky. Then again, 'oh!'

'You've got it,' said Chris, but he spelt it out anyway, in case Nicky had missed the point. 'No practice tomorrow, and no match Wednesday.'

Nicky looked alarmed. A few of the others were wandering over, attracted to the bad news like wasps to a picnic.

'But you could get it finished tonight,' insisted Nicky, 'and then . . .'

'I could,' said Chris, 'but even if I do, Grass isn't going to get it marked for a few days. I'll just have to miss this week's game, that's all.'

Nicky's face was a mask of horror. Just behind him, Jazz muttered: 'What rotten luck.'

At once, the horror was gone and Nicky's face was clouding over. He looked around wildly.

'Where's James?' he snarled.

'You wouldn't let him play,' said Jazz, quietly, and with just a trace of bitterness. 'You sent him over to the lower school playground.'

Nicky knew that was right, but cast his eyes round the group anyway.

'Perfect,' he muttered. 'I suppose you've heard why Griff wasn't around this morning?' he added. Chris hadn't. 'He's got the flu. So he won't be playing either. Honestly, this season just goes from bad to worse.'

Chris shrugged. Nicky eyed him closely.

'You're taking all this very calmly,' he said, suspiciously.

'Well, there's not much I can do about it, is there?' Chris answered. 'It's just bad luck.'

Nicky's eyes took on that diamond-hard quality that normally only came when he was either on the edge of his patience – or well past it.

'Yeah . . .' he said at last, filling the pause with noise, even if he didn't understand Chris's attitude at all.

Chris decided not to leave Nicky in such a grim mood. 'Look at it this way, Nicky,' he said, throwing his arm round his mate's shoulder. 'Wednesday's game should be a sitter. Jinx or no jinx, you ought to walk it, even if we are three or four first team choices down.'

'True . . .' agreed Nicky, his natural confidence returning.

'And now that James has decided not to play at all, it doesn't matter even if he is a jinx. So, tomorrow night should be a breeze, right?'

Nicky's face lit up. With all the bad news there had been earlier in the day, he'd forgotten that he'd talked James out of playing for the 'Brook. His normal grin returned. 'Yeah! In fact, now that we've got rid of you as well, we really can't fail!'

Chris converted his grip into a stranglehold. 'That depends on whether Flea can find someone else who can convert your cruddy passes into goals,' he sniped in return. They both laughed and banged heads in the same way as they normally celebrated a goal.

'I think I'm going to puke,' hissed Fuller, loudly. 'Are we playing football, or what?' He had the ball in the crook of his good arm, and was swinging his broken hand backwards and forwards, the heavy cast making everyone back off. Chris gestured towards it.

'Shouldn't you be resting that? Nothing too strenuous, the doctor said.'

'So much you know, Stephens,' scowled Fuller. 'In fact, they're saying it's nowhere near as bad as it first looked. I might be able to have this thing off my hand in just a week or so.'

'Your hand?' Chris responded, jumping slightly as if he had been caught by surprise. 'I was talking about your brain.'

Fuller took a moment to realise he'd been nutmegged by Chris (though there was nothing unusual in that). He took the ball in both hands and threw it at the striker. In one fluid move, Chris pivoted on his heel, spinning to catch the ball on his right instep. It flashed into the goal from fifteen metres.

'The super-sub makes it nine-seven,' called Chris in his best commentator's voice. He winked at Nicky. 'Never say I don't do my bit,' he laughed as he went off.

That had been easier than he'd expected. Chris gritted his teeth and prepared for the second phase of his making-it-up-as-he-went-along master plan.

In the few weeks he had been at Spirebrook, Robert James had been 'promoted' from the lower school to the middle school playground thanks to his football prowess. Now he was back among the younger guys, involved in a whirling, madcap competition that was mixed up with a girls' skipping game, a sort of cricket meets rounders with no bats thing and a cluster of first-formers who were gathered around two noisy brats squaring off for a fight.

'Pack it in,' said Chris firmly as he went past. The fight died before it had started, not because Chris was such a commanding figure that the younger boys had to obey him, but because they wondered what he was doing on their patch and stopped to look.

Before Chris could find James in the middle of the scrum that passed for a football match, he'd managed to take a catch for the fielding side in the other game. That caused a loud row between the two teams as to whether it counted. The kids who had been crowded round the two boys, came over to watch the new argument instead.

Even if Chris didn't find James, his time wouldn't have been wasted.

Just then, one of the boys, a short, thuggish type with dark brown hair and fists the size (and shape) of house bricks came out of the scrum with a tennis ball bouncing wildly in front of him. As far as Chris could tell, this was a break from midfield. With both sides and everyone else wearing identical school uniforms, he had no real idea where even the goals were, never mind who was playing for which team (or who was playing, period!).

It hardly mattered. Barely a second after the ball appeared, a tall figure stepped up from behind a gaggle of skipping girls and intercepted the ball with one deft touch of his left foot. The dark kid ran straight past him, looking from side to side for the ball, as if it had been snatched away from him by magic.

Which, in some ways, it had.

James clipped the ball a second time, out into a small patch of the playground which wasn't so crowded. He called out to a skinny blond kid who was standing some distance away, picking his nose, then slotted an inch perfect pass which gave his team mate (assuming that was what he was) a clear shot on . . . well, a couple of piles of jackets at the far side which might or might not have been a goal.

The nose-picker didn't get close. Instead he held up his hands and shouted at James for not playing it right at him.

'He's probably poked his brains out through his nose,' said Chris.

James laughed, then looked round realising that this was a voice that didn't belong in lower school territory. In fairness, in the middle of that lot, James looked just as out of place. He was really huge compared to some of the other kids his age, easily half a head taller than the biggest of the others. Two years older, Chris wasn't that much bigger himself.

'Chris!' gasped James, showing he could remember names.

'I need a word with you,' said Chris. 'Do they still run the tuck shop out of the biology lab?'

James nodded, and followed as Chris set off towards the classrooms along one edge of the cramped playground. Mrs Wilson, who taught biology in lower school, never left her classroom. Not for break, not for lunch — some thought not after school or during the holidays either. So, it made a sort of sense to have the tuck shop set up to run through the windows of her classroom, with the stock stored in her cupboard during lesson time. Sure, it meant everything had the faint smell of that stuff she pickled dead things in, but the arrangement sort of worked well.

Chris walked over to the window, expecting to talk to James while they queued. Instead, at the approach of this strange alien from the mysterious middle school, the younger kids stepped aside and insisted he was served first.

'Slumming?' asked Mrs Wilson, looking up from her desk.

'I can't get used to the odd taste the Kit-Kats from our tuck shop have,' Chris replied.

'What taste is that?'

'Chocolate.' Good old Mrs Wilson. There wasn't a better straight man in the whole school.

'Very funny,' Mrs Wilson smirked. She went back to her marking.

'Virgin Cola,' said Chris to the girl behind the 'counter'. He would have preferred the Energy drink, but he couldn't see any. 'You want anything?' he asked James. The younger lad shook his head.

Chris took his drink and paid for it. He stepped away from the window, and nodded to James for him to follow. As they walked off, Chris heard the next lad in the queue, having been offered a Pepsi, turn it down and demand the 'special stuff' he was now convinced they kept only for older kids.

Time was short. There weren't many places Chris could

think of where they could have a private word. In desperation, he tried the library.

'OK, listen,' he whispered to James once they were safely tucked away behind the history shelves. 'I want to try and get something through to you, so don't interrupt, OK?'

James was going to respond verbally, but stopped himself, wondering if an answer counted as an interruption. He nodded instead.

'First off, all this jinx stuff is stupid. I want it to stop.'

Chris waited to see if James would object. He didn't.

'You understand me? I believe in luck as much as anyone, but I don't think it sticks to people and I don't believe you can buy it and wear it like old clothes. You know what I mean?'

James decided that reacting to a direct question couldn't count as interrupting. 'But you're superstitious; everyone knows how you have to be on the field last and how you always touch the badge on your shirt for good luck.'

Chris was caught off-guard. After their phone conversation on Saturday, Chris had decided James was a little on the slow side. He'd picked that hole in Chris's logic easily though.

'That's true,' Chris admitted, 'but what does that actually do? I've lost games even when I've done it, I've picked up injuries . . . It doesn't actually work.'

'Then why do it?' James asked. He had listened carefully to everything Chris had said, but all it was doing was confirming what he felt about Chris lately. The guy could play football, but he was a bit vacant between the ears.

Chris bit his lip, and took a moment to think.

'OK,' said Chris at last. 'I believe in luck. And there was a time when I had a string of good luck at football, and it coincided with me being the last one on the field and touching my badge before I came out. Now it's just like a habit, you know. I don't believe it actually does anything.'

Chris knew that sounded stupid. He just hoped James got the message.

The younger boy was nodding, as if he was considering what Chris had said. 'Right . . . You believe in luck, you follow these superstitions because they brought you good luck, but they don't actually bring you good luck any more.'

That was a fair summing up of what he had said, Chris

realised, even if it wasn't what he meant. He suspected James wasn't going to make this easy.

'Let's start again,' Chris said in a low voice, his patience strained. 'There are times when things go well or go badly, and it's not because of what we do or what anyone else does . . . it's just luck. It's a run of things that go one way or the other for no real reason. And sometimes these runs happen when something else happens at the same time; like with me and the badge thing. They aren't connected. Or if they are, it's only in your head. It's not real.'

Clear as mud, Stephens, thought Chris. He paused to try and get his thoughts in order.

Robert James studied the other boy closely, wondering what all this was leading to. There were more holes in what Chris was saying than in the goal nets on the playing field.

'Why did you start?' James said, to nudge things along.

'What?' asked Chris, completely thrown off-guard.

'Why did you start touching your badge? If you don't believe it works.'

Chris's mouth opened and closed like a beached fish. This was all going horribly wrong. It didn't help that he couldn't really remember the superstition starting; it seemed to have been there all his playing life.

'I don't know . . .' he said.

James's face was blank, as if he was lost on the planet 'Dense'. Chris tried desperately to think back.

'I guess there was this one game when I did it, and I had a really good game. So, next time, I did it again. For luck. And things went well in that game too, and I kept on doing it until . . .'

'But why did you do it the first time?' James demanded.

Chris could feel his temperature rising.

'Look, it doesn't matter, OK? Just stop asking stupid questions and listen! This business with the school team – it's a run of bad luck, that's all! It's just coincidence that it's happening around you.'

'That's not what Nicky thinks –'

'Despite what Nicky tells you,' Chris said quickly, 'he isn't always right. And this time, we're going to prove it.'

James arched his eyebrows.

'How?'

'Two things,' said Chris. 'First, if you don't hang around after school Wednesday, it can't be your fault if things go wrong.'

'But what if things go right?' asked James, with a sad note in his voice. 'If we win, won't that prove I was a jinx?'

Chris sighed. He'd known James would see it that way. 'All it will prove is that we've beaten a team we ought to beat in our sleep. More importantly, once we have a win or two under our belts, people will stop thinking about this 'curse' rubbish and get on with playing football. If we beat King Edward's and then beat Blackmoor, you could turn up having broken a mirror, walked under a row of ladders and run over a black cat, and no-one would notice the difference.'

James looked very doubtful. Chris seemed to think that — win or lose — the matter would be closed after Wednesday. James took a gloomier view.

'Wonderful,' he said flatly. 'Is that it?'

Bearing in mind that they were talking about good luck and bad luck, jinxes and curses, it struck Chris as being a bit rich that he didn't get the chance to tell Robert James the second part of his plan.

'Ho! This is a bit of luck,' said Flea as he came round the corner. 'Fancy finding you here, Robert!'

'Looking for me, Mr Lea?' asked James, poetically stating the obvious.

'Yes,' smiled Flea, who clearly had good news to tell. 'I take it you've heard we won't have Griff for Wednesday's game, as well as Fuller being out — not to mention you, of course, Chris.'

Oh, oh.

'So, I was thinking,' the PE teacher continued in a bright voice, while frowning at the strange, gloomy expression on Chris's face.

'What?'

'I was thinking of playing you in the senior team.'

99

Fourteen

As the bell rang at the end of Tuesday's last period, Chris watched as Nicky, Jazz and Russell disappeared at speed to retrieve kit bags from their lockers and make their way to the gym. They didn't even notice Chris wasn't with them.

In fairness, Nicky had asked Chris to come and watch the training session, but Chris had begged off, using the work he had to do as an excuse.

He packed his books away, and walked slowly to the corridor where their lockers lined the wall. He retrieved his own kit bag, dropped in the English books he needed to complete the assignment, and left Block 1, heading for the gates.

On the way out, he saw Robert James racing towards the gym. For someone dreading the effect he had on the team, he looked very keen.

Chris wondered how Nicky would take the news. Chris had decided not to tell him. He wondered, too, how Griff would react, now that Nicky's original plan looked like it was going to happen after all. Robert James subbing for Griff. It was too wild.

As he came closer to the gates, thinking about the way his own master plan had come to grief, Chris saw Fuller posing in front of some uninterested girls. He could imagine how the news about James would get to Fuller. He'd go mental.

At which thought, Chris decided to tell him.

'Keep your head down!' hissed Chris, angrily. Fuller muttered something but ducked his head down anyway.

'What are we waiting for?' he asked.

'There are still some kids over by the corner of the building. If we try to get in now, they'll see us.'

Fuller scratched his head.

'I thought we wanted them to see us!' he said, puzzled

Chris sighed. It was all very well having found a willing volunteer, but having Fuller on his side, was almost more trouble than it was worth.

'We've got to get in, first,' Chris replied. He looked at his partner quickly, checking to see that Fuller was keeping an eye out behind them. To his dismay, he saw Fuller had pulled a scarf up over his mouth and had turned up the collar on his jacket. Apparently, he thought it helped the disguise. Chris was terrified that his next idea might involve him blacking his face like a commando.

He turned back to the front, peering over the low wall. They had been hiding here for a lot longer than Chris had expected. It felt like a lifetime.

At least they hadn't been caught – yet. To get this far they had crept along back streets and down a footpath, wondering all the time if they might bump into one of the enemy (it was hard not to think of them in those terms, even if it did make everything seem like a black and white movie about World War Two). Their 'disguise' (nothing more than some plain jackets borrowed from a mate of Fuller's who only ever wore black) wouldn't survive close inspection.

Then came the tricky bit, sneaking into the girls' grammar school along the main road from Loam Park.

Fortunately, no-one was expecting intruders to arrive from that direction. Also, a rain shower had driven everyone indoors, so the pair of them had got into the grounds. After a short detour, they had sneaked round to the front, hiding among the bushes and trees around the wall. The ground was a little damp, but the branches provided some shelter from the rain.

It was quarter to six. Chris was amazed that there was anyone about around the buildings across the road, a fact which was putting a severe dent in his plans. If they didn't get a clear run soon, they'd have to call off the attempt and try another night.

He looked over his shoulder again. Fuller was, at least, keeping an eye on what was happening behind them. Chris saw that now the rain had stopped a loud hockey game had started on the field about fifty metres away. Fuller was watching it with glee.

'I wouldn't mind a go at that,' he said at one point.

'Hockey?' wailed Chris in disbelief.

'Looks brilliant, don't it?' smiled Fuller. 'I'd love to play a game where they give you weapons.'

For the sake of hockey players everywhere, Chris hoped Fuller's interest in the game never went any further.

'Here we go!' he hissed urgently. The dopey crew hanging around across the road had been joined by another boy, who had just emerged from a side door. The whole pack of them were moving out of the school yard, talking loudly and lighting cigarettes. A harsh voice came down from an upper window – a teacher ordering the boys to throw the cigarettes away. The black-jacketed posse laughed and hurled abuse, but then ran off. The window slammed.

'OK,' said Chris once the four losers were out of sight. 'This is it.'

Like Spirebrook, Blackmoor Comprehensive had been built in the 1960s, swallowing up kids from a few housing estates and tower blocks in the extreme south-west of the city of Oldcester. Like Spirebrook, it was an ugly place, although it was a different kind of ugly. Blackmoor was a single building, a glass and concrete tower six floors high, parked on a patch of land barely half the size of Spirebrook. It was tucked beside a cut-through that led from Blackmoor 'shopping centre' to the main drag into the city.

The people who planned the school may not have known how to build anything attractive, but they must have had a sense of humour because they put Blackmoor Comp up right opposite a smart girls' grammar school.

The girls' school was very small, there being a limit to the number of intelligent girls in Blackmoor (that limit being about three, according to any 'Brooker). It was dwarfed by the 800-place comprehensive over the road.

Over the last 30 years, every head teacher at St George's High School For Girls had fought a running battle to keep the Blackmorons away from their school and its impressionable young girls, with mixed results. The girls were fine, but the quaint old building which housed the school had gradually become covered in razor wire, barred windows and warning notices promising horrible death to anyone who ever tried to break in.

The one old custom St George's hadn't dropped was the flying of a flag at the front of the school. The pole where it normally lived was just to the side of the main entrance.

Normally. Right now the flag was under Fuller's jacket.

'Let's go,' whispered Chris, and they slipped from their hiding place in the long grass and scuttled out through the gate.

This was the risky bit. They had to get across the road, through Blackmoor's gates on the other side and then into the building without being challenged. Luck was on their side. The traffic had stopped at the zebra crossing between the two gates to allow an old woman with a yapping dog on a leash to cross. They went over behind her, flashing past and sprinting through the gate.

So far so good. Now they had to get into the Blackmoor building. Chris had no idea what time the place would get locked up. He didn't imagine the teachers wanted to hang around for any longer than they had to.

He remembered the boys who had been hanging round the side door. Chris guessed they had been waiting for their mate to finish detention. Would the door still be open?

It seemed the best bet. He grabbed Fuller by the arm and swung him in the direction of the door. Fuller jumped, startled (some commando *he* was). His jacket slipped open and the flag tumbled to the floor.

Fuller yelped out a swear word as if that would help. Then there was a shout from behind them and he repeated it.

'Run,' yelled Chris, with a quick look over his shoulder. The challenge had come from a woman's voice, but he couldn't see anyone except the old woman walking her rat.

'Through the door!' yelled Chris. Fuller hesitated, clearly thinking they should be running away. Chris didn't have time to explain that (1) they were going to be out of sight more quickly through the door and (2) they hadn't come all this way to give up now. He went straight to (3), which involved shoving Fuller through the door.

They were on enemy territory, deep in their half. It was really spooky.

Chris let the door fall shut as he checked out their surroundings. A broad, L-shaped hall stretched away from them, ahead and right. At the end of the hall ahead of them, there was a flight of stairs.

'That way!' Chris called, and they took off along the hall, their trainers squeaking as they sprinted over the floor. Chris slid the last five metres, then jumped up the stairs two at a time. He heard a door bang behind him and the woman's voice, sounding even angrier. He didn't look back.

The stairs went up another flight, doubling back on themselves. Leading the way, Chris raced for the next floor, then kept going. The best way to lose any pursuit, he decided, was to leave it wheezing on the stairs.

By the time he reached the top floor, Chris was sure no-one could catch him. Not even Fuller. Chris could hear him labouring up the stairs.

He took the next few moments to scout out the immediate area. The rooms nearest the top of the stairs appeared to be a library. Chris grinned, imagining some Blackmorons going through their whole school career without ever venturing up here.

A passage led towards the front of the school, matching the layout of the ground floor. Chris ran along to the end of the deserted corridor. Large windows looked out over the girls' school, and beyond. Large, heavy latches held them closed.

Chris looked back along the passage to see Fuller staggering up the last few stairs. He waved him over.

'Why . . . why . . .?' Fuller puffed.

'Save it,' said Chris. He was breathing hard himself, but he was in a lot better shape than the defender. Why had he not noticed how unfit Fuller was becoming? There was a time when Spirebrook's Iron Man had been able to run for 90 minutes and still have the strength to terrorise both teams.

He tried a couple of windows. No luck. Then the third one opened.

'Perfect,' he grinned, turning to Fuller. 'OK, give me the flag.'

Fuller reached under his jacket and pulled out the St George's flag. Chris opened it out and draped it out of the window, trapping the top when he closed it again. The flag fluttered outside the window.

'Why . . . why . . . did we . . .?'

Chris clapped his hand on Fuller's back. 'Time to go. My money is on there being a matching staircase to this one at the other end. Follow me.'

Fuller moaned loudly, but took the first faltering steps along the passage, through a set of fire doors. As he reached the doors, he turned to see Chris leaving something on the floor in front of the window.

'What's that . . . all in aid . . . of?' he asked.

'A little insurance,' Chris grinned.

Fuller shook his head, wondering if he had forgotten the plan since Chris had explained it to him. Chris joined him, and the two of them ran along the passage towards the distant set of stairs.

'Why . . . why . . . did we come . . . all the way up here . . .?' gasped Fuller.

'So no-one could see us,' said Chris.

'But you said . . . we wanted . . . the Blackmorons to see us,' Fuller complained for the second time. He'd fallen completely out of the loop now.

'We do. That's "phase two",' said Chris. 'This is "phase one", where we want people to see something, but not us. This is the sneaky bit, remember?'

Fuller looked at him blankly.

'But we are going to rub the Blackmorons' faces in it, right?' he said, sounding really worried.

'As soon as we get out of here,' said Chris.

Getting out proved marginally harder than getting in. Once they were back on the ground floor, the first door they tried was locked. Chris suddenly realised that running up to the top floor was a great way to lose anyone chasing them (as well as providing them with a great spot to plant the flag), but it also gave time for the angry-voiced woman to arrange to have them locked in and trapped.

He had a moment of panic before they found a fire door. Chris rammed the locking bar and they spilled out into the yard. The wailing siren was actually quite reassuring.

They belted from the playground as if their lives depended on it. They didn't look back.

It was about a quarter mile from the school to the centre of Blackmoor, where there was a brave, bright Asda in the middle of a row of shops selling second-hand electrical goods, cheap take-out food and lottery tickets.

Chris and Fuller ran there as quickly as they could (which

105

wasn't all that fast), checking behind all the time to make sure they weren't being chased. Fuller looked ashen-faced and exhausted.

'This ... had better ... work ... Stephens,' he grunted.

Chris didn't reply, his attention fixed straight ahead, on the look-out for anyone from Blackmoor. At first, all he could see were a couple of girls hanging round outside the newsagents. They may or may not have been from Blackmoor — they certainly weren't St George's — but he couldn't be sure.

Then the paper shop door opened, and two boys came out to join the girls. Chris's heart jumped. He knew one of them well. Very well, in fact.

Just along from the newsagents, on the other side of the road, there was a bus stop. Ideal. Chris nudged Fuller, and they came to a halt in front of the doorway of a second-hand furniture shop. Chris looked along the road. There was no bus in sight.

'What now?' gasped Fuller, grateful for the moment's rest.

'We wait for a moment,' Chris replied. His attention was divided between the road and the newsagents. The timing would have to be spot on; he needed a bit of luck.

The four Blackmorons, gathered in a small circle, were laughing about something, looking down. Perhaps they were looking at a magazine, although that suggested that at least one of them could read. The girls were wearing bright top coats over school uniforms. One of the guys was all in black. Chris was more interested in the second guy, the one with the red hair, the dark green sweater and the faded blue jeans.

Then Chris caught sight of a flash of red in the distance. An Oldcester City bus, making its way slowly along the road. Chris couldn't see where it was headed, but that hardly mattered.

'Let's go,' he whispered. Trying to behave as casually as possible, Chris led his partner along the street.

They crossed at an island, jogging steadily. Chris watched from the corner of his eye to see if they were spotted. At first, the little gang were too interested in their purchase to pay any attention to what was going on around them. But then Fuller banged into a metal stand outside a butcher's shop.

The foursome looked up, staring across the road to see what had made the clattering noise. At once, the guy in the jeans and sweater developed an ugly, rabid expression of pure hate. He and Chris had made eye-to-eye contact.

'You!!' the boy howled, loudly. Along the length of the road, people turned their heads to see what was going on.

Chris grinned.

He didn't know the other guy's name, but they had a long history together. Chris remembered another occasion, after a match against Blackmoor, when he had been ambushed outside another newsagent's, opposite the vehicle entrance into Blackmoor school round at the back of the building. Then, he had been cornered by the same guy after he went to buy a paper. There was no doubt it was him — his bright red hair, virtually shaved along the sides but longer on top, made him stand out like one of those beacons on zebra crossings. He had thick lips, and narrow, squinty eyes. He'd bulked up a bit in the last year or so and he was darker-skinned than Chris recalled, but the Spirebrook striker knew he would recognise his target anywhere.

'Hey, Ginger!' yelled Chris.

'Ginger' wasn't happy to see Chris at all. He wouldn't like the idea of being shouted at across the street by a 'Brooker in the middle of Blackmoor at the best of times, but the fact that it was Chris was a mortal insult.

'Come on!' he yelled at his mate, and ran straight into the road.

Chris's heart missed a beat. It would have been too much if the idiot had been run down. His luck held however.

Avoiding one car that had braked hard to avoid him, Ginger arrived on Chris's side of the road like an express train. His mate was still on the other side, working out what 'Come on!' meant. Ginger didn't care.

On that previous occasion, Chris had first managed to outfox the Blackmoor gang — including Ginger — then he had gone out of his way to provoke them, daring them to take him on. And before that, there had been another time when Stephens had jumped into a rumble they had going with Nicky Fiorentini.

All Ginger could think of, when he saw Stephens in front of him, was that Chris seemed to beg for trouble. Now, here he was, on their patch. Surely, this time, he was going to get what he was asking for.

However, in his rage at seeing Chris, Ginger had become

blind to everything else. He ran into Fuller as if the 'Brooker was a wall that had jumped out from nowhere and planted itself in front of him.

'Ooops, sorry,' said Fuller, grinning foolishly. 'Was I in your way?'

Ginger screeched something from his new vantage point on the pavement that Chris couldn't understand. He looked back across the road, to where his mate was making a not-too-brave attempt to get across the road, wearing a 'it's not my fault; I'm doing my best' look of helplessness.

Ginger realised he was on his own, and tried to scramble away on his hands and feet, like a crab with turbodrive.

'What's your game?' he wailed. 'This is our turf!'

'Really?' replied Chris. 'Looks to me like you're the one offside.' He turned his head and saw the bus was coming closer. A woman with a small child had her hand out to stop it. 'Don't worry,' Chris said, 'we were leaving anyway.'

Ginger's face flooded with different expressions, one after the other. His fear faded once he had scrambled far enough away to be out of immediate danger; then a look of savage anger turned into frustration as he realised Chris and his mate were going to escape.

The bus pulled up. Fuller followed the woman on board and paid their fares. Chris followed him on.

'Bye!' he called, waving to Ginger from the doorway.

As he turned round Chris saw the driver had been watching all this closely. His eyes narrowed as he inspected Chris, paying close attention to the plain black jacket Chris was wearing.

'You're not from Blackmoor . . .' he said. Chris didn't reply — he hadn't expected to be dealing with a bus driver. The guy, who looked about thirty or so, continued to stare at him. 'I bet you're from Spirebrook,' he said.

Chris took a hard look at himself, wondering what had given the game away. The driver laughed.

'Them Blackmorons, eh? They just never learn!'

The driver was still laughing as he closed the door and steered the bus away from the stop, leaving Ginger standing on the pavement, fists clenched.

'You're letting the old school down, getting caught on their patch,' he said as Chris prepared to walk to the seats. 'It never used to happen in my day.'

Chris didn't reply, but went to join Fuller. He was grinning ear-to-ear long before he sat down. It was a good feeling; not only had they managed to put one over on their hated rivals, but they had done it in a way that even previous generations of 'Brookers hadn't thought of. Chris imagined some future Spirebrook students asking themselves what they could do to top the Stephens plan. They'd find it hard. And yet, at its root, Chris's scheme was so simple.

Beside him, Fuller scratched his head and said in a small voice: 'I don't get it. What did we do all that for again?'

Fifteen

Nicky's sixth sense was going off like radar.

'What were you up to last night?' he asked as soon as he saw Chris.

'Morning, Nicky! How was training?'

'Don't try to change the subject,' Nicky snapped, looking hurt. 'I've heard you went off somewhere with Fuller. From what I was told, you looked like you were off on an SAS mission, all black clothing and stuff.'

Chris thought about denying everything, but Nicky would get it out of him in the end. Like most people who could tell a lie with a perfectly straight face, Nicky was a master at spotting when someone else did it.

'We went to pay Blackmoor back for their visit,' he said.

Nicky's face instantly became a mask of horror and surprise. 'You . . .?' he gasped. He stopped dead on the pavement, watching as Chris took another three steps before he realised Nicky wasn't there. People pushed past, glaring at Nicky for blocking their route, but he didn't notice any of them. He was fighting for self-control, staring at Chris as if he was a stranger.

'Are you out of your mind?' he choked.

Chris knew Nicky was getting things out of proportion. He smiled back at his mate, trying to calm his fears, but Nicky picked up the wrong signal.

'How can you laugh about it, Chris? You could have ended up in serious trouble!'

If Chris hadn't been laughing before, he was now. Nicky lecturing him about getting into trouble? That was rich!

'It was no big thing, Nicky . . .' he began.

Nicky stepped closer. He steered Chris off the pavement into the shelter of a chemist's doorway. Through the glass door, Chris saw the shopkeeper notice them and wave them away. He didn't open for another thirty minutes.

'Tell me everything!' Nicky insisted.

Chris sighed, but he was resigned to the fact that he might spend the rest of his life in this doorway if he didn't tell Nicky what he wanted to know. Anyway, Chris was quite proud of the stunt he had pulled yesterday. So, he let the story tumble out, making sure he included every amusing detail, like the old dear with the dog chasing after them and the way Fuller had been gasping like an old woman himself by the time they reached the top of the stairs.

As the story unfolded, Nicky's expression changed from horrified attention to outright disbelief to fury. Chris, watching his friend's eyes, couldn't understand what Nicky was getting so het up about.

'So, why didn't you let me on it?' Nicky said, sounding sorry for himself. 'That whole flag thing was my idea, you know.'

Chris had a sudden flashback to a conversation he and Nicky had had a few weeks back, when they had been trying to come up with a scheme to get the Blackmorons back for the grief they had given James's mum at the cinema. Nicky had suggested they 'borrow' something from St George's and plant it at Blackmoor, so that everyone would think their rivals had done it. He'd scouted it out from the safety of his cousin's car one evening, and noticed the flag.

Chris had come up with the alternative plan, the one involving the ambush at Loam Park.

'Oh, man,' sighed Chris. 'That's right. Sorry, Nicky. I forgot.'

Nicky gave him a kind of half-smile that suggested he accepted the apology, but still didn't understand what Chris had been playing at.

'I thought we'd squared things with them, anyway?'

'Yeah, but . . .' Chris stopped himself going any further. Up until now, he had kept his theory that the Blackmorons had caused the fire at the school to himself. He was frightened some of the others would overreact, searching for revenge in a way that could get really dangerous. Nicky worst of all.

'It just seemed the right thing to do,' said Chris, at last. He knew it sounded feeble, but it was all he could come up with. He glanced through the glass door again. The chemist was still watching them closely as he prepared to open the shop. Nicky saw him too. He made a face through the window.

'Couldn't it have waited?' Fiorentini asked, his quick temper rising again now that the chemist had got on his nerves.

'I wanted to move quickly,' said Chris. He wanted to move quickly now, too. Nicky was getting more and more curious, like a dog on a scent. If Nicky ever got his teeth into the real reason why Chris had acted the way he had, he'd never let go. He stepped from the doorway.

Nicky followed. His brow was furrowed deeply, his brain cooking hotly.

'Why? Why couldn't it wait?'

'Wait for what?'

'Wait for me!'

Chris sighed. If only it was as simple as that.

'You've got football all this week, Nicky. In fact, we have football every night, every week. I just got grounded from school football, remember? So, this was my chance.'

Nicky gave that a lot of thought.

'Yeah, but chance for what?'

Chris was beginning to run out of energy for this discussion. He thought about telling Nicky the truth. He thought about telling his mate that the Blackmorons had torched Spirebrook; he thought about telling Nicky that he had taken Fuller as a poor second choice, but that Nicky had never figured in his plan; he thought about reminding Nicky that it was possible for him to do something without Fiorentini holding his hand.

Any of those was likely to cause a major row. So he settled for shouting at Nicky instead.

'Look – it was just a dumb prank, OK? No big deal. I had the chance to rattle the monkey's cage, and I took it. What's your problem?'

It turned out that Chris had just stated the problem. Nicky was watching him, his stare cold and direct.

'Isn't that the point?' said Nicky, icily. 'It was just a prank. They set fire to our school, so you took revenge by sticking a flag through a window?'

Oh, oh.

There was a huge note of disbelief in Nicky's voice. Chris could see that Nicky didn't know what to think. Was Chris telling him a gag? Or a lie? The one thing Nicky wasn't prepared to accept was that Chris had just told him the plain truth. On the face of it, thought Chris, it did sound a bit limp.

And just to make it worse, Nicky had reached the same conclusion Chris had about the fire on Saturday. Great minds think alike.

'The fire? What makes you think it was someone from Blackmoor?'

Nicky rolled his eyes. 'Don't tell me you hadn't figured that out!' he cried. 'It's obvious! They owed us, didn't they? After that thing over in Loam Park? It has to have been them!'

'I don't know, Nicky . . .' said Chris, limply. They were getting closer to the pedestrian crossing — the same one Chris had used on Saturday.

'Oh, get real! You're supposed to be the clever one!'

Chris ignored the sharp compliment. 'OK, Nicky. Let's assume you're right. What would you want to do? Go over there and torch their place in revenge?'

'No!' snapped Nicky, impatiently. 'I just mean — well, what was the point of what you did? It's just so . . . pathetic!'

Chris looked away, trying not to overreact. That was when he saw Robert James on the far side of the road, hurrying towards them. Even though he was grateful for the distraction, Chris wasn't sure that James was the person he wanted to see right now.

'Hey,' said Chris in a low voice. 'How did he get on last night? Any sign of the curse?'

Nicky knew Chris was pulling his chain. 'Very funny. No, nothing unusual happened.'

'I told you all that bad luck stuff was nonsense,' said Chris quickly, in the last few moments before James came close enough to hear them.

'Hi!' called the younger boy as he fell in at Nicky's side. 'Have you heard the news?'

Chris groaned inside, wondering what it was this time (and wondering how James got to hear this stuff first all the time).

'What?' grunted Nicky.

'Someone nicked the flag from St George's School last night, then hung it from the top floor over at Blackmoor.'

There were few things that Nicky liked better than knowing more than someone else. He didn't get the chance very often.

'Well, of course we knew!' he scoffed. 'It was Chris who did it.'

James appeared suitably taken aback at that piece of news. He looked at Chris with some horror.

'You did it?' Chris started to frame a reply, but James continued before he'd thought of the first word. 'Then you could be in deep trouble.'

Chris's heart missed a beat. 'How come?' he demanded.

'Because they know it was one of our mob,' James explained. 'And the head teacher from St George's is coming over to our school today to find out which one of us it was!'

114

Sixteen

⚽

The best place to hold this particular council of war was behind the gym. They had gathered up as many of the usual suspects as they could find, including Russell, Mac and Fuller.

The word was that a special assembly was going to be held right after registration. The head teacher from the girls' High School was going to be there.

'What's the problem?' asked Fuller. 'She can't recognise us, we were in disguise!'

Chris had already explained to the others that he and Fuller had gone to Blackmoor in borrowed black jackets, hoping that anyone who saw them from a distance would think they were Blackmorons. Apparently, this hadn't worked.

'Maybe the guy you saw at the bus stop grassed you up,' Mac said.

'That's hardly likely, is it?' commented Nicky. Chris dismissed the idea as well. It just wasn't how things were done. And besides, the guy would have to admit that he'd let Chris and Fuller escape. Very bad for his street cred.

'One of the girls, then?' Mac said, determined not to let go of this idea.

That was more possible, but Chris still didn't think it was right. The girls hadn't managed to get a good look at him and Fuller. The only one who knew them was Ginger.

'It's something else,' he said. He felt sick to his stomach. He could be in huge trouble if this all went wrong.

Nicky was pondering another aspect of the affair. 'How come you were seen at all? Was it just bad luck?'

Chris looked up. Nicky was standing right beside James, as if he knew the real root of the problem already.

'No!' he said quickly.

'No,' Fuller was saying at the same time, only with a lot less desperation and a lot more pride. 'We *wanted* to be seen.'

The others looked at him as if Fuller had finally proved once and for all that he wasn't wearing a full kit.

'Not by no teachers or anything!' Fuller explained. 'But we wanted one of *them* to see us, so they would know who pulled it off.'

'Why?' asked Mac, who couldn't understand that explanation.

'So we could rub their noses in it,' grinned Fuller. That was how Chris had attracted him to the plan.

'So, maybe that's why Ginger spilled the beans,' cried Mac, prepared to worry away at his theory until he died.

Chris still didn't see it like that. 'All the other times we've scrapped with the Blackmorons, no-one's ever said anything. Why start now?' Not even Mac could provide an answer for that.

The last few minutes before the first bell ticked away. Chris felt more and more as if he was doomed.

'OK, let's start thinking coolly,' demanded Nicky. 'This woman's coming here to try and find the guys who nicked her flag. Well, she's hardly likely to search through the whole school, is she? So, we just have to make sure no-one can get a clear view of Chris or Fuller in assembly.'

Russell took a long look at Fuller, wondering how they could keep him out of sight. Nicky had seen the same problem.

'You need to have a word with some of the guys in your year,' he told the bigger boy. 'Try to sit in the middle of all the tall blokes. Keep your head right down and don't make eye contact with any of the teachers.'

'Right,' agreed Fuller, who was hardly likely to go eyeball to eyeball with a member of staff at the best of times. He started to move away, searching for some of his year group. The fact that he was looking for a way to hide didn't stop him yelling across the playground to a few of his mates.

'We'll do the same with Chris,' Nicky added, shaking his head at Fuller's stupidity. Everyone started making mental comparisons, wondering who needed to be asked, conned or persuaded into sitting around the striker.

One of the tallest people there didn't figure in his plans. James was very quiet, standing on the fringes of the group, aware that he would be sitting well forward of Chris's class, among his own year group. Looking up, Chris saw James had that pale, sick look around his features once again.

'What's the matter with you?' he asked, standing up and walking over. Chris knew he could leave the organising to Nicky for now.

'Remember telling me how there was no such thing as a jinx?' James said. Chris sighed. 'No, I mean it,' James snapped, seeing Chris looking away. 'This is another disaster. I'm just bringing you one bit of bad luck after another.'

Chris could feel his temperature rising. 'Get real!' he growled. 'Why does everything have to be about you? Maybe we were unlucky – or maybe we were just careless. Why does that have to be anything to do with you?'

James didn't answer, but he hadn't been persuaded. Chris looked him in the eyes and saw that there was a lot of determination inside the younger kid, along with the sadness.

'OK,' said Chris, a little more gently. 'No-one got hurt did they? I mean, a lot worse could have happened to me and Fuller last night. And what about football practice? That went OK, didn't it?'

Still James didn't speak. Chris gave it one last try.

'Look, I knew it had to be someone from Blackmoor who started the fire here. And it wouldn't surprise me if it was the same bunch who stole that stuff from the youth club. So I wanted to try and flush them out last night. When I spoke to you in the library yesterday, I was going to ask you to come with me. I figured if nothing went wrong, you'd see this curse thing was just stupid.'

'But it did go wrong!'

'Yeah, well,' Chris responded, 'we don't know how or why yet. And you could look at things another way. You were lucky Flea found us and invited you to play for the seniors. If you hadn't been training here, you might have been with me. It cuts both ways, Robbie. Sometimes, when one person gets unlucky, someone else picks up some good luck. And vice versa.'

Chris knew it wasn't the clearest argument he'd ever offered, but it seemed to do the trick. The wounded, haunted look on James's face slowly faded away. For just a second, there was a hint of a smile on his lips.

The whole group heard the harsh bellow at the same moment.

'Fuller! Stand still!'

'Aw, man . . .' moaned Nicky. He was first to the corner, but all of the others followed him to see what had happened.

Fuller was standing in the middle of a fast-growing bubble of space. Across the playground, but closing fast, 'Andy' Cole was marching towards him. She didn't look happy.

Chris saw there was someone else behind Mrs Cole, a small, slight woman in a plain blue dress and a navy jacket. She was walking very slowly in Mrs Cole's wake.

No-one was paying her much attention. In fact, there were only two people in the playground who didn't have their eyes on Fuller or Mrs Cole. One was Chris. And the other was the old lady who had been crossing the road when Chris and Fuller had sprinted over, carrying the flag they had stolen. The flag Fuller had dropped before they went through the door.

Chris was certain she had seen that happen. He was also certain that she was looking directly at him now, and had recognised him as easily as she had picked out Fuller across the playground.

There was one other thing he was certain about.

He was in deep trouble now.

For the second time in as many days, Chris had the chance to admire the decoration of Mrs Cole's office. There was a vase of fresh flowers on the corner of the desk today, but nothing much else had changed.

This time, of course, Chris was not alone. Standing beside him, arms behind his back like a defiant soldier on parade, Fuller was making his presence very plain. He insisted he had no idea why he was in any trouble. Mrs Cole allowed him to bluster on for a minute, then shot his defence down in flames.

She wasn't alone either, of course. The frail, elderly lady was sitting at the end of Mrs Cole's desk. Up close, she didn't appear so old. Her eyes were dark, and full of sharp intelligence. There was a determined look about the way she set her jaw.

Deep, deep trouble, thought Chris.

'Just stop there, Mr Fuller,' said Mrs Cole, and Fuller's complaint dried up at once. 'Andy' turned to the other woman.

'Mrs O'Connell, didn't you tell me there was something very noticeable about the bigger of the two boys?'

'He has a plaster cast on his right hand,' the woman said. No messing there, Chris thought. Her voice was like two roof slates grinding together.

'Andy' turned back to face the boys, demanding that Fuller hold out his hands. Chris could feel him struggle for a moment, trying to think of a way to disguise the hard, grey sleeve around his wrist and hand, but he was on a loser. Grudgingly, he held out his hands.

Mrs Cole already knew about the cast, of course, which is why they had tracked Fuller down so easily.

'I recognise his face too,' added the other woman, so there wasn't any doubt. 'I saw him clearly, just before they went in through the door.'

That was the end of Fuller's defence. Mrs Cole stared at him with an expression that could have frozen a volcano, then she waved her hand in a dismissive gesture towards the door.

'Go back to your class, Mr Fuller. I'll speak with you later.'

No-one was more surprised at this turn of events than Fuller. For a moment, he hesitated, flicking his eyes towards Chris as if he was going to ask for advice. Then he was out of the room like Linford Christie. It may only have been a temporary escape, but there was no way Fuller was going to miss the chance to put off facing whatever penalty Mrs Cole could think of.

Chris knew better. This was not good news. By letting him stew for a few hours, Mrs Cole was making Fuller's punishment worse. It also meant she could pick them off one at a time. As soon as the door closed, she faced Chris with an even greater look of calm determination on her face.

This was not going well.

'There's no way that Fuller was the brains behind the prank,' Mrs Cole said, evenly. She was speaking to Mrs O'Connell, but her eyes never once strayed from Chris's.

'A "prank" like this hardly needs much "brains",' the other woman replied. Her eyes were fixed on Chris as well. It wasn't an experience he felt very comfortable with.

'Believe me,' said Mrs Cole, 'someone else actually had the idea.' She paused for a moment. 'Anything to say, Chris?'

He could think of plenty of things. 'Help!' came first,

followed closely by 'Let me out of here!' and 'It was all Nicky's fault!' He doubted any of them would help, so he forced himself to keep calm and just answered: 'No, Mrs Cole.'

The two head teachers watched him carefully. Chris tried to concentrate on a map of the city fixed to the wall behind Mrs Cole's head. Fascinating things, maps. Chris had never been so interested in one before as he was now.

'He isn't denying it,' said Mrs O'Connell, in her harsh, scraping voice.

'I'd like some more evidence than that,' Mrs Cole responded, with just the slightest delay. Chris couldn't help but switch his gaze to meet her eyes. Was there a chance she didn't believe he was involved? It didn't seem likely that she'd be on his side. After all, it was only a few days since he last appeared on school premises when he didn't belong.

Mrs O'Connell's voice became even more brittle.

'As I said to you earlier, Mrs Cole, I didn't get as good a look at the second thief as I did at the Fuller boy.'

'As you said . . .' Mrs Cole echoed, bristling at the use of the word 'thief'.

'But he's the right height, and his hair is the right colour, except . . .'

Chris looked to the side, and knew 'Andy' was turning to face the other woman as well.

'Except?'

'Well, I must admit I thought his hair wasn't so . . . so . . . wild. This lad looks as if he's been dragged through a hedge backwards.'

Chris was happy to admit (especially now!) that his hair was a pretty wild thatch. Within days of having it cut, it sprouted back into being a wild tangle no comb could pass through. The only time it laid flat was when it was wet.

Such as when he had been out in the rain.

Mrs O'Connell hadn't made that connection. The shower that had caught Chris and Fuller as they made their way into the High School, the one that had continued to soak them as they borrowed the red and white flag from its home beside the door, had flattened his hair down, plastering it to his skull. This morning, it was back to its usual, unkempt state.

'So, is this the second boy or not?' demanded Mrs Cole.

Her colleague narrowed her eyes and glared at Chris as if

120

she was hoping to drill through his forehead and find the answer written on his brain.

'I . . .' she began, and Chris sighed inwardly as he realised that all the certainty had slipped from her voice. 'I . . .' He held his breath. Maybe he was off the hook after all. Maybe –

'Yes, it's him.'

Rats.

There was a long, long pause after that. Mrs Cole took quite a while to shift her attention away from Mrs O'Connell and back to Chris. When she did so, she waited for an even longer period to see if Chris would want to say anything.

Even though he was trembling and his stomach was churning, Chris kept silent. Say nothing, he kept telling himself, say nothing.

While he was standing there, repeating that instruction in his mind over and over again, another thought jumped into his mind. The watch. No-one had mentioned the watch. From that, his thinking moved along to wonder why no-one from Blackmoor was here. It was as if the game had ended at half-time, with Chris and Fuller pinching the flag. Nothing had been said about them going into Blackmoor at all.

Coincidentally, Mrs Cole started to explore that very same avenue.

'I take it no-one from Blackmoor Comprehensive saw anything?'

'Them!' snorted Mrs O'Connell dismissively. 'If you could see how they let the children from that school run riot, you'd know the answer to that question already. Every day, there's some insult, some piece of vandalism or graffiti. The staff at Blackmoor aren't likely to have seen a thing.'

Aren't likely to. Now that's an interesting choice of words, thought Chris. Why not 'didn't'? Was it possible that Mrs O'Connell hadn't spoken to anyone from Blackmoor at all?

The older woman seemed to sense that the conversation had taken a turn that she hadn't expected. Just so she could score another goal at Chris's expense, she added: 'I had hoped things were different at Spirebrook.'

The atmosphere in the room dropped ten degrees. 'Andy' bit her lip for a moment before she replied.

'I'm sure they are. Which leads me to ask a question – how did you know the boys you saw were from Spirebrook?'

It was a simple question, and a fair one. If this was as straightforward as Mrs O'Connell had been trying to make it sound, it would have been easy to answer. But she took several moments to gather her thoughts, and there was a shifty, uneasy look about her as she replied.

'I was assured by Blackmoor that it wasn't any of their boys. So I talked to my girls. One of them said she saw the vandals later and recognised them.'

Chris almost called out to deny it. He knew that couldn't be true. They hadn't been seen by any girls at the school. And besides, even if they had, none of the girls could possibly have recognised them; none of them knew Chris (and he felt fairly safe thinking that Fuller didn't mix in their social circles either).

But still he kept silence. The only way to challenge Mrs O'Connell was to admit he was there. His best hope lay in leaving things with 'Andy'.

His head teacher was examining him closely yet again. 'Have you anything to say, Chris?' she asked.

'No,' said Chris, and then at the last moment he added: 'But there's been some mistake.' That, at least, was true.

Mrs Cole nodded slowly, resting her hands on the desk.

'Very well,' she said. 'Go back to class. I'll deal with you later.'

It could have been the same tactic she had used on Fuller, of course, but Chris was hoping Mrs Cole had caught the same hesitancy in Mrs O'Connell's voice he had. Maybe, just maybe, there was a way out of this, provided nothing else happened to muck things up.

He was on the point of turning to head for the door when there was a knock on it. Chris froze, slightly confused.

'Enter!'

The door opened inwards. First to step into the room was Flea, who filled the space so completely it was difficult to see if anyone was behind him.

'Mrs Cole,' he said. 'I think you need to hear this.'

He turned round, beckoning to someone behind him.

'Come on,' he said. 'You can tell the head what you've just told me.'

122

Chris's sixth sense was buzzing loudly. When Robert James entered the room, it wasn't really a surprise.

'Mrs Cole,' the younger boy said, 'there's been a mistake.'

'Really?' asked 'Andy', sitting back. 'And what's that?'

It took James another moment to get the words out. He stood at Flea's elbow, swallowed hard and let his eyes drift to the floor. When he spoke, it was in a small, timid voice.

Everyone heard him OK, though.

'It wasn't Chris who played that joke last night ... it was me.'

Seventeen

It was a long, strange morning. Chris sat in the lessons, and he
knew that words were being spoken, some of them to him,
but nothing penetrated his head. He couldn't remember
anything after he'd left Mrs Cole's office. When the class set
off for another classroom after history, Chris was almost left
behind.

'You asleep, Chris?' laughed Nicky. He couldn't wait to get
out of the room, as usual.

During break, Flea came over while he stood on the edge of
the playground, staring across the field but not really watching
what was going on.

'Good news,' said Flea. 'Mrs Cole has changed her mind
about you playing football. That means you can play in tonight's
match. You have got your kit here, haven't you?'

'No, sir,' said Chris, in a dreamy voice.

'Well go and get it at lunchtime!' suggested Flea loudly, after
waiting for Chris to make the suggestion himself.

Chris nodded, which Mr Lea decided was as good an
answer as he was going to get. He walked off muttering about
whether Glenn Hoddle ever had this much trouble.

During the next double period (physics!), Chris didn't hear a
word spoken by that teacher either. He was starting to be able
to think again, but not about school work. There was only one
problem Chris could focus on – why had Robert James taken
the blame for what had happened at the High School?

After a few moments of standing there with his mouth open,
but no sound coming out, Chris had tried to stop James taking
the rap for the prank Chris had pulled. It was hopeless.

James had rattled off the whole plan. It didn't matter that he had only heard it himself that morning, he knew it perfectly. He told Mrs Cole how they had got into the High School, where they had waited, when they had taken the flag, how they had crossed the road and raced to the top floor of Blackmoor Comprehensive . . . Every single detail except one.

The watch. He hadn't known about the watch.

Chris had kept that secret to himself, part of his master plan that didn't seem quite so masterful any more.

But what good could it do now? There was no point Chris telling 'Andy' Cole about the watch when no-one in the room knew what it meant. It proved nothing. In fact, no-one in the room knew anything about a watch at all.

So, after Robert had blurted out his story – Chris's story, as it really was – Chris had been left trying to save the day without any idea how.

'Wait, Mrs Cole,' he said, 'this isn't right.'

'It sounds right to me, Chris,' the head teacher explained.

'But it wasn't James!' Chris protested in vain.

'But he's confessed to it all,' snapped the old woman from St George's, her voice back to its nastiest.

Chris had tried to explain that he didn't know why James had said it was him, but it wasn't, and that was the truth. Listening to himself, Chris knew it wasn't much of an ex-planation.

'Two minutes ago you thought it was me,' he cried, changing tactics.

'That's because you didn't deny it.'

In school, Chris knew, the right to silence people had in court wasn't a rule any teacher obeyed.

'I still haven't denied it!'

'But this other boy confessed,' the St George's head said again. That was clearly enough as far as she was concerned.

'But that's not what happened . . .' Chris sighed, desperately.

Mrs O'Connell frowned to show what she thought of that, then turned to face 'Andy' Cole.

'Go back to your class,' the head said quietly, but forcefully.

Chris was on the verge of arguing some more, but Mrs Cole lifted her hand to stop him saying anything. 'Go back to your class,' she said again.

Chris felt helpless, but he knew that there was nothing he could do. One part of his mind was saying that he needed time to think, and that there was nothing so terrible could happen to James that couldn't be put right later. At the same time, another part of him wanted to stay.

The first part won. Chris had turned slowly and gone out through the door Flea was still holding open. The last thing he heard as he went out into the outer office was the harsh voice of Mrs O'Connell.

'The way boys stick together – standing up for each other, covering for each other . . . It's times like this I'm glad I work at an all girls' school.'

Then the door had closed behind him, and Chris had been left to try and pick up the pieces of the day.

Leaving the physics class, Nicky was in a very good mood. He was beaming so widely that everyone watching him wondered if his face might crack open. He strangled Jazz in a head lock, threw some screwed-up paper at Russell and even managed to avoid being rude to a teacher who pulled him up for dropping litter. It was scary.

As usual, Nicky made a bee-line for Chris at the end of the lesson.

'Back in the team!' he said. Good news travelled fast.

Chris gave Nicky a half-hearted smile in reply.

'I saw Flea talking to you earlier,' Nicky continued, explaining how he knew. 'So I went to check the new team list in the gym at the end of break. You're in, James is out.'

Chris nodded.

'His luck didn't last very long,' Nicky went on, looking down at the hall floor, his smile fading for just long enough for Chris to wonder if Nicky had changed his mind about their young team mate.

Nicky looked up. His white teeth were dazzling and his eyes were bright. Nicky really was in a *horribly* good mood.

'So I was right about the curse.'

For the first time that morning, Chris felt some of the pressing weight of his thoughts slip off a little. He couldn't believe what he had heard.

'What?' he choked.

'It's obvious isn't it?' Nicky declared. 'Wherever that kid goes, bad things happen. He really is a jinx – even to himself.'

126

Chris wasn't feeling quite himself, or he might have become genuinely angry with Nicky. Sometimes, when Fiorentini got an idea in his head, he twisted everything that happened so that it would fit. This was one of those times.

'Nicky, what are you talking about? James getting into trouble hasn't got anything to do with luck! He *told* Mrs Cole that he and Fuller were the ones who took the flag.'

'Unlucky and stupid!' was Nicky's only comment.

'But it was me!' yelled Chris, developing more of a rage with each passing second. 'You know that, I know that and James knows it. So, why would he tell anyone that it was him?'

Nicky didn't have a quick, easy answer for that. Frankly, the reasons didn't matter to him at all. The result was all that mattered.

'How do I know?' he said, surprised at just how steamed up Chris was getting. It didn't make sense. 'But if it means you can play tonight, I'd say we came out on top.'

There was no easy answer to that. Chris felt his appetite for a row with Nicky slowly disappear.

'I've got to go home and get my kit,' he said.

Nicky's smile came back at full strength. 'See if you can get back before the end of lunchtime,' he told Chris. 'I'll bring you on as a late sub like we did yesterday. Did you see Fuller's face? What a riot!!'

Chris jogged off before Nicky could begin the complete action replay. He knew Nicky would soon find another victim to listen to the tale again, even if it was Russell Jones or Mac, or someone else who'd been there at the time.

Chris stashed his school bag in his locker and prepared to make the short journey home to get his boots and other kit. It wouldn't take long. In fact, if he ran most of the way there and back, he'd probably be on the playground before the lunch-time game had even started.

Leaving Block 1 behind, Chris took the path towards the gates. He was about halfway there when he changed his mind.

The same two girls Fuller had been showing off to the night before were loitering by the gate, eating crisps and giggling loudly. This time, they had a different jester providing them with entertainment.

Seeing them reminded Chris that he wanted to talk to Fuller. It wasn't something he wanted to do while all the others were around – and anyway, Chris doubted Fuller would be playing football with the rest of them that lunchtime. So where else might he hang out?

He wondered if Fuller might be getting dinner – he was a glutton for food and often had lunch in the dining hall as well as bringing stuff to school. It was worth checking.

As he approached the dining room, he saw a small queue winding out into the passage. Evidently, the fact that some of the students might want to eat dinner at dinner time had caught the kitchen staff by surprise and they weren't ready yet. Only a few, older students had been let into the hall so far.

Chris trotted up to the door to take a look inside.

'Hey, Stephens!' came a familiar, but throaty voice. 'No pushing in!'

'Griff! I didn't know you were back.'

Griff was huddled against the wall by the dining room door, his hands tucked under his arms and the collar of his jacket turned up as if there was a chill wind. His face looked pale.

'It was come to school or put up with another day of my mum's fussing,' Griff explained. 'I hoped I might be able to doss around and watch TV all day, but she keeps coming upstairs to keep me company. I'm sick of soup and fresh orange juice and all kinds of healthy food. So I thought I'd come here.'

Chris gave him an encouraging smile. In this toned down, flu-ridden state, Griff was actually quite human.

'You seen Fuller?' Chris asked.

Griff and those around him made various scoffing noises as if Chris must have just stepped off a ship from Mars.

'Where have you been?' asked Griff, pausing to cough wetly. 'Fuller's been suspended.'

'Suspended?'

Griff managed to stop coughing for long enough to stare at Chris in a way that suggested cogs were turning in his mind.

'Yeah, over this St George's thing you and he . . .' His eyes narrowed. 'How come you're still here?'

Chris had suspected Fuller would tell his mates what had happened – that wasn't a problem. What he hadn't suspected was that Fuller would end up in such severe trouble while he was getting off scot-free.

'I've no idea,' Chris cried.

Griff and the others weren't much help. They were now

focused on the fact that Fuller had been carpeted, while Chris was still wandering around.

'Cole sent Fuller home for the rest of the week. That old bat from St George's made such a fuss, she didn't have any choice.'

Griff pushed away from the wall. 'The way I heard it, she'd done the same to you!'

Chris stepped back. He didn't like the way this was going.

Griff turned to face a long, tall, skinny guy with a bony face and a nervous giggle like a hyena.

'That's what you said, right, Dog? Cole sent them both home.'

Dog took a moment to think. Chris decided that he really needed longer – maybe an hour or two – before he pulled that trick off.

'That's what I heard. Spider said Cole had found out who was involved, so she had sent Fuller and the other guy home.'

The other guy, thought Chris. The other guy – not him. That could only mean one person.

Griff was looking more like his old self; mean, spiteful and aggressive. Chris took another step back. It occurred to him that he could just tell Griff there had been a mix-up and that Robert James had been the second guy sent home instead of him. On the other hand, was it a good idea for Chris to admit that *two* other boys were in trouble, while he was still free and clear?

Probably not. Besides, Griff had fastened on a new idea.

'How did Cole know about Fuller so quickly, Chris?'

Griff and the others stepped forward as a group, with the guys at both ends of the line moving out behind Chris. Any second now he'd be trapped. And he doubted that the only punishment he'd have to suffer would be having to eat school dinner with them. More likely, he'd be on the menu.

'That stupid prank was all your idea, Stephens,' Griff was saying. 'How come you've got off? Did you grass Fuller up to save your own neck?'

I'm doomed, thought Chris.

Rescue came from a very unexpected quarter. One of the dinner ladies appeared at the dining room door, pushing it back against the wall with a loud crack and yelling at the queue that the food was ready at last.

The confusion gave Chris the chance he needed. After a long wait for lunch, those people in the queue who weren't interested in taking 'revenge' (plus the ones who hadn't figured out what was going on just yet), surged for the door. Some of Fuller's closer friends froze, trapped between wanting to grab Chris and make him pay and not wanting to lose their place in the queue.

Chris backed away into space quickly. Griff growled at him, but this just made him start coughing again. Deprived of their leader, the others drifted back towards the food line.

'Hey!' called the dinner lady to Chris. 'Don't you want anything?'

Chris looked into the eyes of the group around Griff.

'No thanks,' he said. 'I just lost my appetite.'

Eighteen

'Listen, Nicky, we have to talk.'

Nicky didn't look up from tying his laces. He was much more concerned with getting the fit of his new Predators just right.

Chris waited patiently then gave up for the time being and pulled on his shirt. Around him there was a lot of excited chatter among members of both teams. The juniors were looking forward to extending their good start to the season; the other seniors were looking forward to breaking their duck. No-one gave King Edward's much chance of standing up to Spirebrook.

Jazz caught Chris's eye and gave him the thumbs up; Russell pounded his gloved hands together like a boxer warming up. Even though the senior team's defence was in tatters after the events of the last few days, everyone expected Russell to have a quiet afternoon. In the same fixture the year before, Spirebrook had won 4–0 and Jones had 'saved' two back passes and a corner.

Flea put his head round the door. 'You guys nearly ready? OK, outside and warming up in two minutes, please.'

Chris gave it one last try: 'Nicky . . .'

'Are these great boots or what?' Nicky beamed back, finally emerging from his bubble.

'Great,' said Chris without another glance. 'I need to talk to –'

'A hundred and forty-nine, ninety-nine in the shops, but Uncle Fabian knows this guy who can get them for ninety quid. I bet he'd get you a pair, if I asked him.'

'I can't afford them,' said Chris quickly, hoping to move the discussion away from boots with that flat statement of fact. Naturally, Nicky couldn't accept the first thing he was told.

'Can't afford them? I thought your dad said you could have a new pair of boots this season . . .'

'For Christmas,' Chris reminded his team mate.

Nicky looked up and gestured to show that as far as he was concerned Christmas wasn't that far away. Of course, in the Fiorentini world, almost every day was Christmas Day.

'So you get them a little early,' he said, grinning.

'I don't think so,' said Chris.

Still Nicky didn't give up. 'I get stuff early that I was supposed to get at Christmas every year,' he said, as if he had some secret method he was prepared to teach Chris.

'You have so many relations buying you presents that there isn't time for you to open everything on just one day,' Chris countered, good-naturedly. It wasn't that the Fiorentini clan was rich, it was just that they never paid shop prices for anything. There was always someone in the family who knew a guy who knew another guy who could get a pair of boots, new TV or car at a discount.

Nicky grinned even more broadly. He was intensely proud of his family. He knew Chris thought they were all barmy, but that didn't stop Stephens coming to Nicky's house to watch cable, or muck around on his Playstation. He was even getting to like Italian food.

'What about this job you keep saying you're going to get?' Nicky said. 'If you had some money of your own . . .'

'Yeah, right,' Chris sighed. 'Like there's time. What with training, matches and homework, I just couldn't manage a job as well.' There had been a couple of false starts over the summer, but the shops who gave Chris a chance soon found that he was never available when they really wanted him. What good is a Saturday boy who can't work weekends?

Nicky stood up, and stalked up and down the changing rooms, enjoying the sound of his studs on the tiled floor.

'These are going to be deadly!' he grinned.

'The boots are OK,' said Russell, 'but if they're going to get a lot of goals, they'll need a new pair of feet inside them.'

He and Nicky exchanged thrown towels and loud insults. Chris sighed. At this rate, he'd never get Nicky's attention.

Almost everyone was ready. Nicky sat down to slip his shin pads into his socks, a pointless gesture. Within five minutes of the kick-off, his socks would be round his ankles and he would have flung the shinguards to the sideline.

'Nicky,' Chris insisted. 'I want to talk about Robert James.'

At last he got through.

'Bob?' Nicky asked. 'What about him?'

'He's been suspended.'

Nicky reacted at first as if all that had happened was that James had been yellow-carded a couple of times. It took Russell and Mac together to explain that James had been suspended from school, and to remind him why the younger player was in trouble.

'Right, right, got it,' sighed Nicky, irritably. 'Well, what of it? That just proves that he's got this jinx thing, right?'

Chris fought hard to control his temper. 'Nicky! He's in trouble because he took the rap for me. It's not because of bad luck. Or, rather, it is. He's got himself so wound up about being unlucky for the team that he genuinely thinks he is to blame for me and Fuller getting caught.'

Chris recognised the 'what's your point?' look on Nicky's face at once.

'It's got nothing to do with luck, Nicky. Just like the results we've been having. That's just . . . football. It's just the way things turn out sometimes. You just have to play your best and try and turn things round.'

Nicky shrugged. 'OK,' he said. 'But where does that leave things with James? You tried explaining things to "Andy" Cole, but she didn't believe you. So, where do you go from here?'

Chris had to admit that he didn't have an answer for that. All he knew for sure was that the situation with Robert James couldn't be left the way things were. Plus, of course, there was still the business of getting to the bottom of the fire and the wrecking of the youth club.

It all fitted together, somehow. But how?

On the edge of the conversation, Russell Jones leant forward and tapped Chris on the shoulder.

'Time to go out,' he said.

Chris looked up. The others were already at the door.

Nicky was on his feet quickly. 'Who put you in charge, Russell?' As he said the last word, his face opened in amazement. 'Hey! Who *is* in charge? Has Flea said who's captain?'

It turned out the PE teacher hadn't said a word to anyone. In the confusion, with players dropping in and out of the team every few minutes, Flea must have forgotten to replace Griff as captain.

The boys all looked at each other.

'You take it, Chris,' said Nicky. 'I'm pretty sure Flea would want you to lead us out.'

Jones laughed. 'Chris can't lead us out – he's always last!'

Nicky shot him a hot look. 'You know what I mean,' he snapped.

Chris stood up. The others looked at him and they saw the same thing. A look of steely determination in Chris's eyes that said something had changed in those last few minutes.

'OK,' he said, 'it's about time we got this season started.'

He walked to the door, to the front of the line of Spire-brook players.

'Let's do it,' he said, and he led them out on to the field.

In the last year, King Edward's – a smallish school nearer the city – had come on a bit. From no-hopers they had turned into not-much-hopers.

After a few minutes early on when he had to scamper round a bit, Russell soon found he could take it easy again, just like last year. Even against the unusual defensive line-up the 'Brook had been forced to employ, the Spuds (the name everyone gave the guys from King Edward's) weren't big enough or strong enough to threaten much.

Against Spirebrook's awesome midfield and strikers, they were really out of their depth. From the opening minutes, Nicky started to torment the left back with some of his most inventive dribbling, while Jazz cut the defence open with a precision pass and worked the ball well with Mac in midfield.

It was one of those games where the spectators were expecting to see goals rattling in every thirty seconds. Not that there were many people watching – just the King Edward's substitutes (probably glad to have been left out of the team) and a few 'Brookers hanging around for the show. Most of them would have expected Spirebrook to romp away with a game like this.

But that's football for you, thought Chris. All those thousands of people who watched the 1996 Cup Final or the France/ Czech Republic Euro 96 semi-final – millions, if you included TV

– drawn in by the hype and expecting to see a great match. And what did they get? Nothing. Sometimes, the best games are played at a lower level, between two teams who aren't so packed with stars they cancel each other out.

Not that this was a great game. But it tried hard. And what made it interesting was that it didn't turn out the way everyone expected. The Spuds were hopelessly outclassed, but they had a stubborn, mean character which prevented them just giving the game away. Once they got possession, they hung on bravely, even if they couldn't find a way forward. When they lost the ball, they pulled ten players back in defence, pushing up at the back and packing the midfield. Twice in the first ten minutes they caught Phil Lucas offside.

'We're all over them!' Nicky whispered to Chris while they waited for the second free kick to be taken.

'I know,' Chris replied, 'but it's not going to be easy to score. We've got to find a way to stretch them out.'

Nicky agreed, and he was just the guy to do it. If the Spuds tried to compress play into the middle third of the field, then he'd just go behind them.

They held a rapid chat with Jazz the next time the ball was out of play. 'Through balls behind the defence,' said Nicky. 'Chris and I will run on to them. Phil can keep the centre backs busy.'

'Not too much weight on the pass,' Chris reminded them, 'or their keeper will snaffle up everything.'

'And I'll run at the full back some more . . .' Nicky added with a grin.

Having revised their plans, the 'Brookers went back to the game. Almost straight away, Nicky beat the full back wide and ran behind the defence. The Spuds retreated rapidly towards their own goal, with Chris threading his way down the channel between the centre backs, looking to get on the cross.

Nicky only looked up once. They had scored dozens of goals like this, with Nicky knowing instinctively where Chris would be. They'd done it to King Edward's in past years as much as anyone.

This time, though, as Chris suddenly darted for the near post, knifing through into space, Nicky hit the cross long. Phil Lucas was arriving at the far post, unseen and unmarked.

It was their first real chance. Phil took it on his chest, but that first touch wasn't quite controlled. The ball slipped away from him towards the keeper, who was sprinting across his goal having been fooled by the cross along with everyone else. Phil stretched, snatched his shot and lifted it over the bar.

Nicky yelled loudly, his hands raised to his face like a mask. Phil, stretched out on the ground, threw some loose turf away, disgusted with himself.

Chris clapped his hands, bringing their minds back to the present. 'Good effort, Phil!' he called. He looked across at Nicky. 'Excellent cross!!'

Nicky shook his head, but he knew what Chris was looking for. As he trotted back into position, he managed to put his hands together twice and to signal a thumbs-up to Phil Lucas.

'Unlucky, Phil,' he said.

The ball had gone miles. Chris took a moment to walk over to Nicky for another private word.

'Be positive,' he said.

'I am positive,' Nicky replied sourly. 'I'm positive I should have aimed the cross for you and not Lucas.'

Chris smiled, despite himself. 'Remember what Flea always tells us; remind the player what they did right, not what they did wrong.' It was as close to sports psychology as Spirebrook ever got.

'I know, I know,' muttered Nicky. 'I said he was unlucky, didn't I?'

Chris saw the little flicker in Nicky's eyes.

'And you can pack that in as well,' he told Fiorentini quickly.

The game restarted. For once, the Spuds gave the ball away quickly. Mac, Nicky and Jazz exchanged a series of rapid first-time passes. The ball came up to Chris, who timed his break past the last defender to perfection. He took the ball with one touch, looked up, then volleyed the ball into the back of the net without breaking stride. He spun round, ready to start the celebrations, but he knew at once something had gone wrong. Nicky was looking up into the sky, his face twisted with rage. The King Edward's lads were grinning at each other as if they had remembered they had a 'get out of jail free' card at the last second.

Chris looked to the sideline. One of the parents who had come with King Edward's to run one of the lines was holding up a flag for offside.

'That never was!' groaned Chris, more to himself than in genuine protest. As Mac had played the last pass forward, Chris had rolled around the last defender. It should have been as clear as houses that he was onside, even if he had then sprinted clear.

There was still plenty of time. They were beating the pants off King Edward's. All the same, though, Chris saw a few heads go down. He could imagine the thought creeping into their minds: 'If we can't beat this lot . . .'

That was the problem with Spirebrook that season, Chris knew. It was nothing to do with voodoo or demons or jinxes or bad luck — it was all in their heads. They were talking themselves out of being a good side.

And in that same second, Chris knew why. Everyone in the school knew that he, Nicky and Russell would be gone soon. They were the backbone of the team. He and Nicky had scored the goals for Spirebrook that had made the other teams fear them; Russell had come along and showed that the 'Brook could keep them out too. But when the three of them left to go to the new school, what would be left?

In their minds, the others had already written themselves off as being ordinary, even while Chris, Nicky and Russell were still there.

The shock of realising what was wrong with the team almost numbed Chris's mind. He ambled back towards half-way as if he was stumbling through a fog. The idea had come to him out of nowhere — but he knew that he was right.

What he didn't know was what they could do about it.

The match restarted. From the free kick, King Edward's played it left and right along the back four. After a few seconds of this, Chris and Phil Lucas pushed up, trying to pressure the defenders. At once, the ball was flicked into the space behind them. Mac was a little late coming forward to cover, and the Spuds launched their first attack of the half.

Bruise made one good tackle, but the ball ran loose to another red-shirted Spuds' forward. This was going to be Marshie's first test at centre back.

He seemed to have the guy covered OK. In fact, as the Spuds' striker drew back his foot for the shot, Chris was thinking about how quickly the opposition had been forced

137

into shooting from a long way out.

Then Mike threw his foot out to block the shot, and it took a fierce deflection. The ball was spinning crazily in the air from that moment on, almost wobbling in flight, as if it was rolling down a bumpy slope. It was coming at Russell head high, right in the middle of the goal.

Until, at the last moment, it wasn't.

The spin made the ball swerve and dip, viciously late. Russell seemed to have it covered until the ball dropped behind him.

'I don't believe it!' roared Nicky at the clouds.

It was pretty sick, when Chris came to think of it. It was all very well deciding that Spirebrook's problems were all in their mind, but when something like this happened, you had to wonder . . .

Jazz's head dropped; Mac shrugged and sighed as if he was already sure nothing was going to go their way. Chris knew the whole team was thinking the same thing: 'here we go again; that's four in a row'.

'Come on, 'Brook! Look up!' Chris yelled. 'That's nothing; we can get that back.' He made a special point of grabbing Nicky. 'Don't you dare tell me that was a lucky goal.'

'But surely . . .', Nicky began, confused.

'I know it *was* lucky; that has to be the jammiest goal we've ever seen! But I don't want to hear you – or anyone else – whining about how unlucky we are.'

'I never . . .'

'I mean it, Nicky. We're going to get this game back if it kills us. So, let's see those hundred and fifty pound Predators do something useful, OK?'

Nicky nodded. When Chris went off like this, it was best to agree.

Before the kick-off, Chris got into the faces of some of the others too, making sure they understood that one lucky goal wasn't going to rob them of the game; that they had the rest of this half and all of the second period to turn things round; and that they could put a dozen past this lot if they wanted to.

He seemed to have convinced them. When he tapped the kick off to Phil Lucas, there was only one player still doubting that what he had said was true.

Himself.

Nineteen

Chris was right about how many chances they'd create. Either side of half-time, there must have been a dozen clear opportunities to put the ball in the King Edward's net. They were the sort of chances Chris couldn't fail to score.

Which was a pity. Because not one of them fell to Chris.

He was involved in every attack, spraying passes left and right, putting Nicky clear on the right, knocking the ball sideways for Phil Lucas, laying it off to the midfield. But as for getting a clear shot on goal himself – forget it.

Normally, that wouldn't have mattered. Phil didn't get half the number of goals Chris did in a season, but he was no slouch. Today, though, he seemed slow to get to everything. As the second half wore on, it was clear he'd twisted his knee and was hobbling painfully.

Over half the chances Spirebrook created seemed to fall to Phil. As for the rest, Nicky seemed to develop a red mist every time he had a shooting chance, slamming ferocious shots high or wide; Jazz was robbed twice by good saves; and one glorious header by Mike Marsh came back off the bar. Spirebrook became desperate. Russell Jones was about to come up for a corner before Chris sent him back with seven words.

'Peter Schmeichel, Euro 96, Denmark vs Croatia.'

Chris urged them to be patient, to stick with the game plan, but with every minute, his team mates became more and more reckless. Nicky had his name taken for a two-footed tackle. Chris could see the game vanishing down the drain.

The final straw came when the best chance of the entire game fell to Brewster. In all the games he'd played for Spirebrook, Bruise had found the net just three times; two own goals and a corner kick that had missed everyone and gone straight in.

Nicky had burst clear on the right and sent over one of his rare floated crosses. It was knocked down by a defender. Chris had the first snatch at a shot as the ball landed, just beating another Spuds' player to it. His volley hit the keeper in the chest, nicked off a third defender and bounced, spinning just in front of the line.

Bruise was on his own, standing almost on the line. The only problem he had was that he was turned sideways, with his back almost to goal. Even so, he was almost inside the goal, and the nearest defenders were sprawled on the floor. One of them had even tripped up the keeper.

'Yes!' yelled Chris.

All Bruise had to do was breathe and the ball would go in. Instead he chose to try and send the ball right through the net and halfway to France.

He certainly hit it hard enough. But it went straight up in the air.

Everyone looked up, amazed and appalled that anyone could miss like that. The ball rocketed up vertically, slipping slightly on the wind, before finally dropping towards the goal.

It had spent so long in the air, the keeper, three defenders and two 'Brookers were fighting to get underneath as it landed. The keeper won the jumping contest, covering the ball as it hit the top of the net.

Chris bit his lip hard to stop himself from saying anything. Bruise was looking round, wondering where the ball had gone. Until it landed, he seemed to believe he had smacked it all the way *through* the netting.

In desperation, Nicky was appealing for a corner. He was bright red with frustration and fury. Chris ignored him, picking himself off the ground and wearily preparing to run back into position for the goal kick the ref was signalling.

'Your mate did that all by himself,' the ref was explaining. Nicky didn't let it go.

'The goalie pushed it over the bar!'

'No he didn't,' the ref stated calmly, running backwards as he left the penalty area.

Chris realised Nicky was chasing after him.

'Are you blind???' he roared. His eyes were as bright as searchlights. He ran after the ref as quickly as he had been running the wing all afternoon.

The ref – the Spuds' PE teacher – stopped suddenly, aware that Nicky was still raging at him over the decision. He didn't look angry or anything, but he could tell that Nicky was almost out of control. As far as Chris could see, he was stopping so that he could have a word with Nicky and calm him down.

But he halted so quickly, Nicky couldn't slam on his own brakes fast enough. He slammed into the ref hard.

'Oh, oh,' said Chris. He ran over quickly.

The ref wasn't hurt – he was a big bloke, not unlike Flea, though a few years older. At first, he just looked surprised. But Chris knew the moment the ref stopped to think about what had happened, he would have only one option.

The shock of the collision had disrupted Nicky's rage, but he didn't have enough sense to apologise at once. As the two of them sat there, the ref recovered his wits first. Chris arrived just a moment too late.

'You OK, ref?' he asked, offering the guy his hand to help him up.

'Never mind,' the guy replied at once, his eyes fixed on Nicky. 'Are you stupid, boy, or what?'

'I . . . errr . . .' Nicky stumbled.

'That's a sending off offence that is!' the ref continued. He reached into his pocket.

'Ref – it was just an accident,' Chris pleaded, even though he was only half convinced himself.

Even now, the ref didn't look that angry or anything. He just pulled a small notebook from his shirt pocket.

'Rules are rules,' he was saying. Then he added: 'But seeing as I don't think it was deliberate, I'm only going to book you.'

Chris wondered if the guy knew what he was saying. Nicky, though, was in no doubt.

'Yeah! Like that makes a difference! You've booked me once already!'

'Have I?' said the guy. He flicked open the book. 'Oh, right. OK – off you go, then!'

Chris groaned and turned away, not sure he could trust himself to speak. It wasn't that he was worried about upsetting the ref as well, but he knew that if he said anything to Nicky it could be something he might regret later.

Now that it was too late, Nicky managed to keep his gob shut as well. He stood up and stalked from the field. He slammed the gym door so hard the players in the lower school game thought a gun had gone off.

Chris checked around what was left of his team. The whole lot of them had a defeated look in their eyes now, even Russell, who had been fine up to now. In fact, he looked sicker than any of them.

'Twenty more minutes!' Chris called, clapping his hands. 'Come on, Spirebrook. Wake up!!!'

Once the game was restarted, the others ran around and looked as if they were playing football, but the fight had gone out of them. Chris watched the game falling apart around him, and there didn't seem to be a thing he could do about it. He called and yelled to his team mates, but the creative spark had gone out of them. In fact, the Spuds seemed more likely to score than Spirebrook.

A long punt out of defence by Marsh ended up going for a goal kick at the other end. No-one even bothered chasing it. Hovering on the right-hand side of halfway, Chris was steaming, but nothing he said could bring the 'Brook back to life.

Then, just as he took the kick, the King Edward's keeper slipped. The ball sliced away from the middle of the pitch. There was only one player for several metres in any direction.

As he saw the ball dropping towards him, Chris's mind emptied. It was as if every emotion, good or bad, drained out of him. He felt cold and eerily calm, calculating the drop of the ball perfectly. Even the part of his brain that controlled his football skills went off-line. He had the perfect chance to control the ball on his chest and take it forward. He did nothing of the kind.

Without letting the ball hit the ground, Chris volleyed it right back.

The Spuds' keeper was still sitting on the six-metre line as the ball slapped into the back of the net.

None of the 'Brookers cheered; no-one on the King Edward's side uttered a moan of despair. Chris heard someone mutter 'Crikey', but that was the only comment. The ref, after a moment of watching the ball spinning in the back of the goal, blew his whistle.

Everyone continued to move round in a state of shock for what must have been a minute or ninety seconds. Chris lined up opposite one of the Spuds' players, ready for the kick off. The lad didn't dare make eye contact at first, but then he couldn't help himself, and looked up into Chris's fierce stare.

'Don't you dare call that lucky,' snapped Chris.

The atmosphere in the changing rooms after the game was a little odd. No-one knew whether to celebrate or be miserable. On the one hand, they had only managed a draw against one of the weakest teams in the league. Also, there was the obvious problem of Nicky sitting on the bench, rumbling like a thundercloud.

On the other hand, they had snatched a draw from the depths of defeat. Chris's amazing forty- or fifty-metre 'Beckham' (the distance was growing each time the story was told) was something to celebrate too.

The junior team had won 3–0. Their good mood almost lifted the older boys. Flea was very positive about the way the seniors had played too, and he hated to lose.

There wasn't much chatter among the senior players as they unlaced their boots, peeled off their kit and stumbled into the showers. No-one had much more to say as they got dressed, until Jazz, who couldn't cope with the strain any more, cracked at last.

'Well, we didn't lose that one, at least.'

Nicky fixed his diamond-hard glare on the midfielder.

'Great, yeah. Maybe next week we can arrange a game against Holly Hill Primary and actually win a game.'

Jazz, wounded, suddenly remembered there was something he needed from the inside pocket of his jacket, and turned away for the next thirty seconds.

'Maybe our luck's changing,' said Mac, from the other side. He didn't add the mistake of making eye contact with Nicky, but found Chris looking at him flatly instead. 'No, I don't mean luck . . .' he began.

'He's right,' said Russell. 'We've broken the run. Next week we hammer the Blackmorons, and we're right back on track.'

A few of the others made positive noises to suggest they would happily steamroller Blackmoor, even if they lost every other game this season.

'It doesn't mean anything,' said Nicky. His voice, dark and low, still managed to reach everyone in the dressing room.

'Beating Blackmoor?' Mac asked, unable to believe what he heard.

Nicky looked up. 'Today. A draw against King Edward's is like getting beaten by anyone else. We should have murdered them! We had enough chances to bury the game by half-time!'

His ugly look picked out Phil Lucas this time, who was stretching his leg and wincing, clearly uncomfortable. Flea had disappeared a few minutes before to find an ice pack.

Picking out Phil for blame, bearing in mind that Nicky had fluffed a few chances himself, seemed a little rich, but no-one was prepared to point that out to Nicky. And no-one was ever going to mention the sending off again.

'But we didn't. As far as I'm concerned, that means our bad luck is still with us.'

Chris was tying the laces on his trainers. Hearing those words, he pulled so hard both the laces snapped.

'What?!' he cried.

'You heard,' said Nicky. 'As far as I can see the curse is still with us.'

'Nicky! There's no curse!! Jeez, James wasn't even here!'

He heard Russell make a coughing noise from the other end of the bench. What was that about? Nicky, meantime, was up on his feet, pacing the length of the changing room like a lawyer on the floor of the court.

'Did I mention James? Did I say it was his fault?'

'That's all you've been saying for weeks! But he wasn't around today to put the hex on us, was he?'

Russell made the same interruption/coughing noise again. Chris swung round and glared at him.

'Maybe the jinx works even if he *isn't* here,' Nicky was saying.

Chris whipped back round again. 'Then if it doesn't matter if he's here or not, he might as well be here! Can't you get it through your thick skull, what's happening to us has nothing whatsoever to do with Robert James. Except for one thing; he's providing you with an excuse. You wanted him in, then you wanted him out. The defence was the problem, then it was this freaking 'curse'. The problem was always somewhere else, Nicky.'

Nicky's face fell open with amazement.

'You're saying . . . it's my fault we keep losing?!' he gasped.

'Not just yours. Yours, mine and Russell's. Spirebrook is suffering because we're not giving it 100% any more. We're leaving. And even now, we've got bigger fish to fry.'

Nicky made a strange strangled noise as he tried to find words he could use to argue with Chris. They wouldn't come. All round the dressing room, the other players were equally stunned. Slowly, though, they were all calling incidents to mind as they thought about what Chris had said. They didn't all believe it right away, but every one of them knew there was a simple truth at the bottom of what Chris had said. Spirebrook weren't playing as a team any more. They had lost the spirit that had bound them all together. Nicky's planned tinkering with the defence was a symptom of that.

'So . . . what are you saying . . . ?' muttered Nicky at last.

Chris wasn't sure exactly what he was driving towards. All he knew was that they couldn't hide behind curses and bad luck any more. They had to deal with the real situation.

But how? Chris didn't know what to say.

The long silence was broken by Nicky, who had been staring at Chris all that time. Suddenly, he bent down, picked up his boots and stuffed them into his kit bag.

'You know, you're right. I haven't been feeling right about the way I've been playing for Spirebrook for weeks. I thought these new boots might help . . .'

Mac offered to take them off his hands, as a favour. There were a few quiet laughs from the edges of the discussion.

'Next week it's Blackmoor,' Nicky said quietly, and the fire and steel in his voice was unmistakable. 'We're going to have them. We're going to beat them so bad that when they read the score out, people will think it's a cricket result.'

There were several cries of 'yeah!' and 'we'll slaughter them!'. Given the choice, most of the lads in the dressing room would have voted to start the game right there and then.

Chris — still captain — looked around at the guys he had come to know so well over the last few years. They were still going to split up in a few months, but not yet. Whatever lay ahead, they were still Spirebrook now. Still the best.

Well, still better than Blackmoor, anyway.

'Keep out of trouble,' he told them. 'We want the best team possible next week, even if we're still a bit light at the back.'

'Griff will be back by then,' Nicky reminded him, 'and if we want to play four across the back . . .'.

Chris looked across at his team mate. They both smiled.

'We'll get Robert James into the team,' they said together.

Twenty

Chris was supposed to be going back to Nicky's house for tea, but by the time Chris finished getting changed Nicky and Mac were involved in a heated discussion about the best football boots you could buy. He walked out of the gym to get a little fresh air while he waited.

In ones and twos, the others went past on their way home. Chris could see they were all still fired up. Next week couldn't come quickly enough.

One of the last to appear was Russell Jones.

'Hey,' he said. Unlike the others, he still seemed a bit off.

'You OK, Russ?' Chris asked him. 'You were coughing so much in there I thought you'd caught Griff's bug.'

Russell gave him a weak smile. 'You got a minute?'

'I'm waiting for Nicky,' Chris replied. 'I've probably got hours.'

Russell got to the point immediately anyway. 'What you said in there. You know, about Robert James and the jinx . . .'

Chris was caught by surprise. Of all the guys in the team, Russell was the least likely to believe in any such nonsense. Unless Russell could see it, hear it, taste it or kick it, nothing existed. Show him something about the Bermuda Triangle or aliens abducting humans for bizarre experiments, and Russell said it was far-fetched. He didn't even watch *The X-Files*!

So what was this all about?

'What about it?' Chris asked cautiously.

'Well, after everything that's happened over the last few days, I could see that all the others were really starting to believe this curse stuff. And I didn't think it was fair — to Robert James, I mean.'

Chris agreed with that. But what did it have to do with Russell?

'So, I got wondering about how I could prove it wasn't true. It was obvious, really. They thought the others were losing every time Robbie James was around, but if they *won* when he was watching, they'd see it was nonsense.'

Chris was struggling slightly to see where this was leading. 'What are you saying, Russell?'

Jones took a look around to make sure no-one could overhear them. 'Robbie was watching today.'

'What?!' choked Chris.

'Did you see that kid with the hooded sweatshirt sitting on the wall near the gym? That was James.'

Chris hadn't noticed. The wall was a few metres back from the touchline, and Chris didn't tend to pay much attention to individuals in a small audience like they'd had today.

'But . . .' Chris began. In fact, he had so many questions and comments it was hard to know where to begin.

'I know, I should have said,' Russell said with an apologetic sigh, 'but I figured if we had lost, no-one need ever know. And if we'd won, Robbie could come forward, and everyone would know that this jinx stuff was rubbish.'

It took a few moments for Chris to get this straight in his head. When it did fall into place, it made him feel like laughing.

'So, the worst possible result, from your point of view, was a draw!' he exclaimed.

Jones didn't seem to find it so amusing.

'Yeah. Maybe.'

'In which case,' Chris continued, 'you could argue that – seeing as it *was* a draw – Robert James was a bit unlucky!'

Russell closed his mouth firm and cocked his head slightly to one side, knowing that Chris was poking fun at him.

'What you're saying, then,' he said at last, 'is that I shouldn't tell anyone about all this. If they hear James was here, they'll start wondering again if he didn't bring us bad luck after all.'

At the time, that was what Chris had being saying, but another thought occurred to him now as they both took a moment to think.

'Actually, what I think I'm saying is that you're as guilty as everyone else of taking this jinx business too seriously. And you don't even believe it! What's worse, by acting on your own, you could have made the divisions in the team worse.

We have to start working together, not separately.'

The more Chris thought about it – and he'd been doing little else since the final whistle – the more he became convinced this was the real problem behind Spirebrook's decline. They were no longer a team. They had been pulling in different directions, from the nonsense about the jinx, to Nicky's scheming to change the defence round, to this – Russell Jones (of all people) coming up with a hare-brained scheme to trick all the others into accepting James back into the team. A can't fail scheme that had fallen flat on its face.

Russell ran his hands through his copper-coloured hair.

'You're right, Chris. I was stupid. In fact, I can think of only one person who's been even more stupid than me.'

'Oh? Who?' demanded Chris, slightly annoyed. Didn't Russell get it? This was a time for them to see each other as equals, not to score points off each other. He was sure that Russell was about to say that Nicky was –

'You.'

❁

Russell set off on a rambling story. Chris was delighted. He needed time to get his head round what he had just heard.

'When my brother was around, making me go stealing with him, he was always trying to make it seem like he was helping me, showing me the ropes. Mick taught me how to nobble alarms, how to climb up to the roof without being seen, how to work out where the security guards were, what to nick and what to leave behind.

'It was like Mick thought he was my teacher or something. He used to say that if he ever had to go away, I'd be responsible for looking after the family. You know what my family's like, Chris – dad's too lazy, mum never leaves the house except to go shopping, and Davey and Marie are far too dozy to be any use.

'So, he showed me all these things, and I learnt well. But I also saw stuff he hadn't meant to show me. The first thing I realised is that he didn't take me on jobs with him because he was trying to teach me how to look after myself; he wanted me to do all the dirty, tricky, dangerous work he didn't fancy. And someone the security guards and the police would find easier to catch. That was when I started looking for a way out.

149

'I learnt that being able to hide meant I could hide from Mick as easy as I could hide from a guard; I learnt that being able to pinch stuff from someone's pocket meant I could get stuff from Mick.

'But do you know what the most important thing I learnt was?'

Chris had no idea. He and Jones had first met just after Russell had decided to give up being a thief. He didn't like to think too hard about what Russell's life had been like before — even though he had come dangerously close to being caught up in Mick's web himself. He couldn't imagine what it must have been like to have Mick Jones as an elder brother.

'No, go on.'

'I learnt that the person you should keep the closest eye on, the one you should trust the least, is the one who doesn't trust you.'

Chris could see the sense in that, but not what it had to do with anything. Russell never said much usually. Chris thought he could see why.

'What are you saying, Russell? That you don't trust me?'

'No. What I'm saying is that you don't trust us. You've given the rest of us this talk about teamwork, but you've had a secret all of your own all week.'

A light came on in Chris's mind. Russell spelt the facts out anyway.

'You found something on the floor as we left the Quad. I guessed it was something the blokes who set fire to Mr Palmer's office had dropped. So I dipped it out of your pocket and had a look. It was a tacky Liverpool watch. Then, next day, you showed it to us, but didn't say where it came from. Next, you go off to Blackmoor. Fuller said you dropped something on the floor when you hung the flag out the window. Said it looked like a watch.'

Chris kept silent, but he knew his face was probably betraying the fact that everything Russell had said was the truth. He also knew where Russell was going with this long introduction.

'OK,' he said. 'You've made your point. I should have trusted you guys with what I knew. I just didn't want to get anyone into trouble. I figured I could find out who the watch belonged to by finding which one of the Blackmorons got into trouble when it was found. That's why I wanted to be seen by someone who would recognise us; I figured they'd come looking for us when their mate got into strife. The only trouble is – thanks to that busybody from St George's – no-one looked for anyone from Blackmoor to have pinched that stupid flag.'

Russell considered what he'd been told. Much of it fitted in with what he'd worked out already. Even so, it was nice to get the full picture of one of Chris's plans, to see how his mind worked. Scary, too.

'You know, it's kind of funny they didn't come looking for you anyway. I mean, leaving aside the business with the watch, Ginger saw you on their turf. He must have seen that as a challenge . . . Why haven't they come over here mob-handed looking for revenge?'

Chris had been wondering that himself.

'If only we knew who that damn watch belonged to!' he muttered.

Russell's eyes twinkled and his mouth creased in a smile. 'Maybe we can find out,' he said.

Chris knew what that meant.

'Hang on, Russell, I don't think any of us should take any chances . . . Not the way "Andy" feels about what's been happening.'

'No problem,' Russell smiled. 'In fact, "Andy" is a vital part of my plan.'

'Which is?'

'I'll tell you in a minute. First, though, don't you think we ought to let the others know what's been going on?'

Chris nodded. 'Teamwork. No more secrets. We're in this together.'

Russell repeated those words, singing them to the tune of the anthem from Euro 96. Chris grinned. Someone inside the gym picked up the song, and soon there were three or four voices singing 'forever!' from inside the gym.

'So,' whispered Russell, 'bearing in mind everything we just talked about, do you want me to tell Nicky and the others that Robbie James was watching the game tonight?'

Chris clamped his hand over Russell's mouth, sure he could hear the rest of the team coming towards the door.

'Are you stupid?' he replied.

Twenty-one

The rest of the week and the weekend after passed uneventfully. Chris was in an agony of suspense. By Monday lunchtime, in common with the rest of the team, he was almost crawling the walls.

The game against Blackmoor was on everyone's mind. Even if Spirebrook couldn't achieve much in the Schools League, they had to beat Blackmoor. Finishing the season in the bottom half of the table was one thing; getting done over by the Blackmorons as well would be unbearable.

But the 'Brookers had more than just a football match on their minds. Every day, they waited for something to happen in response to Russell's plan. Every day they were disappointed.

'We've been rumbled, I bet you,' said Mac, pessimistically.

'How?' mocked Nicky. They were in the hall eating lunch, watching driving rain crack against the windows like pebbles.

Mac could think of several reasons. For the moment, though, the look on Nicky's face made them all fly quickly from his mind.

There was a short silence.

'What if tomorrow's game gets called off?' said Jazz.

Nicky had to twist right round to get to the worried Asian.

'Now what? Haven't you heard the weather forecast? This is just a squall. It'll be gone by teatime and then tomorrow it'll be sunny all day.'

Russell and Chris grinned at each other. Russell mouthed 'squall?' at Chris. The striker knew what his team mate meant. Where on earth had Nicky got hold of a word like 'squall'? Perhaps all those geography classes hadn't been wasted.

Turning back, Nicky caught them laughing. 'What?' he demanded.

The two of them put on straight faces at once, which cracked immediately they looked at each other again.

'A nice mudbath game against the Blackmorons,' said Fuller, who chose that moment to walk past them, looking out of the window as he went. He had a set of stereo earphones on his head, from which they could all hear some thrash metal. 'I can't wait.'

'Are you going to be able to play, Fuller?' asked Jazz.

Fuller shot him a dirty look. 'Yes! What, you think I'm going to miss a game like that for the sake of a bruised hand?'

Chris said nothing. If the decision was left to Fuller, he'd play with a broken leg, never mind a 'bruised' hand. However, Flea had already made it clear he didn't want to risk it. Griff would be back, so the defence would be closer to the normal format; they could live one more week without Fuller's help.

'Any news on that other stuff?' asked Fuller, which was as subtle as he could be. Fortunately, they were far enough away from any teachers that no-one heard him, or thought to ask what 'stuff' that might be.

'Nothing,' said Chris quietly, with a warning glance to Fuller to keep quiet. The idea was that there were no more secrets from the team, but that didn't mean they needed to put an ad in the paper.

Fuller shrugged. A frown crossed his face and he pulled off the headphones. 'Batteries are going,' he muttered.

'Here, borrow mine,' said Nicky, pulling his Walkman from his bag. Seconds later, Fuller was plugged in once more. 'Anything for a bit of peace and quiet,' Nicky sighed watching the big defender walk off.

'I don't get it,' muttered Russell. 'Why haven't the Black-morons done anything?'

Chris had no more idea than any of the rest of them. He was wondering if Russell's plan had back-fired, but he didn't want to say anything.

'It's got fouled up somehow,' complained Nicky. 'It's been a week since Chris went over there. If they were going to do anything, it would have started by now.'

Jazz was sitting at the end of the group, an apple halfway to his lips and a thoughtful expression on his face.

'You think they've done something already? Or maybe they're going to try something tomorrow night? At the game?'

153

'Could be,' said Chris. 'But there'll be teachers around all the time and we'll be on our guard. I was certain they'd try something before . . .'

'No-one's going anywhere in this weather,' Nicky commented, peering at the dark clouds outside. 'I think we're safe today.'

They all fell silent, munching through the last of their food. Russell looked even more glum than the rest of them. It was his plan, after all.

'He fell for it, I'm sure . . .' he said. And along with everyone else he went over the call again in his head, trying to figure out what had gone wrong.

The plan had nearly been a non-starter from the beginning. Nicky hadn't wanted to get his cousin involved.

This alone was a bit of a shock. There were four facts everyone in Nicky's circle of friends knew about the Fiorentini family. One, there were a lot of them; two, they were from Italy originally, although Nicky had never been there himself; three, they ate more food than the rest of the city of Oldcester put together (why else had Tescos built a new supermarket in Spirebrook?), though none of them ever put on any weight, and four, if there was any kind of crazy plan on the go, the Fiorentinis would be up to be part of it.

Natalie had taken part in one of their stunning plans just six months before. She was a third cousin with a few removeds (whatever that meant) of Nicky's and had moved into his house after getting a job in the make-up department at the local TV studios in the city.

Nicky didn't like the arrangement. Natalie tended to attract a lot of attention. She sulked to get her own way. She let people down and told lies to cover for her mistakes. These were all things that Nicky insisted were very upsetting to the other members of the family.

None of the guys pointed out the obvious to Nicky.

Even so, Natalie's help had been vital in the spring when the gang had leapt to the aid of an American kid who was visiting Oldcester on a soccer exchange, and who got caught up in the affairs of a crooked American businessman. The businessman had come looking for Jace, and so they had arranged for him to hide out at the Fiorentini house — where one more mouth to feed was hardly a problem. Natalie had used her make-up skills to give Jace the authentic Fiorentini look; dark hair and warm, olive skin. She even borrowed some props that had made the American look heavier.

So, when Russell's plan to flush the villain out of the woodwork this time needed a woman's voice on the phone, Natalie was the first choice.

'She'll want something in return,' whined Nicky.

'So?' asked Chris, trying hard to stop himself from laughing. 'We'll owe her a favour.'

'She's been on at me to swap bedrooms. Says she doesn't have enough room in her closet for all her clothes. Plus, she has to share with Laura . . .'

'That room over the garage is pretty cool,' Mac commented. The others had all agreed, even those who had never seen inside Nicky's house. Nicky had pouted and sulked, but had eventually been persuaded to talk to Natalie.

That had been on Wednesday. It took Nicky until Friday morning to ask Natalie to make the call. The agreed price was the permanent loan of Nicky's portable CD player. He wasn't happy.

At lunchtime, five of them — Chris, Nicky, Jazz, Mac and Russell — rushed up Church Hill to Nicky's house to be there when Natalie made the call. They were all excited, and nearly blew it by making too much noise in the background. In the end, though, Natalie played her part perfectly.

'Hello, Blackmoor Comprehensive? This is Mrs Cole from Spirebrook. Could I speak to Mr Brain please?'

'Their head teacher's name is Brain?'

'Shut up, Mac!'

'But that's a really stupid —'

'What if he knows what "Andy" sounds like?'

'What, you reckon they chat on the phone all the time, Jazz? All Natalie has to do is put on a posh voice and —'

'Hush up! It's hard enough to hear what the other person is saying already.'

'I told you — the recorder will pick it all up. At the end of the call we'll have a complete tape of the conversation.'

155

'Yes, but –'

'I thought –'

Natalie, one hand clamped over the phone's mouthpiece, glared at the five of them. They fell silent.

'If you want me to do this, shut up!' she whispered angrily. 'I have to be able to hear myself think!'

Nicky gave her a weak, encouraging smile. His cousin twisted the wire leading from the microphone attached to the receiver she held in her hand, as if she was threatening to pull it off. Before Nicky could warn her to be careful, Natalie turned away, her back to the boys gathered on the stairs.

'Where did you get that "bug"?' asked Jazz.

'It's something my Uncle Fabian uses to tape calls at work. He's useless at remembering names, so he tapes all his calls to remind him who's rung and why.'

'You can buy them from that weird electrical store in Fair Market,' said Russell, who had a great passion for gadgets. 'They plug into a standard cassette recorder, just like an ordinary microphone.' He indicated Nicky's Walkman lying beside the phone on the small hall table.

Jazz muttered something about tapping phones being illegal, which almost sparked off another loud debate. Natalie hissed at them to shut up. She had closed her eyes, like an actress trying to shut herself off from distraction, but it wasn't working. Mac giggled.

'Hello?' said Natalie suddenly. 'OK. Thank you. Mr Brain? Hel– Sorry? Ah, yes. Brian. It's Andy Cole here from Spirebrook.'

Chris had groaned loudly. Natalie had fallen at the first fence. If Brain was on first name terms with Spirebrook's head, he'd know her real name. Chris had no idea what it was, but he very much doubted it was 'Andy'.

Natalie, though, didn't falter. 'Sorry? Oh, I know. It's what all the students call me – you know, because of the footballer? After a while, I've grown more used to it than I have to my own name!'

She laughed then, but shot another dirty look at her cousin. Chris was starting to fear that they hadn't prepared well enough to get away with this.

'Fine, thank you, how are you? Good. Sorry. Look, is this a

good time to talk? I need to ask you about something, but I don't want to cause you any trouble if you're busy. You sure? No, I won't!'

This time it was Nicky's turn to shoot his cousin a hot, warning look. He tugged at her sleeve and hissed at her to get on with it.

'OK. It's about that business last week with St George's flag. I know, I wasn't going to make a big deal of it myself, but Mrs O'Connell . . . Yes, I agree. I take it you've spoken to her as well.'

Chris tried hard to concentrate on the call, even though he knew (hoped!) it was being recorded. Listening to one side of the conversation was very frustrating. The others had fallen silent at last, but it was still impossible to make out anything of what the other person on the line was saying. It all sounded like Daffy Duck in a wind tunnel with a heavy cold.

'She identified two of my students as the culprits. Yes. No. Well, that's what I hope, too. No problem, but there was one thing I wanted to ask – did you find a watch anywhere near where the flag was flown? You did?'

'All right!' cheered Russell. It seemed to surprise him more than anyone that he had said it out loud.

Natalie gave him a glare that could have frozen boiling water. Russell slid behind Nicky, biting his lip.

'Sorry?' Natalie was continuing. 'Oh, I have the two boys in here with me at the moment, that's why I'm calling. Yes. You mean no-one at your school has claimed the watch? Perhaps they knew it was connected with the flag incident. Ah, I see. Well, yes. In that case it probably does belong to my student.'

Chris's spirits sank. He didn't need to hear what Mr Brain was saying to get what was being said. After all that trouble, planting the watch at Blackmoor hadn't flushed out the owner. No-one had claimed it. The only link to Shell Suit had proved to be a dead end.

'I see. Well, yes. OK, if you could do that for me, I'd be very grateful. I'll leave it with you, then. OK, goodbye.'

Natalie put the phone down, and pouted at Nicky. 'There you are,' she said. Nicky sighed and gestured up the stairs.

'You know where it is,' he said, in a tired voice. Natalie pushed past the clutch of boys at the foot of the staircase and tripped up to Nicky's room to recover her fee.

'What a waste of time that was!' he said. He pulled the microphone off the phone's receiver and pressed the stop button on the recorder.

'Isn't it worth listening to the tape?' asked Mac.

'Why?' snapped Nicky. 'You heard Natalie – no-one claimed the watch. So, we've still no idea who torched Palmer's office.'

'Unlucky, Chris,' said Russell. 'It was a good plan.'

Chris wondered if Russell was trying to be funny bringing luck into it, but he was quite genuine.

'Yeah, well. At least we know now why we haven't heard anything.'

'So, is that it?' moaned Mac. 'What happens now? What if this guy calls the real "Andy"? What if he sends back the watch?'

'He will,' said Natalie. She was coming back down the stairs, clutching the CD player in one hand while she put the headphones on with the other. Nicky uttered a deep sigh. 'That was what that bit at the end was about. He's going to send "Andy" the watch next week if he doesn't hear from anyone at his school by Monday.'

'So, she'll know someone has been making calls, pretending to be her.' Nicky complained loudly. 'Great!'

'I had to make the call seem natural. If I hadn't agreed with him about the watch, Brain would have been suspicious!'

Nicky made a face as Natalie flounced off. He unplugged the microphone and tossed his Walkman into his schoolbag.

'I wish she'd hurry up and find her own place,' he said, grouchily. 'Since she started at the TV studio, she thinks she's going to be an actress.'

No-one was interested in listening to Nicky's complaints about living with his cousin. The failure of the phone call (or, more correctly, the failure of Chris's plan to force Shell Suit out into the open) had made them all depressed.

Even a good weekend result for Oldcester United in the Premiership and an excellent training session with the youth team on the Sunday hadn't lightened the gloom. A wet Monday lunchtime seemed like the final straw.

'Oh, oh, Fuller's back,' said Russell. Now that really was getting close to being the limit.

'What's this you've got in here, Fiorentini?' mocked Fuller as he came closer. 'Some kiddie story tape?'

'I didn't know there was still a tape in there,' snapped Nicky in reply. 'Give it here.'

Fuller tossed the cassette over.

'Who's the bird talking? And why is she pretending to be "Andy" Cole?'

'Shut up, will you!' the others hissed in unison. Fuller's voice had carried over the entire hall. They hadn't told Fuller about the phone call plan, precisely because he was hopeless at keeping a secret. So much for that idea.

'All, right, all right, don't get your boxers in a bunch.' He pulled another cassette from his shirt pocket and popped it into the Walkman. 'So, who's this bloke Brian Brain wants to talk to?'

They were all on the point of jumping on Fuller to keep him quiet when they realised what he had just said.

'Who?' asked Chris.

'Brain. He's on here saying how someone's lost a watch, but it might belong to some other bloke he knows.'

Fuller wasn't the slowest-moving creature on earth, and never would be so long as there were snails, but even someone with the rapier-reflexes of Seaman or Schmeichel would have been caught out by the speed with which Nicky grabbed him and dragged the Walkman earphones off his head.

'Didn't think you squirts liked thrash metal,' he grunted from the bottom of the pile.

Twenty-two

⚽

With two sets of headphones (Nicky's and Fuller's) they could listen two at a time. It took the rest of lunchtime for them all to hear the complete call.

Chris and Nicky went first. This is what they heard:

NATALIE (in what wasn't a bad effort at sounding like Mrs Cole, considering she was twenty-odd years younger and had never heard 'Andy' speak): 'Hello, Blackmoor Comprehensive?'

A WOMAN AT THE OTHER END (probably the school secretary at Blackmoor; she sounded just the same as Mrs Popov; perhaps they were cloned?): 'Yes, this is Blackmoor.'

NATALIE: 'This is Mrs Cole from Spirebrook. Could I speak to Mr Brain please?'

WOMAN AT THE OTHER END: 'I'll just see if I can find him.'

CLUNK. There was a radio playing and the distant clatter of a computer keyboard.

'This is at the beginning,' whispered Nicky, stating the obvious.

'I know,' replied Chris.

They could hear snatches of themselves talking, sounding distant, which was very odd. Then Natalie's muffled voice telling them all to shut up after the thump of her hand hitting the mouthpiece. The silence continued for a few moments afterwards, then the sound of footsteps coming closer and a warning hiss from Nicky's cousin on the verge of becoming Julia Roberts again.

NATALIE: 'Hello?'

WOMAN AT THE OTHER END: 'I'm just putting you through.'

NATALIE: 'OK. Thank you.'

A briefer hush, with just Natalie's breathing breaking the silence.

BLOKE WITH A YORKSHIRE ACCENT: 'Hello?'

NATALIE: 'Mr Brain? Hel –'

BLOKE: 'Hey. What's this? You're very formal.'

NATALIE: 'Sorry?'

BLOKE: 'What's all this Mr Brain stuff? It's Brian, remember. I thought we'd got past all this Mister stuff ages ago.'

'Oh, really?' smirked Nicky. Chris ignored him.

NATALIE: 'Ah, yes. Brian. It's Andy Cole here from Spire-brook.'

This was the part of the call Chris had been waiting for, the moment when Natalie had slipped up. How had she managed to get away with the mistake, particularly since Brain had obviously met her before?

BLOKE: ' "Andy?" I thought your name was Christine.'

NATALIE: 'Sorry?'

BLOKE: 'You just said "Andy".'

NATALIE: 'Oh, I know. It's what all the students call me – you know, because of the footballer?'

BLOKE: 'Aye, I've heard of him.'

NATALIE: 'After a while, I've grown more used to it than I have to my own name!'

BLOKE (after short laugh): 'You probably score more goals, too! Shame there's not a transfer market for head teachers, isn't it?'

Natalie had laughed, and Brain had too. Chris could barely believe it. Natalie had sounded so natural, as if it really was just a joke and not a desperate attempt to get off the hook.

Nicky had a relieved look on his face too. 'Unbelievable,' he said. Chris was about to say he knew what he meant when Nicky sarcastically added: 'Brian and Christine. I reckon he fancies her . . .'

Chris waved his hand to shut Nicky up. The conversation continued.

BLOKE: 'So, how are you, Christine? You sound very . . . jolly.'

NATALIE: 'Fine, thank you, how are you?'

BLOKE: 'All right, I suppose. We've got an OFSTED inspection coming up, as I'm sure you remember.'

NATALIE: 'Good.'

161

BLOKE (tetchy): 'Good? I don't see what's good about it. Bunch of busybodies poking their noses in –'

NATALIE (butting in): 'Sorry. Look, is this a good time to talk?'

BLOKE: 'As good as any. Why is there a problem?'

NATALIE: 'I need to ask you about something, but I don't want to cause you any trouble if you're busy.'

BLOKE: 'Now, you know I can always spare time for you, Christine.'

Nicky put his fingers in his mouth and rolled his eyes up as if he was about to throw up.

NATALIE: 'You sure?'

BLOKE: 'So long as you're not going to make any more funny cracks about OFSTED.'

NATALIE: 'No, I won't!'

BLOKE: 'Fire away, then.'

NATALIE: 'OK. It's about that business last week with St George's flag.'

BLOKE: 'Really? That wasn't anything serious, Christine . . .'

NATALIE (quickly): 'I know, I wasn't going to make a big deal of it myself, but Mrs O'Connell . . .'

BLOKE: 'That woman from across the road? She's just sticking her oar in to make trouble.'

NATALIE: 'Yes, I agree. I take it you've spoken to her as well.'

BLOKE: 'There's not a week goes by that I don't have the pleasure of a visit from her. She came in last week – when was it? Thursday, to tell me I ought to tighten up my security. I had to remind her that it was her flag that got nicked, not mine. But all she was interested in was that the lads who did it had run into Blackmoor and stuck her precious flag out the top window of –'

Chris leant forward suddenly and turned off the machine. 'Thursday!' he said.

'What?!' chorused the others who hadn't heard any of the tape yet.

'So?' asked Nicky.

'It means she went to see Blackmoor *after* she came here.'

Nicky bit his lip, trying to work out what Chris was driving at.

'And this means what, exactly?'

'O'Connell came here straight away, ready to tell "Andy" that two guys from Spirebrook nicked her flag.'

'But there's no mystery there, Chris – she saw you herself.'

'That's how she was able to pick out Fuller when she came here. But how did she know we were 'Brookers? She said Blackmoor told her it wasn't their lot who did it. But she didn't speak to Brain until *after* she came to see Mrs Cole.'

Nicky could see that this meant something, but he had no idea what. Chris felt the same, if truth be told.

'She had to have known right away who we were,' Chris said quietly. His mind raced through the possibilities.

The others were waiting patiently for their turn to listen. Nicky held up the Walkman. 'You want to hear the rest?'

'Yes,' said Chris, realising that he could think about the other matter later. 'Go on.'

Nicky hit the play button.

BLOKE (continuing from where Chris had stopped the tape): '– my school. I said I was investigating it, but hadn't found who was responsible.'

NATALIE: 'She identified two of my students as the culprits.'

BLOKE: 'Really? She never said. Picked them out herself, did she?'

NATALIE: 'Yes.'

BLOKE: 'She makes Miss Marple look like an amateur. You're not going to come down too hard on the lads?'

NATALIE: 'No.'

BLOKE: 'Good. It was just a prank. No reason to get carried away. Just so long as we can make the kids realise this kind of thing can't carry on.'

NATALIE: 'Well, that's what I hope, too.'

BLOKE (quite cheerful): 'It makes a change for your lads to be in the soup, eh? First time in months! Still, I'm sorry you got caught up in my battle with the witch across the road.'

NATALIE: 'No problem, but there was one thing I wanted to ask – did you find a watch anywhere near where the flag was flown?'

BLOKE: 'Aye!'

NATALIE: 'You did?'

RUSSELL: 'All right!'

Chris and Nicky looked across at Jones simultaneously.

'What have I done now?' he asked.

BLOKE (sounding suspicious): 'What was that?'

NATALIE: 'Sorry?'

BLOKE: 'I heard some lads laughing . . .'

NATALIE (very calm): 'Oh, I have the two boys in here with me at the moment, that's why I'm calling.'

BLOKE (relaxing): 'Oh, right! And one of them lost a watch, did he?'

NATALIE: 'Yes.'

BLOKE: 'I'm surprised he held his hand up to claim it. Cheap piece of tat it is. The sort of thing one of my lads used to wear . . . Still, I expect if your boy says it's his . . .'

Chris felt an icy chill in his gut. Brain had been on the point of saying something important, he was sure of it. His mind raced ahead, trying to remember where Natalie had steered the conversation next.

NATALIE: 'You mean no-one at your school has claimed the watch?'

BLOKE: 'No.'

NATALIE: 'Perhaps they knew it was connected with the flag incident.'

BLOKE: 'I wasn't born yesterday, Christine. I didn't tell the kids where it was found, just that a watch had turned up. No-one came forward.'

NATALIE: 'Ah, I see. Well, yes. In that case it probably does belong to my student.'

BLOKE: 'I expect so. I just want to ask one other lad, though. He's the boy I was talking to you about earlier. It's a Liverpool watch, see, and I remembered he supported the Reds. I thought it might be his, on account of him having been expelled. I'd half expected him to cause trouble.'

NATALIE: 'I see.'

BLOKE: 'Only thing is, he's more likely to have burnt the school down than pulled a prank like this. I'd still like to have a word with him.'

NATALIE: 'Well, yes.'

BLOKE: 'But if it doesn't pan out I'll send the watch over so you can see if it belongs to your boy. I'll let you know either way.'

NATALIE: 'OK, if you could do that for me, I'd be very grateful.'

BLOKE: 'He went to Spain with his parents, but I think he's been back for a week or two. I'll try and deal with this today.'

NATALIE: 'I'll leave it with you, then.'

BLOKE: 'Fine. If nothing happens, I'll bring the watch with me when I come to the game Tuesday. Oh – don't forget we have an Arts meeting Thursday.'

NATALIE: 'OK, goodbye.'

BLOKE: 'Goodbye, Christine.'

CLUNK.

⚽

'Damn,' said Nicky. 'He didn't say who it was.'

'He didn't need to,' said Chris, handing the headphones he'd been wearing to Mac. 'I'm pretty sure I know what happened now. I'm pretty sure who our friend the Liverpool supporter is.'

'Yeah? Who? Think we can flush him out?'

'Oh, yes,' said Chris. 'I'm certain of it.'

Twenty-three

The small coach negotiated its way through the gates with care. There was plenty of room, but the driver was worried about the numbers of kids lined up on either side outside. He'd asked to be given this run, and the last thing he wanted was to run anybody down.

Behind him, the boys were sullen and frustrated. They could hear the kids outside, hissing or calling out insults. On board the coach, though, the twenty-eight young lads from Blackmoor were on their best behaviour. Whether they wanted to be or not.

Some of the 'Brookers outside took this restraint as a sign of weakness and jeered even louder. What they didn't know was that Blackmoor's head teacher was riding in the front seat of the coach, and that he had promised to drop from the team anyone who so much as uttered a word. Threats didn't normally stop them, but every member of Blackmoor's team wanted to be part of tonight's game. They kept silent.

The noise levels outside fell sharply soon after as well. Mrs Cole came out of her office like a tornado, blowing away the crowd of kids at the gates and making sure the coach could make its way to the gym unhindered.

The driver chuckled to himself.

Some way towards the back of the bus, Bennett looked out of the dirty windows to the building from where the fiery 'Brooker head had come. He'd been here often enough to know which of the many windows there opened out from her office. If she was going to be keeping an eye on the game this evening, the room would be empty.

Just as he'd been told it would.

The news that his information was right didn't please or delight Bennett. His jaw was set firmly in place, his mouth remained unsmiling. What he had been told was only of interest to those who weren't playing football.

Bennett wanted to get one over on Stephens and his mates as badly as anyone. But he wanted to do it out on the pitch, where it would really hurt. After the trashy start to the season they'd had, Spirebrook were ripe to be taken.

The coach made the turn on to the wide path that separated the school buildings from the playing field, then slowed to a halt outside the gym.

'Remember what I said,' Mr Brain snapped from the front seat, having turned to face them. 'The same rules apply through the game. You will behave in a dignified, civilised manner, or I'll pull you off the team even if the game has already started. I don't care if that means we finish with just three players on the field and losing 30–0. We are *not* here to settle any vendettas!'

The faces looking back at him gave him no reply, but their expressions showed that, whatever the head thought, they were here to settle a point. One way or another.

Mr Brain was first off the coach, walking over to shake hands with Mrs Cole, who had cut across the playground to meet them at the gym. As soon as he had stepped outside, several of the Blackmoor players let out a long sigh, as if they had been holding their breath for fear of saying something.

There was one other teacher in the party, old Mr Sampson, who helped out with school sports when the PE staff weren't available. He'd been at Blackmoor a long time and knew the score better than any of them.

'I've only one thing to add to what the head just said,' he said sternly. 'Get out there and slaughter them.'

The boys clenched their fists and grimaced towards each other. They were ready to do battle with the enemy.

A short distance away, in the shelter of the home dressing room, the 'Brookers were even more ready. Kitted out in the dark blue of their school kit, boots laced, shinguards taped into place, they sat on the benches along three of the walls of the room, listening as their rivals stamped in through the main doors and down the short passage to the other changing area. Someone hammered on their door as they passed. A few of the younger players flinched, but no-one said a word.

Flea was in the corner, gathering flags and other equipment for the two games. But it wasn't his presence that was keeping the 'Brookers quiet. Every one of them was focused on what they had to do that afternoon.

There was a small knot in the bottom of Chris's stomach. He looked around at the other faces in the senior team. They were all quite drawn. Phil Lucas was spinning a ball in his hands, over and over. Russell had his head back against the wall and his eyes closed. Mac was staring into his empty kit bag as if he was looking for something.

In the silence, the grey-tiled, slightly whiffy changing room was more like a church or a library. Every one of the boys was caught in the same mood, like soldiers in the trenches before a big attack. Chris wondered if maybe they weren't too tense. Perhaps there was too much at stake for this to work.

'I've got a question,' said Nicky, his voice suddenly booming out, echoing off the tiles. It caught everyone by surprise. Flea dropped his clipboard, and several of the junior squad jumped as if they had been jabbed with a pencil. One of them made a rush for the loo.

'What should Chris do tonight about his pre-match super-stitions?'

The whole room moved from surprise to astonishment. In the face of everything else, what was Nicky going on about?

'No, no, listen,' he demanded as he realised how they were all gaping at him, preparing to tell him to shut up. 'We all agree that this whole good luck/bad luck thing was all nonsense, right?' He waited for a micro-second to see if anyone agreed. 'Right?' he demanded again, impatiently. This time a few voices muttered words that may or may not have been agreement.

'OK,' Nicky said, satisfied that he had their attention at least. 'Last time out, Chris was captain and he led us on to the pitch. But he's been leaving this room last for as long as any of us have been playing for Spirebrook.' That wasn't strictly accurate (as Nicky's facts usually weren't), and the older guys clustered either side of Griff almost said something, but Nicky didn't leave them time to nit-pick.

'All right,' Nicky continued, 'it may not be lucky, but it's never done us any harm either. It's just part of the team, like these shirts we wear and the way Flea always forgets to turn on the hot water in the showers before the game . . .'

They laughed. Their PE teacher shot Nicky a dirty look and marched to the control valve by the showers. An ironic cheer went up from the players.

'So,' Nicky said, reaching the point at last, 'I say Chris should stick with tradition.' His eyes lit up, as if he had surprised himself. 'Yeah! Tradition, that's what it is. And that's not the same thing as superstition at all.'

Nicky grinned at Chris, delighted with himself. For Fiorentini, that had been quite a stunningly clever argument.

'Actually . . .' Chris began.

His voice was drowned in a tide of voices from all the others. Even Flea joined in. Mac led the chorus demanding that Chris go back to his normal routine; Russell and Griff were the loudest among those who said it was stupid, a waste of time and that Chris could do whatever he liked.

'You idiot, Nicky,' Chris whispered. In that one moment, it seemed, the team's unity of the last few days had fractured once again.

Nicky didn't look worried, turning his head to follow the discussion. In fact, he had a delighted smile on his face. When he heard Phil Lucas suggest a compromise (go out first but still touch his badge), he laughed out loud.

Chris stood up and went over to stand in front of the blackboard. He held up his hands to quell the racket.

'Actually,' he began again, 'I'd already decided to go back to my normal routine. I don't know why – it's just that I've always done it, and I guess I always will. It's like Griff always sits in the corner furthest from the door.'

'That's not superstition,' muttered Griff. 'That's to keep out of the draught.'

'Whatever,' sighed Chris. 'We all have these things we do, that don't mean anything, but just make us what we are. Individuals inside a team.'

'So, what's Nicky's?' asked Jazz.

Chris looked at his team mate and best friend. Nicky was grinning back at him. Suddenly, Chris knew that he had done this on purpose, to break the tension.

'Nicky always causes trouble . . .' he said, and everyone laughed and threw towels at Fiorentini until Flea quietened them down.

'OK, time to go out there. Two things. Mrs Cole has asked me to remind you that you are representing the school tonight. What she means by that is that this stupid feud with Blackmoor mustn't get out of control. You know what she feels about school sports; if there's trouble tonight, she might just ban us from the League altogether.'

The boys all nodded to show that they accepted what he was saying. Even if they didn't believe it was possible 'Andy' would go so far, no-one wanted to take the chance of making this their last game for Spirebrook.

'Second, and this is from me, I want you all to know that I think this is the best school team there has ever been, any time, anywhere. It doesn't matter what the results have been like this season, it's still true. Now, I know we won't all be together for much longer. That's why it's more important than ever to play to your potential. Go out there and show Mrs Cole and everyone else why they'll be talking about this team in twenty years' time.'

With a dramatic flourish, he pulled open the door and the guys leapt to their feet and ran out, whooping and hollering, their studs clattering across the floor. Nicky and Chris were the last to rise.

As they reached the door, Nicky paused, bowing like a royal servant and gesturing for Chris to go first.

'After you!' he said, mockingly, bent low.

'Get lost, Nicky,' said Chris, and he kicked Nicky up the rear end, making Fiorentini stumble halfway through the open doorway.

Nicky stepped back in, coming right up close to Chris. The smile was still there, but his eyes were suddenly diamond-bright and full of determination.

'We're going to slaughter them tonight,' he growled.

'Let's do it,' said Chris, and the pair of them cracked heads the way they had for years after each one of their goals. Flea winced, then watched as Chris touched his fingers to the school badge on his breast as they left.

'They're all barking mad,' he muttered, and he gathered up the match ball and his first aid kit and went out behind them laughing.

Twenty-four

'Number six!' barked Flea. 'Come here!'

His face twisted like a shrivelled grape, the Blackmoor midfielder came over towards the big PE teacher sullenly, a whining complaint on his lips.

'Oh, but ref . . .' he began.

His protests were in vain. Jazz was on the ground, his eyes still streaming as he slowly pulled his socks back up over his shinguards. The whack he had taken had up-ended him so hard he had crashed down on his back. Fortunately, after Flea had checked him over, it was clear he had nothing seriously wrong with him.

'I spoke to you not five minutes ago,' Flea explained through gritted teeth. 'You're booked, and if you so much as look at anyone funny for the rest of the game, you're off.'

Standing just a little way off, Bennett muttered something about home teams and referees. Flea glowered at him and the Blackmoor captain took three or four steps back. It was one thing being lippy to a teacher, but when he was a rugby player the size of a house, even Bennett could see this wasn't a course of action that would help him live long.

'He's booked one of us as well,' said Chris as Bennett walked past him.

'Get lost, Stephens,' Bennett snapped. 'Like I care what you think.'

'I'd say the same,' Chris fired back, 'only I know you *can't* think.'

Flea might have missed the exact nature of the exchange, but he could tell Chris and Bennett were sniping at each other. He marched over, waving Bennett back.

'Blue free kick. Blacks back ten metres, please.'

He sounded impatient. Perhaps having to give eight free

kicks in the first ten minutes had worn away his good nature. The two sides were scrapping away like bad-tempered Rottweilers. Even now, with the ball dead, there was pushing and shoving as Blackmoor's wall retreated and their defenders tried to hustle Phil Lucas, Mac and Bruise, who were looking for space in the box.

Nicky lined up to take the free kick. Meanwhile, Chris paced along in front of the wall. He knew it was driving them mad. One of them tried to trip him, but he stepped on the guy's foot instead.

Bennett was near one end. He pushed at Chris as the striker came up.

'Stay there and you're going to get hurt!' he promised.

'Yeah, yeah,' snorted Chris, his voice rich with contempt. 'I'm frightened.' He turned, and faced Bennett, lowering his voice to a whisper. 'Where's your mate Ginger today? Sure you're up to being brave without him to hold your hand?'

'Who?' asked Bennett.

'You know, that carrot top who follows you around . . .'

Bennett caught up. 'You mean Adam? What about him?'

Chris noted the slight catch in Bennett's voice. 'He normally hangs around when you lot play, doesn't he?'

'Shows what you know,' Bennett replied. 'He got expelled.'

Chris paused, looking straight into Bennett's eyes, searching to make certain that what he was hearing was the truth. In the meantime, Bennett was launching a counter-attack.

'You want to talk about people who ain't here? Where's that squirt Robert James? Too good to play for you losers?'

Chris bristled, but before he could take things further, Flea called out.

'Chris – pack it in. This is a free kick not a staring match.'

Bennett grinned, pleased to see Chris lashed by Flea's tongue.

'Fine, you want me to take a free kick, I'll take a free kick.' Chris ran back away from the wall to where Nicky was standing with his foot on the ball. 'Just like we practised on Sunday,' he whispered.

They both stepped back from the ball, Chris moving furthest away. Flea blew his whistle. Chris took a long hard look at the wall, then came in fast. As he drew back to shoot, the wall braced itself for the impact.

It never came. Chris swung over the top of the ball, falling away to his right. Behind him Nicky was already stepping up. The wall had fractured, all of them flinching away from what they thought was going to be a rocket aimed straight at them.

Nicky chipped the ball through the gap into the space at the near post the keeper had left for the wall to cover. A loud cheer went up from the sidelines as the 'Brookers who had stayed to watch — and there were plenty of them — saw the ball nestle at the back of the goal.

'Suckers,' taunted Nicky. He and Chris bumped heads and high-fived before setting off back to their own half.

Needless to say, a goal like that (along with the celebrations it caused) did nothing to improve the temper of the Blackmoor players. Thirty seconds after the restart, Griff and a tall Blackmoor striker with curly brown hair were down in a tangle after a simple collision came close to being a fist fight.

Flea dragged them apart. 'Enough!' he roared. 'The next one to get involved in something like this, and they're off!'

That took some of the heat out of the tackles, but it was still a rough, hard game. Spirebrook gave as good as they got. Nicky was the next one into the book for a late challenge.

Mac came up to Chris while Flea handed Nicky a lecture that seemed to blow Nicky's hair back. The small midfielder was nursing a split lip, which he touched with his tongue before he spoke.

'What did Bennett say before — this Adam guy has been expelled?'

'Yes,' said Chris. He'd tried not to think too much about it while the game was in progress, but it was an interesting addition to what they knew.

'So, what does that mean? He can't have been involved in the fire. I mean, he's not part of the feud any more, right?'

Chris wasn't sure. Once a Blackmoron, always a Blackmoron. At the same time, was Chris going to carry on feeling the same way about the old enemy once he was at the new school? Perhaps Mac was right . . .

'I guess it depends on why he was expelled,' Chris said.

Mac grinned, and tested his lip with a fingertip. 'I'll try asking somebody,' he said.

In the meantime, the game went on. It was hard to believe

that the first half still had fifteen minutes to run. Chris tried to concentrate on the game.

Nicky, still seething after his booking, was on fire. He did the left back once, stopped to let the guy get up and went round him again just to show him who was boss. Then he hit a cross to the far post like an Exocet missile. All Phil had to do was put his head in the way and the ball was in the net. 2–0.

Chris applauded as the two of them came back. Then he noticed Mac on his way over. The lump on his lip looked even larger.

'He was flogging stuff at the school he'd nicked on holiday in Spain. Guess what the stuff was?'

Chris felt a buzz in the back of his mind.

'Junk watches?'

'Spot on,' said Mac. 'The cops questioned him, and when Brain found out, he slung him out of the school.'

'When was this?'

Mac's eyes opened wide. Chris realised he must have forgotten to ask. The midfielder looked round quickly as if trying to spot someone. His eyes fixed on a stocky kid with fair hair who had a grass stain around his mouth and a lump growing on his cheek bone.

'You found out a lot fast,' Chris said.

'An extended off the ball incident,' Mac replied, calmly. 'I have a feeling there might be another one if that plank with the fair hair elbows me in the mouth again.'

Chris waved him back into position – their opponents were lining up to take the kick off. Two down, the Blackmoor players were starting to look a little deflated. They might be holding their own in the rough-house, but they were being played off the park.

Chris thought over what Mac had said. If Adam and the ginger-haired guy who'd bounced off Fuller in Blackmoor were the same person (and it seemed pretty certain they were), then things started to make sense. Chris guessed Adam must have been expelled around the time of the scuffle in Loam Park – Ginger had been in school uniform then, but not on the day when Chris had seen him outside the newsagent's with the other guy and the two girls.

Chris cursed himself for not having made more of that clue. Ginger had been in ordinary clothes – not his school gear.

If Ginger/Adam was also Shell Suit, things really started to wrap up nicely. Again, Chris was sure this was how it would turn out. He remembered how Shell Suit had been vaguely familiar, even though Chris had seen little more than the eyes. Well, he and Ginger had been eyeball to eyeball plenty of times.

The watch thing wrapped it up for Chris. But it was one thing him believing it, and another for the story to be believable to anyone else. He needed proof. And if Ginger was no longer part of the crew at Blackmoor, that wasn't going to be easy to find.

Chris had hoped Ginger would come along today with his mate, and that he'd be able to flush the truth out. That hope seemed to have vanished.

A sharp call brought Chris out of his daydream. The game had restarted, and Nicky was clear on the right. Chris went forward almost on autopilot. When he cut towards the penalty spot, only Bennett was anywhere near him. As always, Nicky hit the cross perfectly.

Bennett jumped, but he was well short of the ball. Behind him, an instant later, Chris took off as well.

The spectators sucked in breath as the collision occurred. Chris had crashed into Bennett's back, missing the ball by a whisker, but knocking all the air out of his opponent's lungs as they landed.

'Oh dear, missed,' muttered Chris. Bennett was lying on the ground like he'd been shot.

Black-shirted players were rushing in from every direction, but Chris didn't move away. Instead he bent his head to Bennett's ear.

'That's for your mate Adam. Tell him he shouldn't play with fire.'

Bennett made a remarkable recovery for someone who needed surgery a half-second before. He jumped up and got into Chris's face.

'What's that supposed to mean?'

'You know!' Chris yelled back, even though he was now at the centre of a pushing, jostling pack of Blackmoor players. 'Adam and some others were here Saturday before last, setting fire to one of the buildings. For all I know you were one of the others!'

Bennett roared defiantly. 'Are you crazy? Why would I?'

'To get back at us over the Loam Park thing!'

'You *are* crazy! We got back at you for that ages ago!!! Who do you think nobbled that old crock of a bus you use?'

Chris was getting several sharp digs in the ribs and a few kicks too. None of them hurt. He was numb with shock from what he'd just heard. They'd had it all wrong.

Flea was on his way over to yank Chris out of the scrum. 'Half-time,' snapped Chris. 'We have to talk.'

Bennett said nothing, and Chris was pulled clear and given a stern talking to by Flea. The game eventually restarted with (another) free kick.

'Half-time can't come soon enough for me,' muttered the PE teacher as he checked his watch. He made it that there should be at least seven minutes injury time. In the end, though, he called a halt two minutes early.

The two teams didn't get much rest during the break. First, Flea tore into them, then Mrs Cole and Mr Brain came over to add their tuppenceworth. Mrs Cole made it quite clear that if this was an example of sportsmanship, she was prepared to ban senior school football for good. Brain echoed everything she said.

The lower school students listened to all this in stunned amazement. They had no idea what was going on. All they knew was that they were in the middle of a thrilling game, currently 3–3, everything to play for and not a foul in the first thirty minutes.

Leaving the older boys to ponder their future, Mrs Cole and her opposite number walked away.

'I didn't know things were so out of hand,' Mrs Cole admitted.

'Me neither,' said Brain. 'Pranks like the business with the flag are one thing, but this . . .'

Mrs Cole nodded in agreement. 'I've been meaning to call you about that, Brian. You know, of course, that two of my students were responsible . . .'

'Of course, "Andy",' Brain smiled though his eyebrows were twisted to show his confusion. 'You told me yourself.'

'What did you call me?' the Spirebrook head asked, icily.

There was a long silence before either of them spoke again.

Flea normally refereed one of the two games Spirebrook played on a Wednesday afternoon. It was accepted practice that one school's teacher ran one game, while his opposite number took the whistle for the other. It had never stopped Flea being able to talk to his players as their coach before.

This time, though, he took the younger players off to one side, not trusting himself to speak to the older boys. He let them stew.

Which suited Chris just fine.

'I'll be back in a minute,' said Chris and he stood up and made for the gym as if he was going to the toilet. On the way, he caught Bennett's eye.

They met up inside a few seconds later. Chris dragged the Blackmoor captain into the small closet that served as Flea's office.

'OK, let's get this straight. The fire here last Saturday was nothing to do with you lot?'

'No!' Bennett insisted. 'Look, there's no love lost between Spirebrook and Blackmoor, but no-one's ever been that dumb. Only someone really stupid would do something like that.'

'Like your mate Adam, maybe?'

Bennett wasn't ready to go that far. 'You don't know that, Stephens! Besides, why would he? It's not you he's mad with.'

'OK, tell me, who does Adam support? Which team?'

'Liverpool . . .'

'And he went to Spain on holiday, right?'

'Yes. He got into trouble out there for nicking cheap watches from a guy at the hotel. The police over here were told; that's why he got expelled.'

'He tried to sell these watches to kids at Blackmoor?'

Bennett was becoming impatient at all the questions. 'Yes! But they were well dodgy. Westham United — you know, all one word? Sunderland wearing black and white stripes. There were even some that said Spain, Euro 96 Champions.'

'Only a real plank would have thought that could happen,' muttered Chris. He tried to think through what he'd heard.

'Listen, did he keep one of the watches for himself?'

'Yeah, for a bit, only he –'

'– lost it, yeah, I know.'

Bennett narrowed his eyes and glared at Chris.

'What? You really think Adam tried to set fire to your school?'

Chris glared back. 'Would it make any difference if I did?'

They stood like that for several moments, during which Chris had plenty of time to remember Bennett was a year older, several inches taller and much heavier than he was. A while back, Bennett had managed to heave Chris over the bonnet of a car. Chris didn't think much had changed since then.

'Look,' said Chris. 'I can't prove any of this – not without your help.'

Bennett stiffened as he pulled back. 'Oh, sure . . .' he said.

'I have a confession to make,' Chris said.

Bennett waited, all his defences up.

'You had a phone call last night, right?'

'Maybe . . .'

'From Robert James. You know, the loser who's too good to play for us . . .' Chris tried to mimic the younger boy's voice: ' "Hey, Bennett, if you want to get one back at Spirebrook, I can show you how." '

'I knew that was a set-up,' growled Bennett. 'All that guff about how the Spirebrook football trophies were in your secretary's office, how it would be easy to get in today while everyone was watching the football . . .' He laughed contemptuously. 'Think we'd fall for that?'

'You never even considered it?' asked Chris.

'No!'

'Like you never broke into Riverside youth club to steal the trophies from there – just to get back at me?'

'NO! Don't flatter yourself, Stephens. I'm not going to get into trouble with the police just because you're too clever for your own boots.'

'Damn!' Chris knew their plan had gone up in smoke. Bennett hadn't been part of anything that had happened.

Neither of them said anything for several seconds. Chris tried to come up with something – anything – that would turn things round. He knew that Bennett was watching him carefully, trying to work out what was going on in Chris's mind. Keep trying, thought Chris, because I don't know myself.

Finally, Bennett uttered a short curse and a shorter laugh, stepping back towards the door (not that there was much room to move in the cupboard). 'I knew this was some kind of a trick, Stephens. For all I know, this here's part of it, a big act to get me to do something stupid. It ain't going to work.'

'You've never needed any help to be stupid,' Chris said automatically, his voice low and quiet. His heart wasn't really in the exchange any more.

Bennett pulled open the door and went out into the passage leading to the main doors. 'You ready for the second half?' he grinned.

A small spot on Chris's thigh twitched. He'd been kicked there quite hard in the scrum in the first half. Without looking, he knew a bruise was starting to colour itself in there. 'You realise you're losing two-nil?' he asked.

Bennett's smile faded. 'We can get that back,' he snarled.

'Yeah?' said Chris. 'Try.'

Chris rejoined the others. With Flea still absent, Griff was doing his best as captain to gee them up for the second half. Not that they needed any more enthusiasm to get out there and get stuck in. Russell was pounding his right fist into his left glove as if he was preparing to face Mike Tyson.

'Where have you been?' Griff complained as Chris arrived.

'Sorting out some ground rules,' said Chris, firmly. He raised his voice so that he could be heard over all the excitement and chatter around him. 'Now listen up,' he said, checking to make certain that the Blackmorons could hear him every bit as clearly as his own team mates.

'I've just been speaking to Bennett. Seems there might have been a mistake over just who's been messing us around lately.'

He flicked his eyes over towards the black-shirted players again. Bennett had a confused look on his face, a kind of 'is that what we were talking about?' expression. His jaw hung down slackly.

The Blackmorons were alternately looking at Stephens and their captain, swinging from one to the other like the crowd at Wimbledon.

'Now, I'm not saying this makes the Blackmorons our best pals, but it means what's been happening on the field isn't necessary. This doesn't have to be a war. So, second half, we go out there and play football.' He leant forward to make sure his team mates understood that what he said next was aimed directly at them: 'No matter what happens, no matter what they do, don't rise to it. We don't have to kick them off the pitch, we can play them off it.'

Once again, he checked to see how the black shirts were reacting. A strange light passed over Bennett's face, as if there'd been a gap in the clouds for just that moment. He closed his mouth and looked around at his mates.

'If it's a trick, hurt them,' he said rapidly, 'but don't start nothing.'

Chris felt a wave of relief wash over him. He turned back from the other team to face the bemused faces of his mates.

'Two-nil now. Six-nil by full time.'

He could see Nicky had been hovering on the edge of a 'wait a minute' reaction all the time he had been speaking. But even Fiorentini just smiled and clenched his fist with determination as Chris and he met each other's eyes.

'Eight-nil at least,' Nicky grinned.

'In your dreams, Fiorentini,' they heard Bennett reply.

'Let's do it,' said Chris, waving them on to the pitch.

He hung back to be last back out. Griff was the slowest of the others to rise to his feet.

'Why does Flea ever bother making me captain?' he sighed.

The two teams collided again, like huge robots or dinosaurs from a dodgy Japanese film, or impossibly muscled superheroes from a morning cartoon. Some of the tackling was fierce enough to make people three streets away wince.

But Flea didn't have to blow his whistle for a single foul until eight minutes in, when Mac mistimed a tackle. Straight away, Mac offered his hand to the Blackmoor player, hauling him to his feet.

'They've been kidnapped by aliens and replaced by androids,' the Spirebrook PE teacher muttered, unable to believe what he was witnessing.

On the sidelines, those watching – even those who had

overheard what was said — wondered if they had been miraculously teleported to watch a different game. All the same commitment was there, but both teams were playing with an iron determination not to be guilty of starting anything ugly.

As a result, the game was turning into a classic.

A Stephens one-two with Fiorentini, volleyed into the back of the net. 3–0.

Jackson through one-on-one against Jones; the first shot comes back off the keeper's chest, Jackson tucks in the rebound. 3–1.

Lucas heads in a near post corner. 4–1.

Stephens through the offside trap, centre to Jazz, knock down to Marsh. 5–1.

Handball by Bruise under pressure. Bennett steps up for the spot kick. 5–2.

Added to that, Blackmoor hit the post and Jazz saw a goal-bound strike headed off the line. Blackmoor were going down, but they weren't out of the match. Play flowed from end to end, with rapid passing and lung-bursting running keeping the game open.

Chris stopped in midfield, dropped his hands to his knees and panted hard, staring at the grass. All around him, the other players were taking a breather as well, while Nicky made a meal out of going to fetch the ball from under one of the pylons. Just about everyone was done in.

Chris finally felt able to lift his head. It worried him slightly that the Spirebrook players were coming off second in the fitness battle. Griff had been subbed off already — not yet fully recovered from his dose of flu; now Flea was on the point of bringing on a second reserve, which had to be either for Jazz, who looked wrecked, or Mike Marsh, who was limping badly.

Some of the people watching looked almost as done in as the players. Mrs Cole and Mr Brain had been clapping and cheering so hard they were having to lean on each other for support (either that, or Nicky's suspicions were right . . .). No-one dared look away from the game. Even the parents of kids playing in the lower school match were paying more attention to the senior game.

No-one appeared to be about on any other part of the site that Chris could see. The usual hangers-on from the staff room were there; the chess club was there; the sixth-formers who stayed behind to smoke behind the bike racks were there. They'd been caught, but they were still there.

Chris looked back around the players. After a moment's consideration, Flea was taking both Jazz and Marsh off, using the last two subs. There were twelve or so minutes left. Chris imagined Spirebrook might have to start hanging on to what they had from now on.

Finally, he caught Bennett looking at him. The Blackmoor captain said nothing, and his one gesture was a tiny nod in Chris's direction.

Chris straightened up. 'Come on, 'Brook!' he yelled, clapping his hands. 'The last few minutes now. Keep it tight!'

Nicky was back, preparing to take the throw-in. Bennett came over to mark Chris.

'I told Adam,' he said.

'What?!' gasped Chris. He stared at the Blackmoor captain. Bennett's face was quite hollow and drawn. It was more than just exhaustion, Chris knew.

'When your mate called, I knew it was bogus, but I told Adam.'

Chris looked around in alarm. There was nothing unusual in sight, of course. But he couldn't help feeling . . .

He rounded back on Bennett. 'What did you do that for? Adam's nothing to do with Blackmoor any more.'

Bennett shrugged. 'He's still a mate. He and I go back a long way, and he's been part of the feud with you from the first day we went to Blackmoor. Him more than some of the others. He never made the team, you see. I've always known I can get you on the football pitch. Adam, well . . .'

'One thing,' said Chris, hurriedly. 'Does he wear a blue shell suit top?'

'Sometimes . . .' said Bennett.

Chris whirled round. Coincidentally, Flea was looking at him. 'If you lads aren't too busy . . .' he was saying.

'I need to go off!' Chris cried.

'What?'

'I'm injured. I need to go off.'

'Chris, we just used our last two subs; can't you hang on for the last few minutes while we —'

'OK, fine,' snapped Chris, looking away. He ran quickly into space, arm aloft. 'Nicky!'

182

His team mate fired a flat throw right to Chris's feet. Deep in his own half, Chris was completely unmarked and under no pressure. A few 'Brookers in the crowd started to cheer.

That sound died in the dozen or so throats where it had started. Chris had just hit a flat pass straight to Kennedy, one of Blackmoor's midfielders. Stunned by the gift, Kennedy still reacted faster than any of the 'Brook defenders, racing in on goal. Russell came off his line rapidly.

Kennedy entered the penalty area, the ball bobbling awkwardly as he prepared to shoot. The delay was just long enough.

As he threw his foot at the ball, Chris arrived to shove him over. Kennedy hit the ground as his shot was parried out by Russell Jones. A ragged cry of 'PENALTY!' echoed round the pitch.

Chris flicked his head back as he came to a halt, just by the six-metre line. To his amazement, Flea was waving play on.

'Unbelievable . . .' Chris muttered, but he could see why. The rebound had gone straight to Bennett who had a clear shot on goal. Russell was still on the ground and only Chris stood in the way.

Bennett could have blasted it in, but the surprise of such a gift chance made him lob it right at Chris's body.

At the edge of his vision, Chris saw Russell's look of relief as he covered the shot, body behind the ball. The smile vanished as Chris fisted the ball away.

'*PENALTY!!!!*' the Blackmorons yelled in chorus. This time Flea, even though he was utterly confused, managed to blow his whistle and point to the spot.

'Hey – professional foul!!' yelled Kennedy from the deck, forgetting for a moment that he was supposed to be a wounded striker and that it was his job to roll around as if he had been critically injured. Someone else was yelling about 'deliberate handball'.

Flea shook his head sadly. 'I've got to send you off, Chris.'

'Oh dear,' said his striker. Chris didn't wait for Flea to find the rarely used red card he carried in his shirt pocket.

Everyone watched in silence as Chris flew off the field as quickly as if he had been chasing a through ball. They watched in amazement, standing as still as statues, until the gym door slammed.

Twenty-five

Chris kicked off his boots as he went through the door. Moments later, he was hopping towards the rear fire door, pulling on one of his trainers. The delay was unavoidable; there was no way he could run far through the school in his boots.

He stamped his way into one shoe, then the other. There was no time to tie the laces. He'd have to risk tripping up.

The route he chose was the long way round, but it served two purposes (apart from allowing him to change footwear). One, it shielded him from view – the gym was between Chris and the field as he came out through the door. Two, by running across the open space at the back of Block 1, then round the front of the building, Chris could keep the main gate in view.

That had to be the only way in and out. It would take a lot of guts to just walk in through Spirebrook's front door, but everyone connected with the games would be over by the more sheltered rear fence. One individual, if they had enough front, might pass unnoticed as they slipped into the school.

Chris skidded over the greasy grass as he pounded along the front of Block 1, far away from the normal routes students followed in their journeys round the school. On his left, he passed by classrooms fronted by high, wide windows. They were all locked, of course, and the rooms beyond were dark.

But the last few windows, just before the main doors on this side of the building, were lit up. The head's office and the secretary's stood side by side, just off the entrance hall. They'd be locked too.

Chris was sure that wouldn't stop Adam.

He reached the windows and slid to a halt. The curtains at the window of 'Andy' Cole's room were drawn. Nothing unusual in that — she often pulled them closed in the evenings. Chris moved on to the next pair of windows and peered in. Nothing. The secretary's office was empty.

For a moment, Chris wasn't sure how he felt. Relieved? Disappointed? Had he judged the situation incorrectly after all?

That was when he noticed the door between the two rooms was open. It might not mean a lot, but Chris had never known that door left ajar. Perhaps the times he'd stood outside it wouldn't be wasted after all.

Chris went in through the main doors and along the corridor towards the twin doors. If he was right, one of them was probably broken in.

Once again, Chris found his theory fall flat. Both doors were closed and undamaged. For the second time in a few seconds, he wondered if he was completely wrong about everything. On nothing more than a wild hunch, he tried Mrs Cole's door. Locked, of course. Then he tried the secretary's door. And it opened. His heart leapt. He stepped in silently and closed the door behind him.

At once he could hear the sound of someone rummaging through the drawers and cupboards in the other room. The connecting door lay wide open, shadows from within crossing the paintwork. The lock was broken.

As Chris pondered this, the shadows darkened, and suddenly there was a flash of blue and copper.

'Hello, Adam,' called Chris.

The movement in the other room fell silent. Then he heard footsteps as someone took the last few steps to the door. Wild-eyed and slightly breathless, Chris's real opponent stepped through the door.

'Stephens,' whispered Ginger/Shell Suit. His face was twisted into a display of pure hatred.

'Lost something?' asked Chris, innocently. 'You're in the wrong school, you know.' He snapped his fingers as if he had just remembered something. 'Sorry, I forgot. You don't go to *any* school any more, do you.'

'Not at the minute, no,' Adam snarled, 'though I don't suppose that'll last.' He stepped further into the room. 'What are you doing here?'

Chris moved in as well. A large desk lay between them, covered with test papers and files. Chris looked around the room, wondering if anything had been disturbed or taken (and deciding that he'd never be able to tell), then looked up at the other boy.

'Got to see the head,' replied Chris, faking a grimace. 'She here?'

Adam continued to close in. Chris took a step to the side to keep the desk between them. He wasn't frightened of Adam, but he hadn't come here just for the pleasure of a fight.

'You're not funny, Stephens.'

'That's what she said. Seems to think I was responsible for a fire here a week or so back.'

That fact drew an interesting reaction from Adam. He actually smiled, surprised at the 'good' news. 'Really? Now, that is funny!'

He had walked round further, so that he was now closer to the outer door than Chris was. Chris had his back to the windows. Adam squinted as he looked into the light.

'I guess it is,' said Chris, 'seeing as you and I both know it was you.'

Adam's smile vanished as quickly as it had appeared. He was back to his more natural sour expression.

'What you and I know is one thing,' he replied. 'But if you can't prove it, and you don't tell no-one, what does it matter, right? And I think I can persuade you that keeping your mouth shut is a good idea.'

Chris laughed at the threat Adam was trying to attach to his voice. 'Am I supposed to be afraid of you, Adam? Man, you're even funnier than I am.'

'Yeah?' retorted Adam, 'then laugh this off.'

With that, he gave a low whistle. Suddenly three other lads, older and bigger than either Chris or Adam, stepped in from the head teacher's office.

Ha, ha, thought Chris.

'OK . . .' said Chris slowly, backing up. 'Now, what is it I'm supposed to have forgotten again?' He tried to remember where the fire alarm was in here, but then saw it was over by the inner door. The school bell, then. On the secretary's desk.

Just beside where Chris had been standing, but where Adam was advancing now. Strike two.

'Don't forget everything too quickly, Stephens. First, tell us how you knew it was me.'

Chris decided to try an outrageous bluff first. 'Bennett grassed you up.'

Adam flinched, but didn't bite. 'Nah. Try again.'

So much for the dummy. Chris decided to be more direct.

'OK, I found the watch you dropped in the Quad. It took a while, but I managed to trace it back to you.'

'That it? Not much proof, is it?'

Chris shrugged. The four of them had him pretty well hemmed in by now. He looked out of the window but there was no-one in sight. The game wouldn't be over for a few more minutes yet either, so there was little chance of anyone coming back this way.

'It'll do. Your head – your old head – has the watch. He knows where it came from.'

It was another desperate bluff, but Chris figured the situation was serious enough to merit a few outrageous lies.

'You mean this watch?' said one of the other guys.

He was holding up a jiffy bag, which had a sticky label on the outside with Blackmoor's badge on it. He tipped the open end of the bag towards his palm and the garish watch fell into his hand. For the only time in its worthless existence, it had kept perfect timing.

'I found it on the desk in there,' the guy said, nodding back behind him. 'I thought it was funny when I saw the old school badge sitting here.'

Brain must have brought it back, just as he promised, Chris realised.

'Yeah, that's my watch all right,' said Adam. It was just the confession that Chris had been hoping to hear. What a pity that he wasn't going to have any teeth left by the time he got to mention it to anyone else.

'Who *are* these guys?' sighed Chris.

Adam looked around at his accomplices. 'These? Just guys from Blackmoor, old boys. They live near me. They've all been in a jam one time or another, so I knew they'd help me out. And they've no reason to care about Spirebrook, so that was a bonus.'

'Plus the stuff we've nicked!' said the guy holding the jiffy bag.

'Yeah, we've been real lucky,' said Adam. 'Like finding these keys in the office we broke into.' He held up a keyring. Chris knew it had to belong to Mr Palmer, who probably thought it'd been lost in the fire. 'Made up for not finding the cups and things you 'Brookers have won,' Adam added.

'Still, you've got the stuff you nicked from Riverside youth club . . .' Chris replied, fishing.

'And some stuff we nicked from Blackmoor,' Jiffy Bag Boy laughed.

'I take it we aren't going to find the trophies in here, either?' Adam asked. Chris shrugged, trying not to look for the box he'd carried in a week before. 'No matter. At least we have the compensation of hurting you.'

Chris felt the radiator under the window at his back. Out of room. Out of time. 'Hadn't you better be going?' he said quickly. The four of them were very close. 'Someone's going to come soon.'

'We have a look-out,' said Adam. 'We ain't that stupid.'

Oh, thought Chris at once, but you are.

'So, how come this look-out of yours didn't see me coming?' he asked, even though he suspected the answer already.

Adam froze. A slight sign of panic crossed his face, followed by a slight twitch that showed he was beginning to realise that something might just have gone a little wrong with their plan.

'Perhaps he was looking the wrong way,' came a voice.

Chris felt like cheering. He started to laugh instead.

Adam spun round to face the inner door, the one leading into 'Andy' Cole's office. Nicky was at the front, grinning widely. Mrs Cole (her office keys in her hand), Mr Brain and several others were right behind him. In that same moment, the outer door opened and Griff, Bennett, Jazz and several others came in. There was an instant when the four ex-Blackmorons thought about running for it, but when they saw Flea filling the doorway like a large boulder, they decided against it.

'Offside!' chuckled Nicky.

Twenty-six

Adam was crying like a baby by the time the police arrived to take him and his mates away.

'The game still had twenty-five minutes to run!' he complained. Even his own mates were able to confirm that actually it was less than five.

'See his watch?' laughed Nicky. 'It had a picture of Bob Fowler on it.'

'You mean Robbie,' said Chris. 'Robbie Fowler.'

'Not according to Ginger's latest watch...'

They were all still crowded into Mrs Cole's office. It gave them a perfect view as Adam and his mates were driven away.

'Even so,' said Chris. 'You should still have been playing.'

Nicky made a waggling gesture with his hand, the kind that said Chris might have been right, but that Nicky's presence had warped reality as usual.

'You have no idea how many professional fouls there were just after you left...' he began.

'Half of both teams sent off in thirty seconds,' added Bennett.

'I had to abandon the game,' sighed Flea, who was only just catching up with what had been going on. 'They never teach you about stuff like this on the FA's Referee Course.'

'Even so, you found me pretty quickly...'

'You were followed,' said Nicky. He indicated Mrs Cole with a flick of his head.

'Well, honestly,' the head explained. 'Chris Stephens leaves a football match before the end? Get realistic.'

'I think that's "get real",' Brain corrected her.

'Whatever. I've been Chris's head teacher too long to believe that things are ever going to be peaceful wherever he is. So, as soon as I saw you leave, I came back this way as well.'

'Plus,' added Brain, 'we saw through that fake call of yours. I didn't think it sounded like Mrs Cole's voice – so I ran a test. There is no Arts meeting next Thursday. And today, we were able to swap notes.'

'Lucky for me. Lucky for all of us.'

'Not quite,' sighed Nicky, cocking his head sideways as he looked back at Chris. 'Your idea of having two people on look-out – just in case we did flush Adam out – paid off OK. Bob James and Fuller spotted their look-out just after he saw you, and intercepted him before he could get back here.'

'What's unlucky about that?' asked Chris.

'Fuller hit him on the nose,' James explained. 'With his bad hand.'

'He's definitely out until after Christmas now,' sighed Nicky.

There was some muted, sympathetic laughter from around the room. Chris walked over to James and stuck out his hand.

'Thanks,' he said.

'No problem,' replied the younger player.

Chris turned back to face his head teacher. 'Mrs Cole, you do realise that it wasn't James who did that flag trick with Fuller, don't you?'

'Of course,' she smiled.

'So, he's off suspension?'

'He was never really on it.'

'That's a relief,' said Griff. 'With Fuller out, maybe we'd better think about Bob playing in the senior team until Christmas.'

'Not Bob,' scolded Nicky. 'He prefers Robbie. Trust you to be the last to work that out . . .'

Griff was speechless.

'Of course,' said Mrs Cole, her voice rising above the laughter. 'That does mean that you're the guilty party instead, Chris.'

There was a moment's silence. 'Andy' turned to face Mr Brain.

'Unless we can agree to forget the whole thing,' she said. 'Perhaps it would help to bury this silly feud once and for all.'

'Fine by me, Christine,' he replied.

Nicky made a secret face towards Chris, almost splitting

himself open at the tone in Brain's voice. Naturally, Mrs Cole spotted it.

'OK, all of you, out of my office. It's time this place turned back into a school again. Go on! Shoo!!!'

They marched out gradually, slowly making their way back towards the gym so that Bennett and Brain could meet up with the rest of the Blackmoor students. Chris fell in alongside his rival.

'Guess this means we'll have to rearrange the fixture,' said Chris. 'Unless you're prepared to concede seeing as you were losing five-two.'

'Are you kidding?' roared Bennett. 'It was five-three, anyway – we scored that penalty.'

'What?' howled Nicky, quick to join in. 'Chris only gave the penalty away so he could get off and catch Adam!'

'Not my problem,' Bennett answered with a shrug.

'You moron,' snapped Nicky.

'Get knotted, Fiorentini . . .'

'Fine, no problem,' Chris added. 'We'll play you again. Only next time, you'll think five-three was close . . .'

And so it went on, all the way back to the gym. Nicky disappeared to find the bus driver, wondering if he could drop the Blackmorons off away from their school. Like in Scotland. It would go on until the two rival schools could have their rematch. And, Chris knew, it would go on long after he, Nicky and Russell moved on.

I wonder who United have this kind of trouble with? he asked himself.

Donnell upon at the tone in Reilly's voice? That all," Finn Cole snapped it.

"Ok, all of you, out of my office. It's time the place turned back into a school again. Go on! Shoo!"

They marched out, gradually, slowly nearing their way back toward the front so that Ben Cole and Finn Cole could mix up with two of the Black Boys' students who fell in alongside them.

"Oh, we're going to have to rearrange the fixtures," said Chris. "Unless you're going to concede seeing as you were losing two."

"Are you kidding? Inside a minute, it was five-three, anyway," snorted Hal tensely.

"What! Rowan McKay quick to join in. That's only" gave the penalty away so the actual gap on and gap in Acuña.

"Not my penalty," Ramon answered with a shrug. "Your mess," snapped Barry.

Gail moved forward.

"Fine, no problem. Christ, forget it. We'll play you again. Only next time you'll think twice time was close...."

And he'd went along the way back to the gym, Paddy disappeared. "I had that up driven home again that he could drop the Black Boys off away from their school bus in Scotland. It would go on until the two rival schools could have their rematch. And Chris knew it would soon drag after he, at least, had moved on.

I wonder what Ulster have the kind of trouble, he asked himself.

WE NEED YOUR HELP . . .

to ensure that we bring you the books you want —

— and no stamp required!

All you have to do is complete the attached questionnaire and return it to us. The information you provide will help us to keep publishing the books you want to read. The completed form will also give us a better picture of who reads the Team Mates books and will help us continue marketing these books successfully.

TEAM MATES QUESTIONNAIRE

*Please **circle** the answer that applies to you and add more information where necessary.*

SECTION ONE: ABOUT YOU

1.1   Are you?
        Male / Female

1.2   How old are you?   .... years

1.3   Which other Team Mates books have you read?
        Overlap
        The Keeper
        Foul!
        Giant Killers
        Offside

1.4 What do you spend most of your pocket money on?
(Please give details.)

Books _____
_____

Magazines _____
_____

Toys _____
_____

Computer games _____
_____

Other _____
_____

1.5 Do you play football?
Yes / No

1.6 Which football team do you support, if any?
_____

1.7 Who is your favourite football player, if you have one?
_____

SECTION TWO: ABOUT THE BOOKS

2.1 Where do you buy your Team Mates book/s from?
W H Smith
John Menzies
Waterstones
Dillons
Books Etc
A supermarket (say which one) _____
A newsagent (say which one) _____
Other _____

2.2   Which is your favourite Team Mates story and what do
       you like most about it?
       _____
       _____
       _____

2.3   How did you find out about Team Mates books?
           Friends
           Magazine
           Store display
           Gift
           Other _____

2.4   Would you like to know more about the Team Mates
       series of books?
           Yes / No

       If yes, would you like to receive more information
       direct from Virgin Publishing?
           Yes / No

       If yes, please fill in your name and address below:
       _____
       _____
       _____
       _____

2.5   What do you find exciting and interesting about the
       Team Mates stories?
       _____
       _____
       _____

SECTION THREE: ADDITIONAL INFORMATION

3.1 Are there any other comments about Team Mates you would like to make?

_____

_____

_____

_____

Thank you for completing this questionnaire. Now tear it out of the book – carefully! – put it in an envelope and send it to:

**Team Mates
FREEPOST LON 3453
London
W10 5BR**

No stamp is required if you are resident in the UK.